The Finest in Fantasy from Jennifer Roberson

BLOOD AND BONE

Life and Limb

THE SWORD-DANCER SAGA

Sword-Dancer

Sword-Singer

Sword-Maker

Sword-Breaker

Sword-Born

Sword-Sworn

Sword-Bound

*(The Sword-Dancer Saga is also available in the
Novels of Tiger and Del omnibus editions)*

CHRONICLES OF THE CHEYSULI

Shapechanger's Song
(Shapechangers & The Song of Homana)

Legacy of the Wolf
(Legacy of the Sword & Track of the White Wolf)

Children of the Lion
(A Pride of Princes & Daughter of the Lion)

The Lion Throne
(Flight of the Raven & A Tapestry of Lions)

THE KARAVANS UNIVERSE

Karavans
Deepwood
The Wild Road

THE GOLDEN KEY

(with Melanie Rawn and Kate Elliott)

BLOOD & BONE: *Book One*

LIFE

=AND=

LIMB

JENNIFER ROBERSON

DAW BOOKS, INC.
DONALD A. WOLLHEIM, FOUNDER

1745 Broadway, New York, NY 10019
ELIZABETH R. WOLLHEIM
SHEILA E. GILBERT
PUBLISHERS
dawbooks.com

Dedicated to three inspiring women no longer with us

Shera Roberson, my mother

Molly Hardy, my aunt

Pat Hyre, my friend

PROLOGUE

His voice was rich, a much loved, clear baritone, as he handed his seven-year-old grandson a gun.

"All right, Gabriel. First time for everything. Don't expect to be perfect. *I* wasn't. Let's just see what you've got, shall we? See what we've got to work with." A warm hand came down on Gabriel's shoulder, squeezed lightly. "Don't fret, Gabriel."

It was a crisp Oregon day with an afternoon rain abated but lingering in puddles and dampness as clouds receded. Tall, gray-haired Grandaddy, with neatly trimmed beard and vigorous river of thick silvering hair flowing nearly to his shoulders, had driven them out to the country in his white '63 Thunderbird with a box of empty beer bottles in the back seat, and Gabriel remembered the weight of the weapon. How it filled both hands, how it made him tense his arms, how his fingers clung.

How his grandfather slipped a hand under his, eased the gun slightly upward. Grandaddy didn't hold the gun *for* him; he just provided a smidgen of support so that he could stop clenching his entire body with the attempt to hold the gun still. Grandaddy *steadied* him, just a little.

"All right, Gabriel." The same calm voice. "You've got this."

He was nearly breathless with want, with the *need* to please. To excel. "All six bottles, Grandaddy?"

His grandfather's laugh gusted from his chest in a quiet blurt of amusement, blue eyes dancing as the weathered skin next to his eyes creased into a spray of fretwork lines. "If you think you can, of course. But *one* would be a fine beginning, Gabriel. And if you don't get it right the first time, next time will do. Or the next after that. *Baby* steps. Baby steps, son."

But at seven he had gained an inch over what he'd been at six, and he felt strong. His body sang with it. This was, he felt within his bones, a test of some kind, even if his grandfather suggested no such thing. "I'm not a *baby*, Grandaddy. I can do this."

"Perhaps you are not." Grandaddy's hand, once more, briefly touched his shoulder. "Then show me what you've got."

He felt his grandfather remove the support from beneath his hands, the gun. It was a measly little outdated 6-chamber .22 revolver, nothing like the 9-mil Smith & Wesson his grandfather wore in an honest-to-God holster. But it felt big. It felt heavy.

And then it didn't. It felt *right*.

He *focused*. He'd heard that word before, that prompting from Grandaddy. The world narrowed. The world lost definition around the edges, refined itself in the middle. Sound attenuated, died away until all he heard was his own shallow, choppy breathing.

He stopped it, stilled it. Sucked breath again, blew it out on a huffing stream between pursed lips. It steadied his breathing;

smoothed into something akin to a comfortable anticipation. It wasn't excitement. It was the need to do this, to please his grandfather, to prove he could *do* this. And an almighty certainty that he could.

He saw six beer bottles balanced along the pitted, weather-grayed wooden fence rail, six dead little brown-glass soldiers emptied by his father, who liked to kick back after work with two or four beers; bottles appropriated by his grandfather from out of the trash. That was all that mattered. Six bottles. Six targets. Six bullets. Six *opportunities*.

What he wanted to do was what he'd seen in the movies featuring badass shooters: *one-two-three-four-five-six*, one after another, a seamless string of reports as the gun fired, the popping sound of exploding bottles and the cascade of shattered amber glass. But what his grandfather wanted was efficiency.

Precision. Results.

One at a time. *Aim. Squeeze. Take the recoil.* Steady hands. Loosen elbows, shoulders, then do it all again: *one-two-three-four-five-six.*

Efficiency. Precision. Results.

He fired six times. The gun was empty.

He let his arm drop to his side, felt the weight dragging. He was suddenly seven years old again, not remotely a badass, and even a measly .22 felt heavy in the wake of his first experience *shooting* the thing.

"Well," Grandaddy murmured, clearly startled. Then his hand yet again came down on Gabe's shoulder, squeezed. Firmly, man-to-man. "Guess I shouldn't be surprised, with your genetics . . . I think you're what's called 'a natural.'"

Gabe looked up at his grandfather. The words just spilled from his mouth, unwilled; and it was truth. "If you don't get it right the first time, next time may be too late."

Grandaddy smiled slowly, broadly, teeth showing in the thicket of his tidy beard. "Hardwired, boy, is it? All of it? Yes. You'll do. When the time comes." He paused, blue eyes lost in the distances. "And come it will."

Gabe blinked up at him. Grandaddy often went off on stuff he didn't truly grasp, talking about "special Mendelian genetics" and "coefficients of inbreeding," "prepotency" and "outcrossing" and any number of terms in which he staked no interest. He listened, though, because that's what one did with Grandaddy.

"You'll understand, some day," Grandaddy told him once. *"For now, place your trust in me, son, and I'll see you safe. But there is learning to do."*

Well, Gabe liked school, so learning was okay. Loved books. Spent hours lost in worlds created by others. But he also liked to move, to *do*, to not be trapped at a desk in the classroom, or watching educational videos, or viewing documentaries on DVDs at home, or any number of things his grandfather asked of him when he came around. Which wasn't often enough, to Gabe's way of thinking. He loved his parents, loved his younger brother, but he worshipped his grandfather. Life was more interesting, was somehow brighter and louder and sharper and more *real* when Grandaddy came. And it didn't matter that Grandaddy wasn't truly his grandfather, not in blood, but an old family friend, or some weird grownup attachment he didn't quite grasp. Grandaddy just *was*. Gabe knew in the deepest part of his soul that they were linked somehow.

He was eight when Grandaddy came again, and at eight Gabe felt like he was bursting out of his skin, that he might explode were he not given freedom—and yet he knew, too, in some weird instinctive way, that he was utterly clueless. He didn't know what he wanted. He didn't know what he needed. He just knew that he was lacking. That he was lesser. Wasn't badass. That he wasn't truly whole.

He woke up in the midst of a noisy nighttime thunderstorm and knew without a doubt that his grandfather had come. And just as he thought it, just as he *sensed* it, in some incomprehensible way, his grandfather opened the bedroom door and came in smiling, knelt beside the bed. Took into his broad right hand the small right hand of a boy, and stroked back the wayward locks of dark hair with his free left hand.

"God's bowling," Grandaddy said, as all outdoors was loud with angry rumbling.

Gabe stared up at him from the tangle of bedclothes. "God?"

"He's bowling," Grandaddy said. "That's what thunder is, the taking down of the pins."

He frowned. "No, it's not."

Grandaddy's brows rose up beneath a cascade of graying hair. "It's not?"

"No," Gabe said with supreme confidence, because he knew the truth. "That's *Thor.*"

For the first time in Gabe's brief life, his grandfather appeared to be at a loss. "Thor?"

"God of Thunder," Gabe replied. "Thor is *cool.*"

Grandaddy smiled. "Is he, now?" And then he lost his smile, grew earnest and serious. "It's time we had a talk, you and I. You won't remember it, but you need to *know* it." He tapped

5

Gabe's chest. "Bone-deep, *soul*-deep, you'll know it. We'll just let it sit in the back of your head for a while, buried behind everything else—you've a very busy brain, son—and one day, when it's time, I'll call it up in you, and you'll remember all of it. You'll know who you are, what you're meant to be, and what you're intended to do."

That, Gabe found intriguing. "*What* will I do?"

Grandaddy said, as the thunder rolled behind him, "You'll be a soldier, boy. Sealed to it. Life and limb, blood and bone, heart and soul. Not a soldier like others are, for it's not the kind of war most people fight on earth. But because we're not 'most people,' you and I, it will be far more important. The fate of the world will hinge upon it."

Gabe stared at him. "The whole entire world?"

Grandaddy's voice, though soft, carried the weight of thunder. "The whole entire world—and everyone in it."

Remi, awkward boy's limbs asprawl in abandonment on the plank wood of the covered front porch—his father, thank the good Lord, had hung a ceiling fan out here—scooched closer to his companion, rested the back of his skull atop the soft-furred bulk of a blue merle Australian Shepherd atwitch in his sleep. The day was hot, sticky, heavy, promising no relief until nighttime, and even that was chancy. At best the house was cooled by fans of all ilk; evaporative cooling didn't run right in humid weather, and they couldn't afford 'central air,' as it was known, those big units that blew chilled air through all the rooms and gave a man a chance to breathe, to fight the moisture and dry a sweat-damp body.

Remi was used to sweating.

He leaned against the dog, who yipped and woofed in dog dreams, and wondered what the stars thought. That they did think, he knew; they must. They hung up there in the sky, glowering down upon the world, knowing what all men thought. Knowing what *he* thought: Remiel Isaiah McCue.

Son, his Nana had said, not long before she died, *You're meant for larger things. I don't rightly know what those things are, but you're meant for 'em. And one day, they'll find you.*

But when? Remi wondered. And would these things, whatever they might be, manage to find a boy in the treeless, dusty expanse that was West Texas?

He trusted Nana. She said she saw farther than others, deeper; saw beneath the skin to the heart, and swore his was larger than most. Said there was enough soul in him for two people, if he let his light shine. That maybe he'd even share it.

Times he felt like his bones downright *itched*. He couldn't put a name to it. His skin just felt too tight for his bones, like they were growing faster than the rest of him. And it was hard to sit still, at times, like his body just needed to *move*, right along with his mind. That need ran like a river in full spate.

But he got caught up in school, and Friday night football under the lights, and learning to rope a plastic steer head stuck on a straw bale, driving a tractor, crawling out of bed with his big brother in the wee smalls of the morning to open the irrigation ditches so the water might flow to the alfalfa field. He hung out behind the chutes at the local rodeos, and Nana was long dead before he recalled what she'd said about his heart and his soul, and sharing his light, so he never got to ask her what she meant.

And then one day Grandaddy showed up and said it was time for Remi McCue to learn to throw a knife, being as he already knew how to shoot a gun.

Well, yeah. He was a Texas country boy. Shooting a gun came early.

Throwing a knife? Well, not so much. But by the time his old "grandfather" was done with him, Grandaddy said, Remi would understand how horn-and-steel felt in a hand, what balance was all about, and the pure seduction of letting a blade fly to its target.

Hell, yeah. Yeehaw. Though he wasn't sure, then, what *seduction* meant. But that was Grandaddy's way; he didn't treat Remi like a child, or like an adult, either, when he thought about it, but just as Remi.

He was eight when Grandaddy came again after being gone for a couple of years, and that man drove up to the house out of the maw of a big old Texas thunderstorm in his aged white T-bird with red leather seats. Gray hair remained a vigorous crop flowing nearly to his shoulders.

Remi stood on the porch as Grandaddy came loping through the rain, head ducked against the worst. When he reached the porch, he gifted Remi with a display of bright teeth in the thicket of a trimmed beard darker than his hair.

"God's bowling," he said.

Remi shook his head. "No, sir."

"No?"

"It's Thor. God of Thunder."

His grandfather froze upon the step, face blank, and then he smiled. It was a broad, secret smile, with pleased laughter

8

behind it; but not meant to be understood by any, perhaps, other than himself. "Is it?" he asked. "Thor?"

"Bring me Mjolnir," Remi said, envisioning the massive hammer as he raised his hand to grip an imaginary shaft, "and I'll conquer the world."

Grandaddy tilted his head, as if acknowledging something. "It's time we had a talk, you and I. You won't remember it, but you need to *know* it, bone-deep, soul-deep. We'll just let it sit in the back of your head for a while, buried behind everything else, and one day, when it's time, I'll call it up in you, and you'll remember all of it. You'll know who you are, what you're meant to be, and what you're intended to do."

"*What* will I do?" Remi asked, intrigued.

Grandaddy said, "You'll be a soldier, boy. Sealed to it. Life and limb, blood and bone, heart and soul. Not a soldier like others are, for it's not the kind of war most people fight. But because we're not most people, you and I, it will be far more important. The fate of the world will hinge upon it."

Remi stared at him. "The whole entire world?"

Grandaddy's voice, though soft, reminded Remi of a preacher at the pulpit. "The whole entire world—and everyone in it."

CHAPTER ONE

From out of the heat of the day and into looming twilight, I pulled onto gravel and threaded my Harley through a parking lot jammed with pickup trucks. Killed the growl of the engine as I rolled up next to a handicapped spot, stayed straddled as I pulled off my helmet and gloves and let the cool pine-scented air wash over me. Pure tactile, almost atavistic relief after hours on a hot interstate.

I yanked the tie from my hair and unstuck compressed strands from my skull with a couple of quick scrubs so it fell loose to my shoulders again. Unzipped the jacket. Left my ass parked on leather and crossed arms as I surveyed the building before me.

I had to smile. Not exactly my thing.

Now roadhouses, yeah. Definitely. But in the Patrick Swayze/Sam Elliott school. This? Nuh-uh. Pickup trucks, gun racks; a lighted sign boasting live country music. Probably spittoons on the floor, for all I knew. Maybe even a mechanical bull.

The building was a bulwark of massive, stripped pines chinked together rising two stories tall, topped by a rust-patinaed tin roof. Its slab of a front door looked thick enough to bounce cannon balls off of, and the entry steps were framed by a massive split-crotch tree. Behind it loomed the shoulder of a fire-ravaged mountain, and the dying of the day.

I heaved in a breath, blew it out on a sigh as I swung a leg across the seat. "Grandaddy, why the *hell* did you summon me to a cowboy bar in Flagstaff, Arizona?"

I clomped up the low steps in my biker boots and stepped aside as a laughing couple, nearly joined at the hip, exited. I caught the door's edge from the guy, pulled it wide, and the strains of that live country music erupted into the twilight.

I winced, thought uncharitable things about a music genre I cannot abide—all that whine and twang and mud and blood and beer—and prepared myself for an even noisier unwelcome assault upon my ears.

As always in strange places, particularly roadhouses and dive bars, which I tend to frequent, I entered carefully. Eased through the door, let it thump closed, then stepped aside and waited, marking the details of the place. Particularly the exits.

Live band, already established; parquet dance floor; booths against the wall; couple of pool tables in the back. Tables and chairs; long, polished slab of a bar; rough-hewn beams, tree trunk pillars; and so many mounted animals, trophy heads, skins, and antlers affixed to the walls that it looked more like a . . . well, yeah, the place *was* called the Zoo Club. Though it more closely resembled a taxidermist's. In fact, just beyond my right shoulder, crammed into the corner, loomed a ginormous huge-humped grizzly bear with mouth agape to display fearsome teeth.

I did not fit here, not in this place, where I was pretty much an alien. Cowboy hats, boots, plate-sized silver belt buckles, pressed jeans, yoked shirts. Me, I wore a plain black t-shirt, motorcycle leathers, and thick-soled boots meant for the road, not stirrups. I like my bars with chrome and steel and twinned wheels parked outside, where the only hint of horses resides within engines.

A flash of movement at the end of the bar. Seems I'd caught the notice of a young woman. And boy, did I notice back. Long wheat-blond hair was slicked away from her face and tied into a high ponytail hanging down her back. I couldn't see details in bar lighting, but the assemblage of her features collaborated quite nicely, well above the norm. Red lipstick. Her brows, darker than the gold of her hair, arched as her eyes brightened, and she smiled slow and easy, the invitation obvious. She did not appear to care that I was not in the cowboy uniform, or that my hair hit just past my shoulders.

Well, then. I smiled back, raised brows, lifted one shoulder in a half-shrug that told her *Not just now*, saw faint disappointment in the tilt of her head, the regretful twist of her mouth. Maybe later, if she were still around when business was concluded.

"Gabriel."

Even in the midst of roadhouse noise, I heard and knew that tone. With regret I shifted attention from the young lady to the man coming toward me.

Jubal Horatio Tanner, aka Grandaddy, the only one who called me by my full name. Tall, blue-eyed, clear-skinned, with a cascade of springy silver-white hair tucked behind his ears. Imposing man. To me as a kid, he'd seemed old; now, not so much, even with the near-white hair. Ageless, if anything. Rock of Gibraltar type. His brows remained dark, as did his neatly trimmed beard, though it bore a peppering of silver.

He wore, as he always did—for some unaccountable reason I kept forgetting to ask him about—an old-style frock coat, as if he'd stepped out of a Western. Which, inside a cowboy bar in Arizona, struck me as ironically appropriate. He fit. I didn't. Beneath the coat, unless he'd changed his ways, he wore a sheathed Bowie knife and a waistband holster, home to his 9-mil S&W.

We clasped hands, grinned at one another, then stepped close for a quick hug, slap of hands against backs before stepping out again.

"Too long, Grandaddy!" Couple of years, in fact. I raised my voice over the live band. "I thought you'd visit, at least." I didn't say more; he'd know what else I meant.

"Business," Grandaddy said crisply; no apology was included. "You know how that goes. I kept tabs on you." He touched a fingertip to his left eyebrow. "Your dad told me you got jumped."

I almost put my own hand up to that spot in my brow, but dropped it back down. I knew it was there: a thin, pale diagonal line, stitch-free now, but it looked like the hair wouldn't grow back.

I kept my tone light. "Too far from my heart to kill me."

Grandaddy's eyes were unrelenting. "You handle the man who jumped you?"

Handle him? Oh, yeah.

I lifted the scarred eyebrow. "We had us a 'discussion' right there in general population. Nobody bothered me after that."

What I didn't add was that it's tough to bother a man in solitary.

Grandaddy didn't respond, just gestured with a sweep of a broad-palmed hand. "I've got a table in an alcove in the back where we can talk privately. Remi's not here yet; he called to say he was running a tad late. Sorry to say that boy's *always* a tad late; his internal clock runs about as slow as his Texas drawl."

I started to ask who he meant, but Grandaddy'd headed off through the crowd. I followed to the alcove, discovered a pitcher of beer and a half-filled mug, two empty tumblers, a bottle of Patron tequila, and another of Talisker single malt sitting atop the table.

"Unless you've changed your brand of whiskey." Grandaddy flipped aside the tails of his frock coat as he sat down and took up his beer.

I couldn't suppress my grin of delight. "Hell, no. I still drink that whenever I can get it. But it's not usually on offer in biker bars." And anyway, I'd pretty much ridden nonstop to this watering hole with time only for coffee, prepackaged convenience store sandwiches. And, well, licorice. The black stuff. The *real* stuff.

"They don't carry it, so I snuck the bottle in under my coat," Grandaddy admitted, eyes bright with amusement.

Warm affection filled my chest. Damn, it was good to see the man again. I hooked out a chair, swung it around, pushed the back against the wall so I could keep an eye on the bar crowd, then sat my ass down and poured two fingers' worth of fine Scottish whiskey. Lifted the tumbler, let it linger at my lips as the pungent tang of spirits rose to my eyes. Took a sip.

Yeah, there it was, that complex peaty power. I just appreciated it in my mouth a long moment, then swallowed with a grateful smile and a nod of the head. I'd missed this while in prison. "So, this is all your doing, right? Early release, and now I report to you? Maybe the first time an ex-con has been assigned to his own grandfather."

Blue eyes were bright across the beer mug. As always, he *watched* me even as his posture suggested relaxation. "Mitigating circumstances, Gabriel."

I poured more whiskey, enjoyed another swallow. "Now, who's this Remi, and why are we meeting *here*? Why not Oregon, like usual?"

"Remi's coming in from Texas. Arizona splits the difference." Grandaddy drank beer, thumbed away liquid from his moustache, then fixed me with a steady gaze I remembered very well, even if I hadn't seen it for a couple of years. "Pay attention, Gabriel."

Okay, so it's like that. I'd heard those words, that tone, so many times over the years. It always prefaced information Grandaddy considered vital, even if it made absolutely no sense. I huffed air through my nose in amusement, grinned crookedly, nodded.

And he said, by way of pronouncement, "Remi is someone you're going to come to know very, very well, Gabriel. Someone with whom you will form a bond unlike any other. Someone upon whose actions your life will depend, and whose life will depend upon *your* actions."

For a long, arrested moment, drink suspended in midair on its journey to my mouth, I stared blankly at him. Found no illumination in his face. "My life?" I waited a beat; no answer was forthcoming. "As in, life and death?"

"Precisely life and death."

"Uhhh, okay." I set down the tumbler with a muted clunk, scratched at my bisected eyebrow. It itched now and then. "Can you kinda elaborate on that? Just—" I waved a hand in an indistinct gesture encompassing worlds of nothing much "—you know, for the sake of me knowing what the hell you're talking about?"

The eyes were penetrating. "He will have your back, and you will have his, pretty much twenty-four, seven, three-sixty-five."

I contemplated that announcement, knocked back more whiskey, then opted for candor. "That still doesn't tell me shit, Grandaddy."

Now he was quietly amused. "Not yet, no. We'll wait till Remi arrives, and then I will, as you say, elaborate."

I opened my mouth to question further, but gave up, knowing it was pointless. Grandaddy was often cryptic, and he could not be rushed. I'd learned not to push or things got more obscure. I could tie my brains into knots trying to sort out the man's intentions. "This Remi got a last name?"

"McCue. And—*ah*, speak of the devil." Grandaddy laughed softly. "Or not." He shoved his chair back, rose, extended his hand. "Remi, good to see you, boy."

I raised my brows. Unlike me, Remi McCue fit right in with the crowd. Dark denim western shirt, tucked in; neatly pressed jeans, leather belt with big silver buckle, cowboy boots, even an honest-to-God *hat*.

This was the man Grandaddy thought I'd *bond* with, what-ever the hell that meant. Upon whom my life was to depend.

A *cowboy?*

The booze warmed my belly. I gusted a laugh and sat back in my chair, grinning. "No offense, but . . . you gotta be shit-ting me!"

The stranger gazed down at me a long moment, registered that he was himself the target of the irony, and raised one elo-quent dark brow beneath the brim of his cream-colored hat as he made his assessment of me. In a clear tone he drawled, "Well, boy, looks to me like you're wearin' one of my steers in all that biker leather, so I wouldn't go sayin' much, was I you."

Ah. Okay. Like that, then. "You weren't me the last time I looked."

Grandaddy laughed. "Oh, in a way he is, Gabriel. While you're not related in a normal sense, there is a common genetic background. Take a harder look."

I did. Okay, yeah, the cowboy was around six-feet, one-eighty, so we were pretty much within an inch and five pounds of one another, and he had dark hair, too, but his eyes were a clear blue, not my brown. He was tanned, I wasn't; prison leaches melanin. Still, I had to concede we were of a similar physical type.

McCue smiled as he was given his second inspection. "Well, if Grandaddy says we resemble one another, then I'll have to say you *are* a handsome devil." He paused, lips pursing. "Might could do with a haircut, though."

Beneath the hat, McCue's hair was neatly trimmed and did not remotely approach the vicinity of his shirt collar, let alone his shoulder blades. I smiled back, not meaning it; you learned

18

to do that in prison. "And you're a poor man's Matthew McConaughey."

That, too, you learned there, to challenge before he did.

But the cowboy, patently unoffended and offering no return challenge, grinned slow, then drawled in deep tones, "All right, all right, all right."

"Remi, sit down and have something to drink," Grandaddy told him, before it went further, "and Gabriel, have another. You'll need the alcohol. I'm about to embark upon a foray into the expositional—and I guarantee you won't believe a word of it. All I ask is that you suspend your disbelief and hear me out."

I employed a booted foot to shove the empty chair toward the cowboy. He caught it, settled it, took his seat. We eyed one another in brief male-to-male consideration and evaluation, smiled blandly, poured drinks. My second went down easily. McCue drank Patron.

Grandaddy meanwhile assessed us like he was weighing our worth, marking things about the two of us I couldn't grasp. This was a man who *knew things*, who always struck me as a secret-keeper, but not out of ill-intent. Out of privacy and a wish to control what he said when he said it. Of what he viewed was *safe* to be said.

And just now, Grandaddy appeared to arrive at a conclusion. His smile was a brief, sardonic twitch. "Forgive me the melodrama, but I do promise that at some point, some day, all will come clear. I ask merely that you keep your minds open." His smile broadened. "I did train you for that."

Much as I wanted to, I didn't swear in frustration. Yeah, you don't push him, but Grandaddy could be more than a little frustrating at times. And a sideways glance at McCue suggested he felt the same as he smiled crookedly at me and twitched a shoulder, tilted his head in shared resignation.

But we waited. It's what you do with Jubal Tanner: you wait for pronouncements to be declared from *on high*.

He spoke quietly beneath the whine and twang of the music, but we heard him easily. In fact, everything else seemed eerily distant, muted. "You boys will go to bed tonight wiser than you are at this moment, yet ignorant of much more. That, you will learn as you go, if you survive—and yes, I mean that in the literal sense." The back of my neck prickled; Grandaddy's eyes were insanely compelling. "You know me as a close family friend, someone who *approximates* a grandfather. The relationship is complicated, but in truth we're all related."

The cowboy and I exchanged baffled glances. Related? What the hell?

Grandaddy smiled a little. "Not by blood or birth, as humans count it, but by birth*place*, and by certain bonds of that birthplace." He turned his beer mug in idle circles upon the table. "Where we come from, where *our kind* comes from, we are all of one body, but not biologically linked. Not as humans know it."

I stared at my—whatever he was. What the hell?

Grandaddy—it was the only name I'd known him by, and hard to shake—stared back. There was no tension in the man's body, no indication of anticipatory concern for the reception of his words; his attitude was that he'd merely stated the obvious.

And I heard him in my head again, saying, *All I ask is that you suspend your disbelief.*

CHAPTER TWO

I finally managed the question in a carefully calibrated tone. *"Our kind?"*

McCue's body language shouted that he was equally taken aback, but he'd latched onto something else. "Not as *humans* know it?"

Grandaddy nodded. "The long and the short of it is—neither of you boys were born entirely of mortal man and woman."

And then the music got real loud in my head, and I couldn't say a word. Couldn't *think* a word. All I could do was double-down my focus and stare fixedly at the man while my brain froze solid.

Remi McCue, after an equally paralytic moment, poured more tequila into his glass and sucked it right down. Then he cleared his throat and said, in a tone surprisingly casual under the circumstances, "Lick that calf again?"

Distracted, I shot him a look. "What the hell does that mean?"

McCue accommodated with a cheerful translation. "It's Texan for 'Excuse the fuck out of me.'"

Grandaddy just rolled on. "You are not entirely human. You were born of *heavenly matter.*"

The bar got louder yet. I blinked hard and slow, feeling empty of everything other than a turgid disbelief, an odd unsettled tautness in my belly.

I leaned forward, stuck my face into hands as I propped elbows on the table, and rubbed my forehead roughly. Replayed the last two sentences.

Uh-huh. Yeah. Right.

Of all the people in the world I'd have bet money would *never* lose his shit, Grandaddy headed the list. He, meanwhile, just sat there very quietly with gentle humor in his eyes and the faintest of smiles evident within a silver-peppered beard. He was, despite everything he'd stated, unaccountably and utterly relaxed.

The sky is blue. The sun sets and rises. Oh, and by the way—you're not human.

Okay, I'd inhaled legends, folklore, and mythology, grew up on science fiction and fantasy novels, movies, and TV shows. It was therefore a completely natural extrapolation from that background to wonder if maybe I'd slipped through a wormhole into another dimension, or crossed over into the *Twilight Zone*, or hopped aboard the TARDIS. For entertainment purposes, I'd learned long ago to suspend disbelief, just as Grandaddy asked.

Well, hell. Things had gone so far sideways as to be off the planet entirely. I might as well allow myself a Mulder Moment.

I lifted my head from my hands. "Are you an alien?"

"I am not," Grandaddy answered gravely.

After a pause, I nodded and poured another drink. I hadn't eaten for hours; I wanted *effect*, not flavor, and knew I could get it. I knocked it back fast, which was an abuse of fine single malt, but seemed called for under the circumstances.

I shot a hard glance at McCue, who gazed back in a sort of frozen consideration. I didn't know the guy, couldn't assess his thoughts, but it seemed that the cowboy was asking my opinion with a single arched brow.

I could do it. He could do it—the Spock brow lift. I wondered if we shared other habits, being sort of related, in a celestial kind of way. Which sounded—uncomfortably kinky.

It was easier to focus on a stranger than to contemplate what my—*our*—Grandaddy had said, even if he was sitting right there. "This is all kinds of batshit crazy," I told McCue, watching him closely for reaction, "and you don't even seem to be thinking *twice* about what bullshit we've just been told."

The cowboy shrugged, shoulders lifting the seams of his pressed denim shirt. He flicked a glance at Grandaddy, settled his focus back on me. "I'm listening to the man. That's how you learn. Open mind, he said." He hooked a thumb in Grandaddy's direction. "Besides, this man's been nothing but good to me. I owe him the courtesy of hearing him out. And if he taught you anything—and I'm betting he did—so do you."

I noted how the slow drawl softened, was less pronounced. And a spark in blue eyes suggested maybe McCue was taking this more seriously than I'd thought.

Grandaddy had never, in my life, lied to me. I knew it bone-deep. I *did* owe the man the courtesy of hearing him out.

But . . . *not born entirely of mortal man and woman?*

Open mind was one thing. Doable. Suspension of disbelief was another. Doable. But *this* was just utter, complete, absolute, one-hundred percent bullshit.

And I, who tolerates no bullshit for very good reasons, had learned that life does not always allow for open minds and

23

suspension of disbelief no matter how much you'd like it to. I'd been out of prison a matter of days. I'd just ridden over a thousand miles. Hadn't eaten in hours. Plus, I'd had just enough to drink, *felt* just enough of the alcohol to allow frustrated impulse to take over. From somewhere inside, from a crack in the wall I'd built a couple of years before, anger seeped in.

I shoved my chair back with a scrape of wooden legs on wooden planks, offered him a brief acknowledging tilt of the head, and set my palms against the table and started to push to my feet.

But then Grandaddy just *looked* at me, and I found myself somewhat vigorously reapplying ass to chair.

It hadn't been by choice.

And no one had touched me.

I sat because *physically I could do nothing else.*

I stared at Grandaddy in shock. Nah—well, maybe. "Did you just . . . did you just *whammy* me?"

"Have yourself another drink," Grandaddy suggested lightly, freshening his own beer.

I seriously considered flatly refusing. Came close. Did not. Under the circumstances—he had somehow *forced* me to sit my ass back down—it seemed the safest option to acquiesce. After a moment's subtle testing of whether my limbs obeyed again, and discovering they did, I had that drink, fast and hard. I craved the burn, the buffer bought by liquor that could be dropped between what I couldn't grasp and my own inner denials.

Or is it inner demons?

Just as I opened my mouth to ask a question, I became sharply aware of a new arrival at the table. At first I thought it was a cocktail waitress, then realized that no, it was someone else entirely: the ponytailed blonde I'd briefly communed with as I first entered the roadhouse.

I sat up and took notice. *All* of me noticed.

The alcove boasted one modest, muted light glowing down from the wall. It highlighted the exotic angles and planes of her face, the slant of her brown eyes. She glanced briefly at Grandaddy, at McCue, offered them a red-lipped smile, but focused her attention on me.

"Sorry to intrude . . . well, I lie: I'm not sorry at all. But since there are no ladies with you, I thought I'd take the bull by the horns, so to speak—" She slid a sidelong, amused glance at Remi's hat, then returned her attention to me, "—and see if you would care to dance."

I took a closer look than I had upon entry into the roadhouse. Tall, slim, simple red tank top, wheat-colored jeans, red boots that in no way could be considered cowboy, a doubled loop of gold chain around her throat to match hoops in her ears. In all circumstances other than those at present, I would have been happy to depart the table for the dance floor. She was most definitely my style.

But I'd just been told *I wasn't even human.*

I was not so drunk as to be dismissive of a woman, particularly an attractive one. I'd been in prison awhile. Instead, I smiled up at her from my chair, reached out a hand, took hers into it, leaned forward and pressed my lips against the back of it. "What are you drinking?"

Something flickered in her eyes. But she simply cracked her glass down against the table and said, "Whatever *you're* having."

I was markedly aware of how both Grandaddy and the cowboy watched us. McCue's crooked smile was slight as he drank tequila, but unquestionably present. Grandaddy merely waited, expression bland. I knew that look.

I ignored them both and poured two fingers' worth of scotch into her glass. "Let's look forward to a refill," I promised. "*Later.*"

Without breaking eye contact she scooped up the tumbler, knocked back the scotch, then turned and walked away from the alcove. The ponytail swung like silk against her red-sheathed spine.

"Huh," McCue said, with a world of complexities in that syllable. "Here we are in a cowboy bar, and it's the *biker* who draws the attention of a woman like that."

I offered a slow, broadening smile; the earth felt firmer beneath my feet. This dance, I knew. "Shit happens."

Remi grinned back, saluted me with a quick tilt of his head, then focused again on our grandfather. "So, Grandaddy . . . you were sayin' something about us bein'—*heavenly matter.*"

My amusement fled with that, as did lingering thoughts about the woman. Remi McCue seemed much too open to the bullshit, even if it was a man we'd known all of our lives saying it. Maybe the cowboy was batshit crazy, too.

"*Of* heavenly matter," Grandaddy clarified. "*Of* is not *it.*"

And sometimes a cigar is just a cigar.

Loose and lazy from the liquor, I sat back in the chair, slumping with one leg stuck out. I briefly considered trying to leave again, dismissed it even as I rubbed my brow; the last time hadn't worked out so well. And Grandaddy had that *look* on his face.

Infernal, that look. Dammit.

So. Okay. I'd play along. "But I'm still me?" I hooked a thumb in McCue's direction. "And he's still—him?"

"Of course." Grandaddy's tone suggested possibly I was an idiot. "You're flesh, blood, bone, brain, like everyone in this room. The fundamental difference in you both lies at a much deeper level. It's not physical. It's *essence*."

"Essence," McCue echoed blankly.

"When our kind is born," Grandaddy explained, "we are made of matter, of essence. Celestial energy, if you will. We do not have bodies. We're not human. But many of us are intended to exist on earth, and to do so we need hosts. In certain instances when a human newborn fails to thrive, or is too ill to live and the parents pray for intercession . . . well, heaven intercedes. And the newborns survive because the dying soul is replaced with the living spark born of heaven." He smiled. "Yes, you are indeed Gabriel Jeremiah Harlan, older brother of Matthew, who was born in the perfectly ordinary human way to Will and Elizabeth Harlan; and *you* are Remiel Isaiah McCue, younger brother of Lucas, born to Jack and Clare McCue in the perfectly ordinary human way. You didn't arrive in a clap of thunder, or spring fully formed from Zeus's brow. Your *flesh* is human. Your bones. It's just that your souls are not."

Struck again into silence, I noted the live band was, once more, really very loud, as if increasing whenever Grandaddy laid his weird bullshit on us. So was the crack of cue ball at the break, a scattering of stripes and solids. All sound seemed filtered directly into my brain, filled it up. There was no room for anything more. Certainly not the ability to suspend my disbelief and simply *accept* what we'd been told.

"Well, hell . . ." McCue said after a moment, seemingly at a loss.

"Not exactly," Grandaddy said with nuanced clarity. "Do you remember—and now, finally, I *mean* you to remember—when I said to you both, on separate occasions, that we would have a talk, but you wouldn't remember it until one day when I'd call the memory up in you? That you'd know who you are, what you're meant to be, and what you're intended to do?"

The memory, now bidden, came sharp: Yes, I did recall Grandaddy had said that, and apparently so did McCue, because he nodded as well. But I didn't remember what the topic of the talk was, just that we'd had one.

I shared a brief glance with the cowboy, then looked back at the man who claimed that he was after all our grandfather of sorts—but somehow wasn't, you know, human. Minor detail.

"Now is the time," Grandaddy said, "and I'll call it up in you—but it will be done gradually. The learning curve is steep."

I asked, wanting to be very certain that the alcohol, for all I desired its buffer under the circumstances, was not completely altering comprehension, "*Heaven* heaven? *Heaven*?"

Grandaddy silently lifted his hand in the air and pointed an eloquent forefinger upward.

Christ on a cracker. Or, so to speak. I scrubbed a hand over my face, trying to massage comprehension into a brain that preferred denial. Learning curve? How about utter craptastic bullpucky. "But—why?" I asked, trying for a neutral tone. "You're saying people just pray because their babies are dying, and all this little newborn heavenly matter gets stuffed down their gullets?"

28

Remi McCue laughed. "Now ain't *that* poetic?"

"We need human hosts," Grandaddy said, "but we don't *take* them. We're of heaven, not hell. We don't possess people. We answer prayers."

I cast him a skeptical glance, brows raised. "Every single prayer?"

Grandaddy's regret was sincere. "I wish it were otherwise, but that's not possible. There is a plan, you see . . . there's a grand design, but it's chaotic, not straight-line. Rather like evolution, it hops around, divides, ties itself into Celtic knotwork. To effect that design, to untie those knots, certain things are done. Certain things are allowed to be *und*one. Some prayers are answered, some are not." His eyes softened. "It's not always fair, what is undertaken, what gets set aside. We make difficult choices that are often incomprehensible to humans."

McCue's tone was overtly casual, yet I heard an edge. "But you need *babies*."

Grandaddy nodded. "Yes, we need human hosts. Adults generally don't ask or desire to be—*inhabited*. Naturally they don't want to give up their souls, to have them be replaced with another. But desperate parents with dying infants *do* pray for heaven to save their children, and newborn souls are merest threads that all too easily break." He spread his hands on the table, palm-down. "So, as they fray to the edge of breaking— and they do break all on their own; we force nothing—those threads are replaced with new. It's a matter of reciprocity. The babies survive, grow to healthy adulthood, and most bring great joy to their parents—when otherwise they die within an hour, a day, a week, and cause much grief and desolation." His eyes were brilliant even in soft light. "That is heaven's mercy, to give those parents a child. Then, at need, when those children are grown and on their own, we call on them."

I tapped the fingers of my left hand against the tabletop and glanced at the cowboy. "What was that you said earlier? About licking a calf?"

Rabbit hole time. Through the looking glass.

Grandaddy had said we wouldn't believe him. Damn straight.

I squinted into the bottom of my empty tumbler, noting a thin amber glaze of whiskey dregs. Maybe it would be easier to digest all of this if I was drunk off my ass.

McCue looked thoughtful as he drank more tequila, then absently tipped the tumbler on edge and rolled it in slow circles against the tabletop. He ventured a question. "So, we two had our so-called heavenly matter stored in dying babies, which saved them; and then we grew up like normal kids doing perfectly normal things . . . and now you *need* us?"

"Heaven does, yes," Grandaddy agreed. "But there are other reasons. You turned twenty-eight human years old a second past midnight, the both of you. It is of significance."

McCue frowned, but I shook my head decisively, certain of *this* much. "My birthday isn't for another week."

Grandaddy's brows twitched in dry amusement. "That's what you were told, yes. It is untrue. You were 'born,' as much as we ever are, in different states, to different families, but on the same day at the same hour and within seconds of one another. That's rare, especially for us—no one can gauge the instant heavenly matter coalesces into a soul—and it binds you." He shifted in his seat, leaning forward to compel our attention. "You are twenty-eight. Two, and eight. The numeral 2 governs certain attributes: harmony and rivalry, but also partnership and communication, shared ideals. As for the 8—" he closed one hand around the beer mug, raised it, "—it represents other elements: you are armed to lead, to direct. These things are what heaven needs of you both."

I caught back a blurt of laughter, but could not control skepticism. "Biblical numerology." I shook my head. "But aren't there other bits of heavenly matter out there? Other heaven-made babies now grown to adulthood? Not just us, right?"

"Of course. And we're calling—we've been calling—upon them all, and will continue to," Grandaddy replied. "Other souls, other birthdays, other numbers. Today it was you. Tomorrow, others."

McCue's laugh rode a choppy gust of breath. "In other words, you're saying we're not fish, and this isn't a mass spawning."

Grandaddy's brows rose briefly. "Colorful but accurate. No, in fact we skew the other way. Fewer, rather than greater numbers. That's why it was so unusual that the two of you were born almost simultaneously, and why we believe you may be of significance. But we don't promise you a rose garden because of it; in fact, there is danger in it for you, because now you'll be tracked. Targeted. You need to know this."

Grandaddy said it all very casually, without the weight of portentousness, of pretension. Which meant it was important, because I had learned to read him years before, much as I could: simple statements often meant more than others.

I cleared my throat. "Tracked how, and why?"

"By hell. *For* hell." Grandaddy downed more beer. "To simplify, the best way might be to say you have beacons inside you—"

31

Despite the booze, I felt sluggish alarm kindle. "Now we have *beacons* as well as essence?"

"—or internal GPS units, if you'd prefer, and at 12:01 last night—or, more accurately, this morning—they began the process of coming online."

I leaned down and smacked my forehead into a palm in disbelief; Grandaddy could be inexorable, once on a conversational path, and I had learned to stay out of his way.

"And to keep the metaphor consistent," he continued, "that means anyone with the right kind of receiver will be able to track you. Including hell."

I didn't even bother pouring myself a drink this time. I simply picked up the bottle and began to chug.

CHAPTER THREE

Under the noise of the bar, McCue's tone was intent. "In this case, a beacon, this GPS unit, is a light? Or maybe a shining soul?"

"You could put it that way," Grandaddy agreed.

"Uh-*huh.*" The cowboy smiled. "I guess Nana really could see under my skin."

"She had the Sight," Grandaddy confirmed. "And I believe she had an inkling of who I might be. Or *what* I might be." His brows twitched together briefly, as if he recalled something slightly less than pleasant. "I told you, we don't *possess.* But there are times we have to massage memories. I can't very well be everyone's actual grandfather . . . old family friend works nicely, but the adults must be *guided* to that understanding." Blue eyes flicked to McCue. "Your Nana saw more deeply than most."

McCue smiled. "Well, she said my soul shone brightly enough for two people. So maybe she sensed something about me, too." He looked at me, assessed briefly, raised his brows. "Of course if he keeps drinkin' like that, he may just drown all *his* light." He leaned forward, grasped the bottle in my hand, yanked it away and thumped it down upon the table out of my reach. "*Uisge beatha* like that is meant to be savored, not guzzled like it's horse piss. That's a dishonor to fine whiskey."

I squinted at him, startled the Texas cowboy pronounced the Gaelic correctly: ooishkay-bah. The booze was running in me, and the question just slipped out as I flicked a glance at his hat. "*You* know about *uisge beatha*?"

"Whiskey," McCue said. "Water of life. *Aqua vitae*. Yeah, I know all kinds o' shit. I was a Rhodes Scholar. Attended Oxford University and everything." He resettled his hat, smiled slow. Something in his tone suggested he'd found offense in my blurted question. "That would be Oxford, England, by the way. I may be just a redneck country boy to you, but I'm a damn *smart* redneck country boy."

Apparently I'd gotten under his skin. Equally apparently there was steel reinforcement underlying his good ol' boyness. "I do know what a Rhodes Scholar is," I pointed out. "I've got a Master's in folklore."

"Doctorate trumps Master's." The cowboy resettled in his chair and said cheerily, "Comparative Religion. And are you *always* this much of an a-hole to people you've just met?"

Well, after prison, yeah, probably I was. Especially being halfway to drunk. But *why* I was an a-hole wasn't any of his business.

I opened my mouth to answer, but Grandaddy cut me off. "You boys done pissing? Or do you want to keep whipping it out and measuring? I know I said rivalry goes with the birthday territory, but right now there's no time for this *mano a mano* malarkey."

I sighed, blinking one eye, then the other to clear my

booze-blurred vision. Realized I should have eaten when I had the chance. "Can we cut to the fuc—" But I broke that off, because I caught the hard look in a hard blue eye; Grandaddy did not approve of vulgar language. "—chase?"

Grandaddy reached inside his frock coat, drew out two small leather boxes. "Happy Birthday. Put them on: right hand, middle finger. Then shake on it."

"And what happens then?" I asked with suspicion, rubbing my brow. Most of my face felt numb. "We go to Oz? Hoth?"

Grandaddy laughed. "You'll power up your beacons out of sleep mode, punch them to 100 percent. As I said, consider them heavenly GPS units."

McCue looked thoughtful. "I thought you said hell can track us through these beacons."

"Yes, though not at every instant. But heaven can as well. That will come in handy now and then."

I, too, wanted clarification, even inside my booze-addled head. "Are we supposed to *do* something with them?"

Grandaddy smiled widely and bared white teeth. "Use them to save the world, boys. That's what you'll do with them. And it's time you two got down to business, because when you watch the news and read the papers you may think things seem bad now, but they're going to get a whole lot worse. Because this place has just become the devil's playground." He paused. "And I do mean that, boys. *Literally*, Lucifer's playground. Because he's coming. The war has already begun."

McCue snorted. "You don't look much like him, but you're sounding an awful lot like the preacher back home."

"Jacob Tarnover," Grandaddy said promptly. "I know him well. A devout man."

The cowboy was startled. "You know him personally?"

"I know many people. I travel a lot." Grandaddy nudged the leather boxes closer. "Open your presents. Do as I said: right hand, middle finger. Shake on it."

I took up the small box closest tome, flipped back the hinged lid, saw the heavy signet ring: silver pentagram embedded in a matte black stone, silver bezel and band. A glance at McCue's showed the same.

We stared at one another. My mouth twitched even as his brows rose. It was just too damn obvious. Low-hanging fruit. I saw a glint in his eye.

Simultaneously, we intoned, *"One ring to rule them all."*

Grandaddy grimaced. "You are the children of pop culture, I see. Well, I can play, too: *'One ring to bring them all and in the darkness bind them.'* And that's *exactly* what you're going to have to do to win this war: in the darkness bind *him*. For good. Throw Lucifer back into the pit."

"This is all kinds of bullshit," I insisted, but knew, somewhere along the line, I'd lost the battle to make any kind of impact on the proceedings. Probably when Grandaddy sat my ass back down without moving a finger.

McCue grinned, held his ring up in the light. "Well, boy, you ready for this rodeo?" He had a way of slurring "boy" into two syllables, forsaking the hard "y."

What the hell. Grandaddy clearly expected something to happen. I figured it would, or it wouldn't, and I felt the whiskey enough to be willing to give it a try.

I shoved the ring on, held out my hand. McCue took a little more time, seating the ring carefully on his finger, then extended his hand. We met one another's eyes. No doubt he felt as foolish as I did. But we closed, clasped. Silver clicked faintly as the rings met.

My heart thumped hard. Ears buzzed. I was blind, then not. The world spun. Stilled.

"Shit!" I cried, even as McCue did.

I felt like I was in the middle of a marathon and out of breath. Was I glowing? Were we glowing? Were our damn beacons shining? Were we transmitting to hell?

Hands joined, silver rings touching . . . I definitely felt something. And McCue felt it, too; I could see it in his eyes. Deep inside, I sensed a certainty. A comfortable acknowledgement of . . . something. *Some*thing. Some *thing*. Hell, I was out of words.

Maybe I'd never had words for a moment, an awareness, like this.

And I disliked it intensely. You don't just go around binding yourself to a total stranger to fight with the host of heaven to stop Armageddon. You just *don't*.

Grandaddy seemed to think you do. "This is how it shall be," he said quietly. "Always. You're bound now. Life and limb. Blood and bone. You are not immortal. You are not superheroes. Your bodies are wholly human. It's the beacon—the *soul*— that's the heavenly matter. So look after one another. Keep yourselves alive. It will not always be easy. But you are needed. The Adversary has loosed his vanguard. Now it's our turn to do the same before the End of Days."

I wanted to accuse him of invoking Charlton Heston at the Red Sea. I did not. Images filled my head.

Satan. Lightbringer. Son of Morning. Son of Dawn.

Fallen archangel, thrown down from heaven itself.

I released McCue's hand, stared at the ring hugging my middle finger. Even drunk, I remained aware of—whatever it was. Indefinable, but, again, *something*.

McCue inspected his own adornment. "Beelzebub. Belial. Diabolus. For real?"

Grandaddy nodded. "None other. This rose, by any name, doesn't smell sweet at all. Because it's corrupted, and it is *foul*."

The cowboy thought that over, dark eyelashes hiding most of his eyes. Then he nodded, sighed. "Well, *that's* about as welcome as an outhouse breeze."

I rested my head in one hand, elbow propped against the table, and contemplated the half-empty bottle of single malt. A vague thought drifted through that in the morning I might be convinced none of this had happened, so long as my brain did not bleed out of my head on a river of *uisge beatha*. I was so far gone now I figured I had nothing of worth left for the hot blonde who'd drunk my scotch.

I considered mourning that—and it was worth mourning, I was certain—but my unmoored attention drifted onto another topic. "So, it's Good versus Evil, is it?" I side-eyed McCue, then shifted back to my grandfather, who had said of the cowboy: *He will have your back, and you will have his, pretty much twenty four, seven, three six five.* "You want us to work together? Him and me?"

"Because of the synchronicity of your birth, it was always the intent. And now you're sealed to it." Grandaddy's eyes glinted. "Rivalry, as I said, but also harmony, partnership, shared ideals."

Again I shot a glance at McCue, noted his closed expression, returned my attention to Grandaddy. I knew what I was about to say would be considered rude, but I had a point to make. "Look—and yes, I know I sound like an a-hole—but I don't even *know* him, Grandaddy. We're strangers to one another. Now you say we're responsible for one another's lives?"

"Everyone begins as strangers," Grandaddy countered, "except in heaven. We are of one host, boys. We're made of the same matter."

"Resistance is futile," I quoted in derision. "But, you know, I'm not really into the whole assimilation thing."

McCue smiled. "Hell, boy, you might could find me a downright sociable man."

"Oh, God," I muttered, too drunk to mind my tongue. "He really *is* Matthew McConaughey. Or Sam Elliott. Or—" I waved a hand in a circular but nonspecific direction "—anyone else who talks that Hollywood cowboy talk."

"West Texas," Remi McCue corrected. "Never been to Hollywood."

I fixed Grandaddy with a stare bordering on stink-eye. "So if my new bestie and I are made of heaven's matter, what the hell are you? Some kind of, I don't know . . . *angel?*"

Grandaddy smiled. "Let's just say I'm an agent of heaven."

I pressed the heel of my hand against my brow and swore, but beneath my breath so Grandaddy wouldn't hear it. Then muttered, *"Please* tell me you're not going to grip me tight and raise me from perdition."

Remi shot me an amused glance. Grandaddy just rolled on. "You're the weapons I've prepared, the grenades we'll hurl, the landmines we'll place. But in the meantime . . . well, let's tug on Superman's cape just a tad, shall we?"

McCue grinned and actually *sang* the next line about

spitting into the wind, which was a downright unhealthy thing to do as well as being messy.

I stared at him, refused to sing the next line of the Jim Croce song, because I didn't want to think about the Lone Ranger and his damn mask, and I never sang in bars. Especially if they were playing godawful country music.

I shifted against the chair back, propping a boot more heavily against the floor to keep from sliding off my ass. "Just *how* do we go about tugging on that cape?"

"By killing things."

Holy hell. The back of my neck prickled.

The expression in Grandaddy's eyes told me he knew exactly what kind of impact that simple sentence had on me, and why.

The cowboy stirred uneasily. "Grandaddy—"

"I said *things*," Grandaddy said clearly. "Not humans—well, unless certain humans insist; there *are* evil people out there. No." He looked at us both for a long moment. "I told you. Lucifer has loosed his vanguard. Well, he was never stupid, that archangel. Just too proud, too arrogant, too ambitious. He had, shall we say, an overdeveloped sense of entitlement."

McCue's smile hooked sideways again.

"And it cost him heaven," Grandaddy went on. "So, if *you* were a smart, devious archangel stuck in hell and wanted to begin softening up the world for your long-prophesied return, how would you go about it?" He leaned forward, tapped a forefinger on the tabletop. "You would exploit *disbelief*. You would exploit *skepticism*. You would *use* all those things people believe don't exist. Legends, stories, myths." He looked at me. "You're the folklorist. Don't you believe?"

Oh, this was undoubtedly a trap. I recognized it from childhood. With care, I allowed, "Much folklore has roots in some *portion* of reality. Something happened, or existed, that inspired the stories."

"Same with religion," McCue agreed.

"But that doesn't mean every detail is true," I continued, launching into a lecture mode I hadn't used in years. "We're here in the Southwest, so let's take the urban legend of the chupacabra, the Mexican goat-sucker. Is there really such a beast? I don't think so. What I believe is that someone saw a big-ass feral dog, or an oversized coyote, probably mange-ridden and half hairless, killing a goat for a meal." I hitched one shoulder into a shrug. "Well, hell, *that's* boring. And maybe the guy was drunk, or high on weed or peyote, so he made a tall tale out of it."

McCue was nodding. "We have that legend in Texas, too. Reports of sightings crop up from time to time, and animal deaths that are believed to be caused by a chupacabra."

"Sure," I agreed. "That's because these kinds of stories are like contagious infections. And there are always gullible people, or hoaxers; or total whackjobs, too, who buy anything." I paused. "And conspirorists."

McCue stared at me. "Conspirorists? That's a thing?"

"Conspiracy theorists." I shrugged. "Saves a word."

Grandaddy said quietly, "And so, too, are there skeptics who dismiss everything." Despite the pallor of bar lighting, his eyes burned brightly. "There was a man, a French poet, who understood. It's a famous quote, and you'll undoubtedly recognize it, or some form of it. Charles Baudelaire said: *The greatest trick the devil ever pulled was convincing the world he didn't exist.*"

After a long moment, I expelled a chuffing sigh. This was going nowhere at hyperspace speed.

"I'm an accommodating man," McCue said, in a more circumspect tone, "and I like to think of myself as open-minded. But. You know there has to be a 'but.' Convince me."

"There were several earthquakes in the last month," Grandaddy said quietly. "Japan, Turkey, South America, Russia, New Zealand, Northern California, other places as well. The ground opened up in each of those places, and things came out."

I had been somewhat aware of the news in prison, if not intimately acquainted with it, but became more familiar on the ride down the coast via overhearing snatches of conversation in bars and restaurants. *"Things?"* I quoted, wary.

"The devil's surrogates. And they have assumed many guises." His look on me was intended to be quelling. "Yes, Gabriel, it is indeed just as you said: everything in folklore, everything in the tallest of tales, in all the myths—even religion, as Remi noted—has roots in reality."

I wanted to clarify. "I said *portions* of reality."

Grandaddy nodded. "Which assumes at least a spark of it. Even a minute speck of reality is still reality."

I was too drunk to parse semantics with a man as clever as this one, so I just squinted at him.

"When hell's vents opened," Grandaddy said, "our reality was altered. It's been expanded upon. Those minute specks are now much larger. Therefore all those ghosties, ghoulies, things that go bump in the night, are now very real, and have been for some time. So are werewolves, vampires, black dogs, poltergeists, even your goat-sucking chupacabras, plus countless other members of the dark hierarchy. But worse than that—"

"Worse?" I yelped.

"—many now host surrogates, or will. And if a surrogate climbs inside any of those so-called mythical hosts, the threat is trebled. They are all of them *Lucifer's* creatures, made of *hell's* matter, not heaven's. Far worse than the stories."

"*Surrogates?*" I repeated. "I take it you're not talking about political mouthpieces and spin doctors."

Grandaddy said, "Another name is *demon*. But we avoid that in public."

McCue said after a moment, as if in passing, "Well, that's handy as a latch on an outhouse door."

I grunted. "I think an argument could be made that political surrogates might actually *be* demons."

Grandaddy ignored me. "Faith is certainty without evidence," he said. "Faith is safety. Disbelief? Well, these days, that's a doorway to surrogates. It allows them to enter. To wreak havoc among unbelievers."

I stared at him. If Baudelaire had nailed it, Lucifer was indeed one damn smart fallen archangel. But . . . "That's a narrow mythos, Grandaddy. There are more religions in the world than Christianity, and more holy books than the Bible. Folklore is of all cultures."

"A rose by any name, Gabriel."

"And every religion has a villain," McCue said. "Don't matter what he's called. Or she. Or it. Evil's evil."

"There are questions to come, and answers," Grandaddy said, "but regardless of the name of the belief system and its own rituals, whatever they may be, the war has begun. The harbingers have risen. They've come to pave the way, to destroy. So we must destroy them. As of tonight, you two are being employed. Being *de*ployed." He swallowed beer, brushed moisture from his mustache, then gazed benignly upon us both. "Childhood's over, boys. Happy Birthday. Happy *Re*-Birthday. You're now in the vanguard of the heavenly host."

After a moment, McCue grinned slow, though something in his eyes spoke of an emotion other than amusement. "Well, ain't that just sweeter than stolen honey?"

I blinked hard, tried to clear my vision. He was wearing two hats. Had two faces. But I had to ask. "Is that for real? That accent?"

"I am Texas born and raised . . ." And then he broke off, appeared to reconsider that this claim, in view of what our grandfather had divulged, perhaps needed amending. "Texas *raised*, at least. It sticks to you. And ya'll better get used to it."

"But it—" I flipped a hand back and forth, "—waxes and wanes."

McCue smiled. "Depends on when it's good ol' boy affectation or just me talkin'."

I, with a mind not as sharp as it had been before so much whiskey, decided against continuing that topic and turned to Grandaddy and cut to the chase. "Since we're angels, do we at least get wings?"

Grandaddy shook his head decisively. "You're not angels. Not yet. For now, you're almost entirely human. Baby steps, boys. It will take you time." His eyes were on me. "But as of tonight you will begin to recall certain things, and those memories will guide you."

"Almost entirely human," I quoted dryly. "Almost entirely? Isn't that an oxymoron?" When Grandaddy didn't answer, I heaved a sigh. "So, I'm an angel-wannabe. Except I don't wanna be."

And McCue, for no reason I could remotely begin to decipher, began quietly to sing. Again. But it wasn't what the band was playing.

My head was throbbing. "*Now* what are you singing?"

"It's a country song. Charley Pride. 'Kiss an Angel Good Morning.'"

I gazed at him in frank disbelief. "A guy we believed was our old family friend is *an agent of heaven*—and *I'd* call that an angel, myself—we've got heavenly GPS units inside us, we're supposed to save life, the universe, and everything—and you're singing *Charley Pride?*"

McCue shrugged. "I can sing Willie Nelson, if that floats your boat into calmer waters. Maybe 'Angel Flying Too Close to the Ground.' Which might could be really appropriate, if things are fixin' to go sideways."

I grabbed up the whiskey and began chugging straight from the bottle again.

CHAPTER FOUR

I awakened hard and fast with the thick, acrid taste of sour bile in my mouth.

Whiskey. Too much. I'd drowned in it, bathed in it, soaked my brain and gut in it. I had a hard head for booze, but not like this; not so much *gulped* in so short a time, especially being off booze for so long thanks to an unexpected vacation behind bars.

What was it Grandaddy had said—?

Oh. Yeah. Angels and babies and heavenly matter and *beacons*.

And hell.

And Lucifer.

Shit.

I had no clue where I was. It was dark, but a glint of light pierced the room along the junction of blackout curtains. Beyond, I heard traffic. I rolled out of bed—literally—and a quick glance proved it was a motel room. But I didn't recall *getting* a motel room.

Nonetheless they came with bathrooms, did motels, and bathrooms came with toilets, and I resolved then and there to pray to the porcelain god. I hastened to make heaving obeisances, rinsed out my mouth when my belly stilled, then lay sprawled upon the tile floor and welcomed the coolness that soothed my face.

And then, despite the muddlement in my head, *memories* swarmed in.

It had happened so long ago—I'd been twelve—but I remembered it clearly because it hurt like holy hell.

It hurt my little brother, that is. At first. Then it hurt *me*.

It was an accident, but also an example of manifest stupidity. And it nearly got Matty killed.

After the out of control bike with its ten-year-old blindfolded passenger crashed into the neighbor's car parked at the bottom of the hill, I went tearing to the house screaming for Grandaddy, who was babysitting while our parents were away, who came out the front door with a frown upon his face asking what on earth I was yelling about and did I want to wake the dead? Not a wise thing, waking the dead. They were not pleasant companions.

Whereupon I poured out the whole story, ending with the frenzied claim that it was an accident, a terrible, horrible accident, but I appeared to have killed my brother.

Matty, as it turned out, wasn't dead, just knocked half-silly and had a broken arm. Grandaddy scooped up his disoriented charge, carried him into the house, set him carefully upon the couch, examined his injuries.

I, panic-stricken, could barely stand still. And when Grandaddy at last said that my baby brother would survive and turned his clear blue eyes upon me, I blurted, "I'll do anything to take the pain away. Give it to *me*! It's my fault!"

Grandaddy asked, in a very soft voice, "Why on earth did you tell him to wear a blindfold while riding his bicycle down a hilly street?"

I hugged myself, shoulders thrust nearly to my ears. "It was just something to do. I don't know. I don't know. It just was a dare. It was stupid, I was stupid!" I looked fearfully at my brother. "Matty, I'm sorry!" I thought the pain and the dull bewilderment in my brother's eyes might kill me. It hurt me to my soul. "Make it stop," I pleaded. "Make him better. Give it to me. Please."

Grandaddy stared hard at me, weighing me against something; I just wanted him to hurry up. "There is a way," he said after a moment, "that serves two purposes. One will relieve him of his pain."

"Do it, Grandaddy!"

"The other will teach a lesson to a very foolish older brother. One who should know better, who should always protect his younger brother. It's a stewardship, Gabriel."

I knew I'd broken a trust. While my father didn't spare the rod, Grandaddy had never laid a hand on me and never would. But his disappointment mattered terribly.

And Matty?—Matty didn't deserve what had come of his ill-advised journey down the hill with a blindfold on his eyes as his older brother laughed like hell, a journey only undertaken because he worshipped me and didn't want to let me down.

Matty was crying and his eyes looked weird, like he couldn't see straight.

I nodded frantically. "Anything, Grandaddy. Take the pain away."

His voice remained quiet, but compelling. "Will you bear it for your brother?"

I looked at Matty sobbing on the couch. "Always, Grandaddy. I will." I nodded hard. "I'll always take his pain. I don't want Matty to hurt. I don't want him to be hurt. Let it be me. Let me bear it."

Grandaddy's hand was gentle on Matty's dark hair, but he looked at me. "You consent to this?"

I nodded decisively again, and felt the weight of his gaze. I wanted to look away, but Grandaddy did not tolerate any display of submission. Obedience was required, yes; never submission.

"Do you understand?" he asked. "If you do something stupid, if you do something wrong, there are always consequences. You might have killed your brother."

I looked at Matty again, then wiped at my own welling eyes. I thought my chest might burst apart. "I know," I whispered. "I know, Grandaddy."

"Do you understand, Gabriel?"

I nodded fast and hard.

"And do you understand the concept of primogeniture?"

"All passes to the firstborn son," I answered promptly; I'd learned that from Grandaddy years before. "The eldest inherits all."

"Including the rights and responsibilities of his siblings," Grandaddy said. He looked down at Matty, ran a gentle hand through his hair. "It's far more than land, than wealth, than material goods. It's the stewardship of the younger. Matthew is yours, Gabriel, as much as he is your parents,' and mine. Do you understand?"

I nodded.

"You're old enough, now," Grandaddy noted, meeting my eyes once more. "Perhaps you're ready."

I realized then he was thinking about something deeper, something more than just healing his youngest grandson and teaching his eldest. "I'm ready."

Grandaddy wasn't quite Grandaddy anymore. He was other. He was *more*. He wore the face of a man, but reminded me of a story where a man bore the soul of something ancient, and far more powerful.

"Do you accept this responsibility willingly?" Grandaddy asked. "Even all the pain that accompanies it? It's a binding, son. A very powerful one."

I knew it soul-deep, in the parts of me that bore my name, my selfhood. "I accept it, Grandaddy. Willingly."

Grandaddy smiled, teeth glinting briefly in the beard. "Don't gird your loins quite so hard, Gabriel. It's not like that. No trumpets, no white light. You'll just know. It's duty, and honor, and love, and loyalty, and utter devotion. It's what no man can take from you. But you can surrender it should you choose."

I was certain. "I never would."

Grandaddy marked his sincerity. Nodded. "Hold out your arm, Gabriel."

I did so, and Grandaddy touched it even as he touched Matty's, and the pain passed from my brother to me.

It hurt. It hurt bad. Against my expectations, against my will, I gasped noisily and tears slipped free.

I'd done this to Matty. I'd done this to my brother.

Grandaddy didn't heal my arm once I assumed the pain. Grandaddy made me bear the consequences of my own actions: a broken arm, and a concussion.

But neither mattered. What mattered was my brother, and

even as I inherited Matty's pain, stunned by its force, my brother fell asleep right there on the couch.

"Primogeniture. Or, as we say, *primogenitura*," Grandaddy told me. "It's now coded into your soul."

As I sat upon the bathroom tile and blinked myself out of the *then* and back into the *now*, I heard the door open. Despite the protests of stomach and head, I heaved myself upright, made it to knees, reached for the knife sheathed once again at my spine—except it wasn't there.

"Hey," called a voice. "Is it alive?"

I climbed to sock-clad feet—where the hell were my boots?— clung to the door jamb. Steadied myself, took one step into the room. Saw a man silhouetted briefly against the daylight beyond the open door. A man wearing a cowboy hat.

Okay, probably didn't need a knife with him.

"You are a walkin', talkin' example of 'rode hard and put away wet,'" announced the hat. "Though maybe talkin' is a bit beyond you just this minute." He closed the door behind him, shook the paper bags in his hand. "I picked up some grub. You want anything to eat? Grandaddy'll be here soon."

I frowned, rubbed at my brow. Picked grit out of my eyes. Heard Grandaddy again, inside my head.

"Do you accept this responsibility willingly? Even all the pain that accompanies it? It's a binding, son. A very powerful one."

I knew it soul-deep, in the parts of me that bore my name, my selfhood. I'd said, *"I accept it, Grandaddy. Willingly."*

I now stood upon the cusp between bathroom and bedroom and stared at the stranger. Grandaddy had said I would remember things. And I had. I recalled the day I caused my brother to crash. But this guy wasn't Matty.

"Food?" he asked. "Or maybe hair of the dog? We found a flask of whiskey in your saddlebags."

"Primogenitura," Grandaddy had told me. *"It's now coded into your soul."*

I blinked hard, thinking about Matty, an older Matty, then pushed those memories away with a hard inner thrust of denial. Not now.

I ran a hand through tangled hair, snagged some in the ring I'd donned at Grandaddy's behest. Stared blankly at it a moment, then looked back at the cowboy.

McCue? McCue.

"My bike," I rasped, throat sore from vomiting. "Where is it?"

"Outside," he answered. "Grandaddy and I hauled your ass here, dumped you on the bed, then went back and fetched your bike."

I was appalled. "You rode *my bike*?"

Remi McCue set bags and cups upon the table, moved into something approaching daylight, though dim. Then he ran open the blackout curtains, and I winced away from the vicious assault of daylight.

"Son, I been ridin' roughstock for years. Bulls and broncs. A Harley's downright polite compared to them."

I stared at him. A stranger who wasn't, quite, according to Grandaddy. And there was definitely a strong resemblance between the two of us.

"Everyone begins as strangers—except in heaven. We are of one host, boys. You're made of the same matter."

I felt a chill touch the base of my spine. "I didn't dream it,

53

did I? Any of it?" Well, except for Matty's childhood incident, which I hadn't thought about in years.

"Nope, not a dream," the cowboy said. "Well, unless we had us the *same* dream. He gave us a plateful, Grandaddy did. While you were snoring off the whiskey, I did me some thinking. The man has *never* lied to me. Not in my life. And this—" he raised a hand into the air, displayed the ring, "—well, I felt something. And so did you."

"You're bound now. Life and limb. Blood and bone."

I gazed again at the ring on my right hand. The middle finger, not the ring finger. Symbolically, the longest finger represented Saturn, the Balance Wheel, a sense of right and wrong, the law, the search for truth and propriety, self-analysis, secretiveness.

Yeah, I figured being born of *heavenly matter* maybe led one to self-analysis and secretiveness.

Silver pentagram set in hard black spinel. Five-pointed star contained within a doubled circle. Co-opted of late by some as representative of black magic, but in early Christian symbolism the basic upright pentagram represented the five wounds of Christ and was considered *protection*. Alpha and Omega. A spinel, in lore, supposedly boosted energy to power up a spiritual quest. Silver was a precious metal representing purity, purpose, vision, and strength.

Well, couldn't be a whole lot more symbolic than all of *that*.

Something flew across the room. I caught it out of instinct. "Hair of the dog," McCue said. "Settle that head. Grandaddy wants to go hiking. Has some more to explain, he says."

It was my own flask, silver, embossed with a Celtic cross. I unscrewed the cap, raised it briefly in thanks, sucked down whiskey, then gazed at McCue. I had most certainly been drunk the night before, drunker than I'd been in a long time, but an alcoholic blackout was not numbered among my experiences, not even last night. And I remembered this guy.

Then I focused on what McCue had said. "Hiking? Does the man not know what a hangover is?"

Remi laughed. "Well, that's what he announced. *We'll go up the mountain, gaze upon the world, and listen.* That's what he told me last night, when we dragged your ass in here." He smiled. "Pretty much what I've always done when Grandaddy came calling, though we don't really have mountains to speak of in Texas. So mostly we walked along the arroyo. You?"

There were mountains in Oregon, and I had climbed some with my grandfather. But I didn't say so. Just stared at him. He stared back, expression bland. *I don't know you*, I thought. *And I don't want to know you. I've lost too much. I can't invest again.*

And Grandaddy was in my head once more. '*Remi is someone you're going to come to know very, very well. Someone with whom you will form a bond unlike any other. Someone upon whose actions your life will depend, and whose life will depend upon your actions.*'

"You know what this reminds me of?" McCue asked.

I shook my head.

"Movies where aliens show up, or elves, or witches, and no one seems ever to have heard about 'em. Like it's all *new.*" He shrugged. "I mean, yeah, I'm a little skeptical about Area 51, but at least I'm *aware* of it."

"The UFO crash at Roswell," I added.

"We *know* about angels," McCue said. "We know about Lucifer and Armageddon. The concept isn't new. It's just—disbelieved. As reality, I mean. As possibility."

I blew out a noisy breath. "Yeah."

"*Maybe* Grandaddy's lost his mind," McCue observed. "Maybe he's senile—unless of course he is what he says he is . . . I don't rightly think heavenly creatures possess the capacity to *go* senile, do they?" He shrugged. "Hell if I know. But I'm going to listen to the man."

I leaned hip and shoulder against the door jamb. I hated admitting any kind of weakness, and muddled memory, in my view, is indeed a weakness. But I got no vibe from Remi McCue that suggested the man was looking for an edge, for leverage. What I sensed was calmness and possibly an inability to take offense. Which might come in handy if we really *were* meant to work together.

I'd been alone a long time. And this guy is not what I'd pick for a shiny new bestie. Nothing against him, but—a biker and a cowboy?

I looked at him, thinking back to something Grandaddy had said. "What's your name again? Your full name?"

"Remiel Isaiah McCue," he replied. "Remi for short. And you're Gabriel—what?"

"Gabriel Jeremiah. Gabe."

The cowboy grunted. "Makes more sense, now, though, don't it? Biblical names. Seems we were named after some big-hat celestial beings."

I cast my line carefully, with single-word bait. "Grandaddy's an *angel.*"

"Agent of heaven," McCue corrected. "Or so he said."

"Come on, man, seriously? Like a sports agent? I don't think so. Angel in disguise, maybe."

Remi shrugged. "He can call himself whatever he likes, I

guess. I got on my phone last night, did some browsing. I'm somewhat acquainted with the whole angelic hierarchy thing, thanks to schooling, but never thought of it in terms of *family*." His eyes were steady. "You buyin' what he said?"

I frowned. "Sure sounded like *you* were last night."

"I got no reason to disbelieve the man," McCue said flatly. "If you look at various cultures and religions, there are commonalities of context that suggest such things as celestial beings—or whatever you want to call them—exist."

I drank more whiskey out of the flask. "Maybe."

"You're a folklorist. Master's, you said?"

I nodded.

"But I take it from what you said last night that you don't believe everything you read."

I gusted a cut-off laugh. "Hell, no."

A corner of his mouth twisted. "But I'll bet you believe that much of folklore has arisen out of 'commonalities of context.'"

I smiled, tipped the flask, then screwed the cap back on and deflected again. "I'm guessing you do."

McCue picked up one big cup, offered it. "Coffee. I don't know how you like it; I brought back creamer and sugar, too."

"Black. Thanks." I unwound myself from the door jamb, tossed the capped flask to my bed, took the steps necessary to place myself within reach of nirvana. Even fast food coffee was better than none at all, though the room likely offered a whopping two whole servings via sealed foil bag and cheapo coffeemaker. A glance at the other bed showed me a somewhat rumpled bedspread. "You sleep here?"

McCue smiled. "Grandaddy and I weren't sure you wouldn't choke on your own puke last night, so yeah. We did you the courtesy of removing your boots, but that was it. So your virtue's still intact."

I grunted, peeled back the hatch on the plastic cup lid, sucked down coffee. It had often crossed my mind that this brand was more like 3,000-mile motor oil than actual coffee. Now, in the Pacific Northwest? *That* was coffee. And it needn't be pussied up with various flavorings, either.

"*'Commonalities of context,'*" I said after a few swallows, quoting Remi.

McCue sat down in the chair beside the small table, opened a bag. "Kind of like saying a vast multitude buys into all the bullshit."

I smiled; I'd been in conversations like this before, in class and out of it. "But it's hard to deny when so many cultures share similar backstories. Bits and pieces, I mean. Look at all the cultures that've included stories of a Great Flood in their oral and written traditions."

McCue dug out a cardboard box holding something approximating a burger, only it was ham and sausage and egg instead. "Your Master's is in folklore . . . my PhD is in Comparative Religion. You see any parallels there?"

I captured the other bag, sought my bed. "One can always make an argument that religion *is* folklore."

"I'm talkin' about you and me." Remi drank coffee, smiled his slow, crooked smile. "You any good with knives?"

I frowned. "Handy enough. Where's this going?"

"Grandaddy ever show up and teach you how to throw? I mean, how to use actual throwing knives?"

I shook my head. "We spent most of our time shooting."

McCue nodded. "I'm a good shot. Rifle, handgun; I'm a

Texas boy, and I grew up on a ranch. But Grandaddy always wanted me to work special on knife skills."

I remembered my grandfather suggesting I learn how to handle a knife. But then, my father—my *human* father—was a former soldier, current cop, and it was natural the man would want his sons to be skilled. I had indeed learned. Wore a knife at my belt, carried another in my Harley's saddle bags.

But Grandaddy had always taken me shooting. "You're saying he specifically targeted our training."

"I'm saying it's an *idea*," McCue clarified. "And something worth asking about when we're up on the mountain."

My brows rose. "You don't trust him."

"No, no . . ." He lifted a belaying hand. "I trust that man with my life. I just want to be sure I understand what he intends for me to do with it."

I lifted one shoulder in a half-shrug. "The battle of Good versus Evil. Isn't that what he said?"

Remi tilted his head, and the hat went with it. "*Is* there such a thing?"

I'd thought on it throughout my life. I'd thought on it long and hard. *Before* I went to school, *at* school, when I wrote papers and my thesis, before walking away from my future. In talks with fellow students, fellow teaching assistants, even with professors caught up in the esoterica of academia.

My intellect claimed it was an exercise in freedom of thought not necessarily moored to reality.

My gut said otherwise.

I looked at McCue. Made no comment, but I had the feeling he'd follow.

Remi's blue eyes were bright. "If you accept that . . . then maybe there's truth in everything Grandaddy's ever said—and ever will."

Grandaddy an *angel*—or, well, an agent of heaven.

Lucifer, *real*.

The run-up on earth to the End of Days.

Surrogates—demons—walked the earth, and put on the guise of legends, and myths, and campfire stories.

"So," I said, "we're ghostbusters?"

Remi McCue's smile broadened. "I'm thinkin' more like Michaels."

I squinted. "The craft store?"

"No, asshat, as in the *archangel* Michael. Otherwise known as the Sword of Heaven."

"He's only one archangel," I said, "of the four we know best. Maybe we're Raphaels, or Uriels, or—" And I stopped dead.

Remi's tone was dryly amused. "Gabriels?"

Shit. "I *do not* want to be an angel. Or even a proto-angel."

"Archangel might be nice, though." McCue sounded downright philosophical. "Remiel, well, he's not so high and mighty as the Big Four, but he's a good guy."

I frowned, perplexed.

"Angel of hope," he said, "and I'm sure *hopin'* we can win this rodeo."

I squinted at him. "I'm too hung over for this."

CHAPTER FIVE

The trail was called Fatman's Loop, for no reason I could determine, and it wound up the stony, fire-ravaged flanks of what was, Grandaddy told us, Mount Elden in the San Francisco Peaks on the northern outskirts of Flagstaff, once an active volcano. It was a rough skein of a trail attended by sentinel Ponderosa pines, scatterings of oaks and aspens, and other scrubby vegetation. An elevation of 7,000 feet sucked a fair amount of oxygen from the air, and a man working through the effects of a hangover knew it. I felt aged beyond my years, thirsty, fatigued, and sweat trailed down neck and chest and stuck the thin cotton weave of my black t-shirt to my torso.

Motorcycle leathers had a purpose—for motorcycles. They provided a tough layer against the onslaught of asphalt or gravel, should a bike go down. Not so good, though, for a man hiking up a mountain in thin air, in summer, no matter how attractive the surroundings, though at least I'd left my jacket at the motel. Here it was very dry, unlike the moist, rain-laden environment of the Pacific Northwest. The trails were no more challenging, but when hiking with Grandaddy in Oregon I hadn't been wearing motorcycle boots, or sweating whiskey out of my pores, or wrestling with the announcement made the night before that I was a part of heaven.

That I was *born* of heaven.

That I now had some kind of celestial partner and was *destined*—and how the hell had my life become weighted with words like that?—to be a soldier in the front lines of an angelic army intended to fight evil. To keep Lucifer from returning to take over the whole damn world.

My so-called grandfather, who *knew things*, as I had always viewed it, offered no intel at the moment. Grandaddy climbed the mountain with a walking staff in one hand, lacking Gandalf's robes, perhaps, but none of the gravitas, the secrecy, the seeming awareness of *portents*, of *knowledge*, of *elements of information* held apart from his own grandsons—or, well, whatever the hell we were to him these days. Amoebas, maybe, in the celestial pecking order.

Grandaddy went up first, with McCue just behind. I toiled at a slight remove, thinking I'd really rather be back in a motel room; or, better yet, in a sports bar, watching men meet on the fields of *athletic battle*, rather than being aimed as weapons in a heavenly war.

It was a popular trail, and we were not alone on the mountain. But brief meetings with others consisted of water breaks, or viewings of where they'd come from and where they were bound, and the occasional curious dog.

Mountain lions, one older gentleman warned, he of the mashed hat worn against the sun; the crumpled khaki clothing; the browned, aging flesh and a sparse gray ponytail. Don't let your dogs run loose, he said pointedly, gray eyes fierce, because lions might take them down from the heights.

Since no dogs accompanied us I was not certain what this kind of suggestion actually meant, but McCue thanked the man with immense charm and courtesy, exchanging pleasantries, said farewell with a polite tip of his hat, and did not bother to point out to the gentleman that we had no canines with us that might be at risk of being taken by lions.

Not even by fleas, I reflected, though possibly flies.

Up we went again, until Grandaddy called halt at a cluster of granite boulders just beyond a crowded cluster of immature oaks in the midst of massive pines, and bade us enjoy the view.

McCue perched his jean-clad ass atop a pile of boulders, set his booted feet, removed his hat to scrub a forearm through neatly trimmed hair, hooked the hat over a knee and smiled into the day as he stared across the distances. I, on the other hand, simply stopped walking, pulled a plastic bottle from a back pocket, sucked down water. I could smell the whiskey exiting my flesh on perspiration. So much for the shower.

"Well?" Grandaddy said. "What did you notice?"

"That man," McCue observed, "was not entirely a *man*, now, was he?"

I frowned at him. "Which man? We passed several."

"The old man. The one who warned us about mountain lions." Remi's brows rose. "You didn't feel it? He wasn't warning us about *dogs*, you know. That was meant for us. Be careful where we go, because danger awaits."

I found it baffling. "You got that from an old man you talked to for, like, maybe five minutes?"

After a moment, McCue turned to gaze up at Grandaddy, standing amidst the sunlight in the bright backdrop of the day.

"I would like to say his mama didn't raise a fool, but I'm beginnin' to wonder."

Grandaddy smiled. "Don't underestimate Gabriel. His strengths lie elsewhere."

"Who was he?" Remi asked, ignoring my side-eye.

"An angel; and yes, that was a message. You'll find the world is full of messages—and full of angels—now that you're awakened. Some will be clear; some won't be; some will be wrong. And, if I may be permitted to wax Biblical a moment, false witness shall be borne." A trace of breeze stirred Grandaddy's hair. "You've been around them all your lives, but no one knew you, either of you. Hide in plain sight, as I said. But those beacons I mentioned? Your heavenly souls? They are the seat of your strength, the homeplace of your spirits, but they are also the lodestones that others will follow to find you. There is much benevolence in the world, fragments of heaven made whole as living beings, if not wholly human; but just as he warned you, there *are* lions upon the heights who will try to take down the dogs."

I gusted air through my nose. "Can I at least be a big tough Rottweiler? Not a wussy little Chihuahua?"

"Shows you know nothin' about dogs," McCue observed. "Those are tough little suckers. They'll chew your toes clean off your feet and then grin at you."

Grandaddy's blue eyes were bright. "You, Gabriel? Pit bull. Most certainly. But carefully bred, socialized, well-trained . . . and your purpose will come clear."

I pounced on it. "Just what *is* my purpose, Grandaddy? *Exactly* my purpose. Spell it out. You laid a lot on us last night."

His gesture guided our view beyond the mountain flank. "Take a look out there, boys. Tell me what you see."

It was a sun-rich day among the pines, with skies so blue it nearly hurt my whiskey-buffered head because I'd stupidly left my sunglasses in my saddlebags. Below lay a ribbon of road, and a massive lone hill of red volcanic cinders that had once been mined. Half the hill was eaten away. Beyond lay vast expanses of flat earth and occasional convolutions of cinder hills. The Peaks themselves were a huddled cluster of an extinct volcano's cones and craters, overtaken by Ponderosa, aspen, oak, various scrub vegetation, grasses.

"I see forever," McCue said, voice smooth and contemplative. "The unending earth."

"He appears to be a poet," I said with dry amusement, without rancor or sting. I didn't know the guy, but we were stuck in the same whackoid shit going down. "Yeah, it's a big world. But why is that hill so torn up? Looks like a big ol' shark chomped on it."

"They don't use salt on the roads in winter, here," Grandaddy answered. "They lay down cinders . . . which, lacking the protective nature of salt, consecrated or not, makes this area ripe for activity of the unnatural kind. But they don't work that hill anymore. Cinders for the roads are hauled in from more distant cones." He paused. "Gabriel, I want you to think about where you are. Tell me what you feel. What you *sense*."

I was hung over, tired, short on oxygen. But this was nothing new from Grandaddy; he suggested this whenever we'd gone exploring on his visits. So it was with nostalgia and a certain ease of spirit, of familiarity, that I loosed my awareness of the here and now and let the sense of the immediate environs come to the fore.

I closed my eyes, made my heart slow, allowed my awareness of *self* to be at peace.

A bright day, warm but not hot; clean, fresh air; the sound of insects, of birds, of air in the grasses; the rush of wind among the trees. My inner self caught a flash of yellow color, a reflection off something opalescent, the watery blurring of pastel colors layered one upon the other.

It rose like a tide within me, the sense of calm, of quietude, of a deep, earth-anchored spirituality.

I smiled, opened my eyes. "It's sacred. To the Navajo, Sacred Mountain of the West. Abalone Shell Mountain. *Doko'oosliid.* And to the Hopi, a home to spirits. *Katsinam.* Kachinas. A place to find a way through *koyaanisqatsi,* life out of balance. Up here on this mountain, we're safe."

"Huh," Remi said after a moment. "That one of those strengths you were talkin' about, Grandaddy? He's a sensitive?"

"To places, but not to people. He's not an empath. People, for Gabriel,"—Grandaddy smiled a little—"remain something of a challenge. You, on the other hand, do understand people. You are an empath. You balance one another, Remi; and yes, *koyaanisqatsi* is indeed life *out* of balance, and that is exactly what is happening now. Your job is to help restore the balance." He looked at me. "You dreamed, did you not? Last night?"

I was unsurprised he knew. I nodded.

"That stunt you pulled putting Matthew's life at risk."

I winced; stated like *that* it sounded so very much worse . . . but, well, yeah. I had indeed put my kid brother's life at risk.

"It was a test I knew would come in some fashion," Grandaddy said. "Matthew was your brother in flesh, so there was a bond, but not in soul. Nonetheless, you had the instinct. Some recognize it, embrace it. Others duck it, or just never awaken to it. I didn't doubt that you'd awaken to it and consent."

I frowned. "Awaken to what?"

"The stewardship of the younger. It's what you did with Matthew all of his life. *That* day, though—that was for Remi."

I was aware of McCue's hatless head coming up sharply as he, too, stared intently at our grandfather.

"*That* day?" I echoed. "The day I nearly got Matty killed? How the hell was that day for *this* guy?"

"Matthew was Remi's proxy. He represented the younger brother you needed to have, to trigger the drive to protect." Grandaddy smiled. "There's always an alpha, Gabriel. That's the role of the eldest, because he or she is first. The first precedes the others, prepares the way, makes smooth the path for the younger to follow. Your instinct was always to protect Matthew no matter what, regardless of any danger . . . because that's what you'll do for Remi. That's what *primogenitura* is."

I shot a quick glance at McCue, switched back to Grandaddy and waited for more. More always came, with Grandaddy.

"Find two soldiers who fought together," he advised. "Ask them about the bond battle creates. They are far more than 'besties.' As for you and Remi, that instinct you had for Matthew is the instinct you have, or will have, for Remi. You just don't know it yet, don't *feel* it. That day when you offered to carry your brother's pain, begged me to lift it from him, to give it to you, I knew you were ready. And you consented. But you weren't *sealed* to Matthew that day, Gabriel, because he wasn't heaven-born. That day prepared the way. Last night, when you put on the rings and clasped hands, you and Remi were sealed to one another."

I looked sharply to McCue, saw the cowboy staring back, equally startled. We neither of us knew what to do with the information. I could only see Matty in my head, in my memories; I had no clue what McCue was thinking.

Sealed to one another?

I lifted my right hand and examined the back of it, studied the ring upon my middle finger. Rubbed the ball of my left thumb over silver pentagram, black stone. When I raised my eyes, I found McCue staring back. While his face appeared relaxed, the expression in his eyes was a myriad of complex thoughts I couldn't define.

But then the cowboy smiled crookedly, looked back at Grandaddy, an angel from on high. Regardless of semantics. The surface of Remi's tone was casual, but there were undertones within it. "So, I'm the beta, am I?"

"There's a reason you grew up with an older brother, Remi," Grandaddy said. "Birth order affects development. You're not *lesser*. Beta merely means second. Younger. Gabriel's spark simply quickened before yours. That doesn't make him *better*. Remember: even with twins, one is born first."

McCue considered it in silence, then nodded slightly. "Primogeniture is known mostly as a medieval concept. But it extends farther back than that. All the way to Biblical times." He looked at me. "Predisposition. Predestination. Guess we'll find out if they apply, won't we? Bein' together *in the trenches*, and all."

So, Remi McCue was not entirely an amiable beta soul. I

looked at Grandaddy, found him smiling faintly. I asked a silent question.

"It will come," Grandaddy promised. "It's a *process*."

I shook my head. "We have lives. Hell, I just got mine back. You can't expect us to walk away from everything."

Grandaddy's voice took on an edge unlike anything I'd heard from him before. My skin itched, and I stared at him in shock. He was *doing* something again.

"That's exactly what I expect, Gabriel. This is the *End of Days* I'm talking about, with the fate of the world at stake. *Everyone* born of heaven must answer this call, if we're to succeed. Is it a sacrifice?—of course it is. But there is nothing in your lives that is of greater importance than this." His eyes were steady. "You have never disappointed me. Don't do so now."

I looked for compassion. Found none. "What about our families?"

Grandaddy didn't even attempt to hedge. "I said we could massage things. Well, I have massaged the minds of your parents and brother. They believe you are in prison finishing your sentence."

"But that's only six more months."

"And your father's reaction once you're out? Would you be welcome in his house?"

After a long moment, I said no. Because I remembered what my father had said—even if *he* didn't because of Grandaddy's brain massage. That night on the porch, as I rolled my bike out of the garage, felt like a death-knell. My mother stayed inside, and Matty was probably out getting high.

"And what would you do, Gabriel?"

"Get on my bike and head out. Maybe for good."

Grandaddy nodded. "Well, we will free you of that. They will remember no hostilities, only that you, once your sentence is served, are on the road. And so you are free to do your duty without interference for however long it takes."

"Just cut them off like that, huh?" Though I wouldn't much miss my father. I glanced at the cowboy, looked back at Grandaddy. "What about him?"

"Remi is traveling the world undertaking research for the book he plans on writing. And he may, from time to time, call home to reassure his parents. But the calls will show overseas locations, nothing in this country. You, on the other hand, may drop postcards to your mother once your sentence is completed. Your father's a son of a bitch, but she's a worthy woman."

And there it was, all tied up in a neat little bow. The present. Our futures. An explanation for it all.

McCue sat rigidly on his rock. "But what about—?" Yet he broke it off abruptly, as if he'd seen the answer in Grandaddy's eyes.

After a moment freighted with tension, he reached down, pulled tough prairie grass from the ground, began to plait long strands. Whether he was thinking alpha vs. beta, or blue vs. red, or cat vs. dog, I didn't know.

He asked, "We have any start-date for Lucifer's return?"

"No." Grandaddy was decisive and yet regretful. "There are signs, of course. Indications. But no timeline. The world doesn't run like clockwork, despite humans swearing it does." He nodded slightly, staring into space. "I've dumped a great deal on your plates. But trust in your hearts, follow your souls, and know that I would never set my grandchildren upon a false path." He turned, reached into the pockets of his frock coat, drew forth items. One he tossed to Remi, another to me.

I caught what was thrown, frowned. Looked at my grandfather in bafflement. "A shotgun shell?"

"Powdered iron load," Grandaddy said. "The best means of dispersing or destroying a ghost. Birdshot works, so does buckshot, if it's silver, or iron. Same with bullets. Remi, show him what you've got."

McCue, smiling crookedly, held it up into the light. Displayed between thumb and forefinger, it gleamed pure and clean and silver: a .45 caliber bullet.

"You can take down a werewolf with that," Grandaddy said, "and a passel of other things. Now Gabriel, I do know you're aware of the lore, of the legends. I taught you, and so have the halls of higher learning." His smile was wry. "Even TV, movies, novels, and comic books. But what you have to remember now is that these are no longer tall tales. These beings are surrogates. They *wear the guises* of fiction and folklore."

"Grandaddy—" But I broke off as he held up a hand.

"There's a woman in town," Grandaddy said. "Her name is Lily Morrigan. She's expecting you. She'll provide you with details of your first job, as well as with some items you'll find helpful in the coming days. She's unconventional, but completely trustworthy."

"'First job?'" I echoed.

"Why can't *you* tell us what we need to know?" Remi asked; and I heard the first hint of tension in the cowboy's tone. "You've been doing it all our lives."

Grandaddy smiled. His eyes were ageless. "Because you're not my only grandchildren. There are others we're preparing.

Go to Lily. She'll keep you updated, and I'll contact you when it's necessary."

I longed for scotch. But I longed more for the uncomplicated ignorance of two days earlier, before stepping foot inside a roadhouse in Northern Arizona and out of a life that was in no way perfect, or even comfortable, but was nonetheless free of such encumbrances as saving the world.

"How do we find this Lily?" McCue asked.

"Have drinks at the Zoo tonight," Grandaddy said. "She'll find you." He turned away from the vista then, stood with his back against the sky and a staff in one hand. He put me in mind of Moses on the Mount.

Or, yeah, Gandalf.

"You're trained," he told us. "You're ready. But it won't be easy. Trust your instincts. Trust what I've taught you. Believe in what you're doing. Commit, and never waver." He smiled, and a glint was in his eyes. "Fight the good fight."

I realized then what was in the offing. "You're *leaving*," I accused. "You drop all this apocalyptic bullshit on us, then walk away?"

Grandaddy marked me. Weighed me. Flicked a glance at Remi, who waited in the silence of tense expectancy. Then he nodded his head with its wealth of flowing silver hair. "Fair enough," he observed. "You're not boys anymore, to idolize every word I say without questioning it. I've never steered you wrong, but you've got minds, and were trained in school to accept nothing on faith." He bared teeth in a broad smile. "Even if that is the key to all. So. Do this job. Then decide if it's bullshit."

I was all out of patience, but schooled my tone into matter

of factness. "Look, all this is normal to you. I get that. But I barely know this man you say I'm now *sealed* to and you expect me to trust a woman I've never met to explain to us a job we're to do in order to serve heaven. Heaven! Cut me a little slack about being slow to buy into all this without questioning it, okay?" Without stirring a hair, he suddenly loomed extremely large against the sky. His shoulders stretched the seams of his frock coat. Behind him the world, the air, blurred into something like pixels. Pixels under a sheen of oily rainbowed water.

Holy crap. Those were wings. I couldn't see them, not clearly, not beyond impression, but those were *wings*.

McCue's tone was dry. "You want to ask that again, do you?"

I did not.

"It's a broken road you're on," Grandaddy said, as the pixilation died, "and you'll stumble, and you'll fall, and you'll likely be hurt, even badly hurt. Your bodies are human. You're mortal. You can die, because soldiers do. But just spit out the blood, pick yourselves back up—*pick one another up*—and do the best you can."

I let that settle a moment. "God," I muttered finally, "we're verging on an Army commercial."

McCue quoted, "'*Sancte Michael Archangele, defende nos in proelio; contra nequitiam et insidias diabolus esto praesidium.*'"

I shot him a glance. "Seriously? Latin?"

"Timing seems appropriate. '*Saint Michael the Archangel, defend us in battle, be our safeguard and protection against the wickedness and snares of the devil.*'"

I squinted. "When Latin evolved as a language all those four thousand years ago, I don't think it was *ever* intended to be spoken with a Texas accent."

Grandaddy threw back his head, and his rich laughter rolled out into the day like the tolling of a bell. Maybe the voice of heaven? I shivered.

Our grandfather grinned at us both when the sound died. "Yes, Michael would approve of you both. Most assuredly." He drew in a breath, released it, and there was memory in his eyes. "I said this to you both many years ago. You needed to know it, to nudge you in the right direction, but it wasn't necessary that you recall it then. Now, it is." He looked at us both, one at a time. "There was a thunderstorm."

I smiled as memory snapped into place. "You said God was bowling."

"But he wasn't," McCue noted. "It was Thor."

I nodded firm endorsement. "God of Thunder. Damn straight."

Grandaddy looked large against the sky. "I say again what I said that night: 'You're sealed to it, now. Life and limb, blood and bone. The fate of the world hinges upon it.'"

I remembered it so clearly. And I heard Remi's Texas-accented voice overlay my own, as we said together, "'The whole entire world—and everyone in it.'"

Grandaddy nodded. "The information you'll need to survive is everywhere. Much of it you've studied, much you'll need to learn. Look to all cultures, all source material, judge for yourself what is evidence when you've experienced it—or when you're certain you can trust whoever provides you with the intel. Sort out what is empirical, what is allegory, what is metaphor. Because even the writing on the wall may be false, or intended to mislead. Remember that dead languages are *dead*, and that a book written by many men, in many tongues, may be misunderstood, may in fact be mistranslated. And most certainly may be misquoted to serve agendas."

And then he turned away, set his staff, and began to walk down the mountain.

I squinted, closed my eyes, rubbed my brow. But I looked at the cowboy, the only man left on the mountain who understood this confusion; hell, *shared* this confusion. And probably shared my inclination to disbelieve, which was, apparently—if one were to believe a man he'd trusted all his life—a doorway to the devil.

"You know," I reflected aloud, "he really should just *do* it. Grandaddy."

McCue raised brows. "Do what?"

"Plant his staff and announce to Lucifer: '*You. Shall. Not. Pass.*'"

The cowboy laughed, then held up an object that glinted in the sun. "A silver bullet . . . *for werewolves.*"

I inspected the shotgun cartridge I held. "A powdered iron load for *killing ghosts.*"

Remi shook his head. "Makes me wonder if we're supposed to cut our own stakes for, you know, *vampires.*"

I sighed, tucked the cartridge into a back pocket. "Life just got a whole lot more interesting."

McCue rose, stretched, stared thoughtfully into the sky as he put his hat back on and, unexpectedly, quoted Shakespeare: "Cry 'havoc' . . . and let slip the dogs of war."

Well, if the Rhodes Scholar was going *that* way . . . I rolled my shoulders, cracked my neck. "And I'm no damn Chihuahua."

Remi smiled, and I smiled back. For that brief flash of a moment, even as strangers, we were in complete accord.

McCue nodded, pocketed the silver bullet. "Come on, pit bull. Let's go see a veterinarian, make sure you're up to date on your shots."

I followed, heard McCue start singing—*again*—as he led the way down the mountain. After a moment of disbelief, I raised a question over the sound. "That more Charley Pride?"

Remi broke off long enough to call back, "Rascal Flatts. 'Bless the Broken Road.' Grandaddy says we're on one now—figured we might need every blessing we can get."

I couldn't help the plaintive tone. "But does it have to be *country*?"

"God's music, boy. God's music!"

I wondered if maybe I could get a WiFi signal through my phone's mobile hotspot. Because then I'd download a glorious oldie, all seventeen minutes of Iron Butterfly's 'In-A-Gadda-Da-Vida,' and play it as loud as I could, even if it drained the entire battery. That song, too, was quasi-Biblical, since the song was *intended* to be 'In the Garden of Eden' when it was written, before it got totally booze-mangled.

"Or I can sing a hymn, if you'd rather," McCue called.

I scowled at the cowboy's back. "How about we just go with the sound of silence?"

Which prompted McCue to shift to Simon and Garfunkel's "Bridge Over Troubled Water."

Well. At least it wasn't country.

CHAPTER SIX

S aturday night McCue and I grabbed quick showers in our motel rooms, steak dinner at a place called Horsemen Lodge—it, too, featured mounted dead animals, leaving me to wonder if this was required decor for Arizona; very different from the coffee bars of Portland—then on to the Zoo Club.

It was crowded and noisy as I preceded Remi McCue inside. Live country music once again reverberated within the massive roadhouse: drums, guitars, and the broken nasal croon of a tenor voice sliding all around the notes.

Crying in his beer, I reflected sourly, forcibly resolving not to insert fingers into ears. They were always crying in their beer about a woman. Or maybe about their dogs. Or their trucks.

I worked my way through the crowd but shot a brief glance over my shoulder at Remi. I raised my voice to be heard above the music and crowd noise. "You ever cry over your truck? Or a dog?"

McCue's brows knit as he called back, "Am I supposed to?"

"You're a cowboy, aren't you? Into country music?"

"I'm more likely to cry over my *horse*," McCue said. "And do you really think a cowboy bar is the best place to debate the merits of what country people do or do not do? Especially when it's obvious you're *a biker*?"

Well. Possibly not.

At the back near the pool tables, I found us an empty two-seater table shoved up against one of the tree trunks serving as load-bearing support for the beamwork overhead. String lights dangled, illuminating the glass eyes of a snarling stuffed bobcat as it crouched overhead. It put me in mind of the lions the old man on the mountain had mentioned.

"I'll get drinks," I said as McCue dropped into a chair. "What do you want?"

Remi was evaluating the surroundings; maybe checking for surrogates? "House draft'll do."

I made my way through to the long slab of bar, ordered and fetched two brimming mugs, worked my way back. Handed one down to McCue, but paused as my attention was caught by the pool tables beyond, near the back exit, as someone indisputably female bent over the table.

I do like a woman with a stick in her hand.

Smiling, I wandered closer with mug in my fist.

It was the young woman from the night before, the one who'd asked me to dance, then knocked back a share of my Talisker. Still with the blonde hair pulled back in a waterfall of ponytail, but tonight she wore black tank top, black jeans, silver at both wrists and in her ears, a doubled string of chunky turquoise on silver wire around her throat. And she wielded a mean pool cue.

She played a man, and she beat him. The game had attracted onlookers; there was laughter, cash exchanged, elbows planted into ribs, muted jokes at the expense of the cowboy she'd defeated. Was she a hustler? Or just good at pool?

As she looked up and met my eyes, I smiled. Inclined my head just a tad to acknowledge her win. Sent the invitation. Hell, Grandaddy'd said nothing about ignoring the attractions while we waited to meet whoever this Lily woman was. Hell, for all I knew, *she* was Lily.

The light over the pool table was better than in the rest of the bar. I saw now that in addition to brown eyes, she had the faintest dusting of freckles across her nose. Other than bright lipstick, makeup was minimal; but then, she didn't need it.

It was hard to look at anything other than those red lips. Probably, she knew it.

I saw the spread of her pupils as she stared at me across the table, the loosening of her mouth. She looked nowhere else as, with a slow smile, a lifting of brows, she handed off the cue stick to the man nearest her, who happened to be the cowboy-hatted man she'd just defeated. She hesitated an instant to keep my eyes on her, then turned and quietly slipped out the back exit.

I was no fool. I damn well followed.

As I stepped outside into the darkness beyond, as the door swung shut behind me, I smelled a hint of perfume. And then she surged close and her hands were on me, one reaching between my legs to cup, to tease, the other sliding up beneath my t-shirt to spread against my chest. She moved in close, stepped me back until shoulder blades and ass were against the logs of the roadhouse, and let me discover what those lips were all about.

Well, alrighty then. If this was Lily, I'd be sending Grandaddy a Candygram.

"What's your name?" she asked against my mouth.

At that particular instant I didn't know. I didn't care. My mind was on other things, such as all the blood heading south.

"What's your *name*?" she insisted.

I smiled against her mouth, then cleared my throat. Was mostly breathless. "Hell, woman—whatever you want it to be."

This was—really fast. Like, holy shit fast.

Motel. Motel would be good. Or a car, if she had one. Hell, even McCue's *truck*, if I could get her around to the front of the roadhouse.

Or maybe right there was good. Yeah, this could work. Even against the rough logs of a wall.

Then her breath was unaccountably cold against my mouth. "You *lit it up* last night. I felt it. And it shines so bright, it does. It's so very pretty. But now I'm going to extinguish it. I'm going to extinguish *you*."

What the hell—?

"Call me Iñigo Montoya, for all I care," she said, "I go by them all. Hell, call me Legion."

Well. Not Lily. And the woman had a *knife*.

I caught her wrist as she thrust hard with the blade toward my belly. It was all instinct, pure reaction, to catch and snap that wrist, to thump the heel of one hand against her breastbone in a short, sharp pop of impact that knocked her backward. I'd learned the hard way never to underestimate, never to hesitate, never to give anyone with a weapon in their hands the opportunity to use it—and I decided on the spot that gender damn well didn't matter when outright murder was a real possibility.

She'd have gutted me. I saw it in her eyes as she staggered, then backed away. She'd have opened me up, reached inside, yanked out my intestines.

"I'd have *tap-danced* on them," she said through bared teeth, clearly following my thoughts. "Or maybe fried them like pork rinds and chowed right down on them."

I'd hurt her. She backed off farther with her wrist clasped against her abdomen, breathing hard. Between us on the ground, glinting in fitful light, lay the knife.

She glanced at it, looked at me. Her eyes remained brown, but the pupils stretched into an alien verticality, like weird-ass slitted cat eyes. The accompanying smile was feral. "Welcome to the war." And she stripped off the necklace and flung it at me before she turned and ran.

I ducked aside, but not before one of the silver and turquoise loops coiled around my neck and closed. I felt the throttling pressure, felt the stones bite into my flesh, felt the wire on which the chunks were strung close down hard on my throat, squeezing flesh.

I caught at it with both hands, tried to dig fingers beneath the wire. All breath was banished, and black spots crowded in from the edges of my vision.

Then my ring—Grandaddy's ring—made contact with the wire. Silver on silver.

Even as I heard the back door creak open, heard a Texas-accented voice questioning what the hell was going on, the necklace fell away. It spilled to the ground and lay beside the knife, silver wire all melted, charred turquoise chunks unstrung and scattered across the dirt. I sucked air in, gasped it back out again.

McCue was beside me. "You okay?"

I massaged my neck, cleared my throat. Swallowed painfully, sucked in and blew out a breath. "Shit," I expelled on a gust of air, "I guess—" I hacked a little, sucked air again, but the voice still came out broken, "—guess Grandaddy was right."

"About which?"

"All of it! Including the thing that old man said up there today—" I coughed, cleared my throat, flipped a hand toward the ravaged mountain looming behind us, "—about lions taking dogs from the heights. She damn near took *me* right off. Shit." I rubbed my neck again. No blood, but very sore.

Remi bent, collected the knife, examined it in bar lighting. "Huh. SOG Seal Strike." He turned it over in his hands, admiring the weapon. "Damn near ten inches over all, and a blade almost five." He looked at me, brows lifted. "Yep, she was goin' for you, all right." He bent down in muted light, scuffed at the shattered necklace with the toe of one boot as he studied it. "What'd you do to piss her off so fast?"

I intended to answer, but the door opened again. I twisted away from it even as Remi stepped back, flipping the knife in his fingers with ease, clearly prepared to use it.

Another woman, but vastly different. Elegant inked spirals and angled geometry ran in a rainbow of colors up her bared forearms wrist to elbow in sleeve tattoos, twisted silver bands clasped her biceps, and she wore her two-toned hair in a modified Mohawk. It was dark and cropped close to her head on the sides, though not shaved; choppy and red on the top. The end of her right eyebrow sported the twin glitters of silver hoops, and a torc—an actual Celtic torc, worn in the correct manner—hugged the back of her neck as the coiled, knotted ends rested on her collar bones. Even in poor light, her eyes, set at a slight upward tilt, were a very clear green.

"So," she said, and a lilt colored her tone, "you boys outside to see a man about a horse, or got something more on your mind?"

I rubbed my throat again. "Do what?"

McCue was laughing. "That's country speech, son. She's asking if we're drainin' the lizard."

I reflected that the ponytailed blonde very nearly *had* drained the lizard, if of something other than piss. And it sent an uncomfortable quiver through my gut. God, those *eyes*.

"You Jubal's boys?" she asked. "You look like it. You look like a lot of them." She pursed her lips, nodded. "Jubal and his grandkids. I've seen many of you. Come on, then. Let's go next door. My rig's parked over there."

McCue actually tipped his hat to her. "Would you happen to be Lily Morgan, miss?"

She seemed amused by his Southern courtesy. "Morr-*i*-gan," she emphasized. "Not Morgan."

Morrigan. Hah.

Remi caught it, too. I found it clever and amusing as he ran with it. "Your sisters around? You come as a trio, don't you?"

Her eyes sharpened on him, accepted his challenge. "They're in the rig," she said. "Come on along and meet them."

Remi was deadly serious. "Yes ma'am."

I watched the woman continue striding ahead. "You're not suggesting she really *is*, are you?" I asked, sotto voce. "*And* her sisters?"

"Well, I don't think it's the Kardashians, no," he said dryly, "but you just met someone who claims to be Lily *Morrigan*. You tell me."

"Irish mythology in all its beauty," I answered, grinning. "The Morrigan is the Goddess of Battles, heroes, the dead. She's either herself and independent, or one of three sisters. The stories differ."

The woman swung around, walked backward with tattooed arms hanging loose. Her torc and arm bands glinted in starlight. "So, which do you figure you boys will be? Heroes? Or the dead?"

I cleared my throat, neck still sore. "Very much alive and victorious," I replied. "Every damn time."

"Well," she said, smiling, "that is what I'm here for. To make sure you survive to *be* victorious."

"Where exactly are we going?" I asked, looking ahead of her to the building some distance away. "Or are you living in the bowling alley?"

"Right here." She paused, stepped aside, swept an illustrated arm out to indicate a massive black-and-red bus-like vehicle that had a front end on it like an 18-wheeler cab.

"Whoa." McCue was patently impressed. "That is one honkin' big rig. Garage unit?"

She nodded approval. "Sixteen feet of work space at the back end, the rest is all for living. Come on in. I've got whiskey." She tossed a bright glance at me. "Though it's Irish, not the Scottish Jubal says you prefer. Might help that throat."

I was astonished. "*You* live in a motorhome?"

It was, I felt, complete cognitive dissonance to link her with the giant vehicle. Lily Morrigan, with tattoos and Mohawk, was most decidedly not what one might think of behind the wheel of an RV, based on what I'd seen at rest stops. She tilted her head a little, assessing me. "The battlefields don't generally come to me, I go to them. Now, come on inside. I'll show you a few things, find out what you know, ply you with whiskey until you're babbling like babies, and then you can crash here after you've done the job." She pulled open the door, climbed steep steps, disappeared inside.

Oh. Yeah. The job Grandaddy had mentioned.

Remi went up first, took off his hat as he entered. I waited a beat, ducked in behind him. Stepped into the impression of warm lighting, rich wood, leather, brushed metal fittings. Music was playing, something robustly Celtic.

And then the crow on its perch croaked, and the huge Irish Wolfhound rose up from the floor.

Lily Morrigan said sweetly, "Meet Nemain, the crow. The bitch is Macha. My sisters." Her smile was very wide and it set her eyes alight. "*Céad míle fáilte* from the Goddess of Battles. A hundred thousand welcomes."

CHAPTER SEVEN

couldn't help myself. I was pretty sure I knew the answer, but something in me needed to ask. A couple of days before, no. But after what Grandaddy laid upon us and my encounter with the murderous Iñigo Montoya/Legion (or whatever her real name was), I was no longer so certain how the world was ordered.

"You're not . . . really," I said, and knew it sounded weak. Better I should scoff, or deny. Or simply be polite about it and say nothing. But . . . "From *mythology?*"

Then Remi McCue stepped in. "I am a man prone to belief in many things, but this, well . . ." He let that trail off, seemingly at a loss for more. Then he tacked on, "Who are you *really?*"

I thought *what* was she might be a better inquiry, but at least McCue had asked a sensible question. More than I had.

Her bright eyes amused, Lily Morrigan said, "This from a man whose soul is born of heaven." Then she shrugged. "Need to know basis. And what you *need* to know, right now, is that I can set you boyos up with what's required to undertake the task. Follow me."

We followed. McCue seemed unfazed by the surroundings, by the fact we were inside what approximated, to me, a decidedly up-style hotel suite. I noted good wood, granite countertops, rich leather upholstery, flooring a split between tile and carpet. Everything was sized with infinite care to optimize limited space. Couch, recliner, big U-shaped dinette. Stove, oven, sinks, refrigerator, and freezer. Entertainment center over the front cab with speakers, flat-screen TV, CD and DVD slots.

I'd passed plenty of motorhomes on the road—always, always wallowing in an interstate lane where they did not belong. I'd seen them at campgrounds with awnings put out along with yappy dogs, but I'd never been inside one before; had never anticipated this kind of quality, of detail.

And certainly I had never expected to walk through a kitchen and into an actual *garage* that made up the entire back end of the huge RV. It housed banks of utilitarian white-faced cabinetry, a metal ladder running up to a hatch in the roof, diamond-plated chrome flooring, plus a ceiling fan and skylight, and a roll-up door.

A rectangular platform of sorts was folded inward and fastened against one big wall, beside banks of drawers; I realized it was a bed that could be lowered and leveled. I saw, too, an oxygen tank, monitors for blood pressure and heart, a tangle of tubing that suggested IVs could be hung. On the other side, where Lily Morrigan led us now, was a stack of drawers topped by cabinet doors, and a counter.

"Jesus," I muttered, rubber-necking. "Livin' large." Certainly larger than my prison cell.

She flipped latches, pulled open foam-padded, compartmentalized cabinets and drawers, began taking items out of storage. Two handguns, an assortment of sheathed knives, even two short-barreled shotguns. She also stacked plain cardboard boxes of ammunition, various tubes and flasks, plus small dyed-leather bags with mouths snugged closed by thongs and ribbon. A motorhome that was, I realized, a combination of living quarters, field hospital, armory.

Remi voiced what I was thinking, though the vocabulary differed: "Might could come in handy, rig like this, at the end of the world."

Lily picked up two revolvers, one in each hand, held them out. I took one, McCue the other. I was conversant with handguns in general, knew these after a fashion, but had never fired either style. Mine had a short, fat, 3-inch barrel, long cylinder, a striated grip that felt like rubber. Probably 7.0 to 7.5 length overall.

I broke it open: five chambers. The one McCue held had a longer barrel; 6.5, I judged, and an overall length maybe 9.5 inches.

Lily watched me. "Well?"

I shrugged. "Taurus Judge. Two different models. Both hold .410 shotgun shells—bird- or buckshot—or .45 caliber rounds simultaneously."

She nodded. "In our line of work it's silver rounds, of course, just like the bird- and buckshot. Or powdered iron cartridges. Even consecrated salt will do, though that's only a temporary hold that gives you time to reload, or get the hell out of there."

"Only a five-round chamber," I pointed out.

She shot us both a hard look. "If you can't put down something in five, maybe you deserve to be dead. It's a revolver, not a semi- or auto, so reloading in the midst of battle is a challenge, but maybe that'll convince you to get the job done within a couple of shots."

I swapped out with McCue so he could inspect the short-barreled model. Other than the reloading in the midst of battling demons thing, I was familiar with the weapons and their features.

Lily picked up a shotgun, tossed it to me; I caught it, tucked it automatically under one arm. "Well?" she asked.

I set down the revolver, put the rifle through its paces. "It's a Remington 870. Started with an 18-inch barrel, modified with a police tactical barrel swapped in. Plug is pulled, so you can load it with five or six shells." I grinned. "It's a James Bond movie, right? You're our Q setting us up with all the cool weaponry? Where are the gadgets? The Aston Martin?"

She smiled briefly, shoved unmarked ammo boxes toward both of us. "Silver-dipped birdshot, buckshot, powdered iron, silver rounds. Keep in mind that you can't just walk into any old sporting goods store and buy this. You'll be with me a fair amount of the time, and others can resupply, but you'll need to learn to *make* what you need. You can buy many supplies online, but you can also go to pawn shops and estate sales for silver. You can obtain silver shot online from APMEX—they're the top gold and silver retailer—but it's very pricey. Melt down your own, make the shot. Or dip what you buy."

McCue studied the gun in his hands, then looked up at her. His blue eyes held respect, but also concern. "You're serious."

"It's a *war*," she said evenly. "*I'm* here, am I not—the Goddess of Battles? Wake up, boys. You're part of it, now." She picked up a sheath, tossed it at Remi. "Tell me about this."

He caught it one-handed, set down the revolver. He slid

three knives out from the sheath, spread them like a fan. They were slim, elegant, oh-so-sharp, with slightly curved handles. "Hibben throwing knives." His tone was worshipful. "Gen 2. Blades four and a-half inches, give or take; overall is almost nine. Just under six ounces apiece." His grin lit up his tanned face. "Works of art, these are. Three to a sheath."

"Dipped in silver and holy oil. Get it done in three," she said, "and you don't need more. But—a little backup. For you both. Here."

McCue set aside the throwing knives as she slid a big leather sheath across the counter to me. I put down the revolver, shotgun, pulled the knife from the leather. Steel blade glinted light and dark in whorls and tangles like oil atop water.

"Bowie," Remi said, standing close. "Twelve-inch blade, almost eighteen inches overall. Serious business. Full-tang Damascus steel; look at that patterning. My God, she's a gorgeous thing."

Light glinted off Lily's piercings as she continued. "Buffalo horn handle, brass fittings; both are protective materials when it comes to certain unnatural beasties," she said. "Always, always use consecrated holy oil when cleaning. And do it every day."

McCue and I exchanged a glance, brows raised. *Holy oil?*

Now she touched the leather bags, the silver flasks. "Herbs. Oils. Some for protection, some for stopping, dispersal, or killing. Holy water; but you'll learn to make your own there, too. You can mix in a little colloidal silver for an extra kick. Consecrate the salt, bless the water, you're good to go. Holy oil: it's abramelin, made of equal parts myrrh, calamus, cassia, plus a little essential oil of cinnamon, and seven parts pure olive oil.

Add a blessing, it's ready. You can burn bones with it, take out a surrogate, depending on what's needed."

"Stop." I raised one palm in a belaying gesture. "Just—slow down." I looked at the supplies laid out on the counter. Herbs, flasks, ammo, knives, guns . . . "You keep talking about 'holy,' 'consecrated,' and 'blessings.' Are we supposed to haul all this to a priest, ask him to pray over it?"

Lily's eyes were bright as her brows rose. "Doing so would probably result in your being arrested."

"No shit. And I can't really afford that. So, we have a priest on our team?"

Lily looked at McCue, then back at me. Her expression suggested she believed we were perhaps blithering idiots. "That's right," she said in tones of dry discovery, "you're newbies. My bad. Okay, so there are rituals and rites. I'll give you both cute little booklets containing those you'll use most often. Learn Latin."

"Got that down," Remi said quietly.

She looked at me. I shook my head. "A few lines here and there."

"Then you learn it, too," she advised. "Don't depend on Remi to be right there when you need it. Memorize the rites, because in the midst of demonic confrontation you're not going to have time to draw out a booklet and find the right page. In the meantime, remember something very, very important."

We waited.

Her expression was quite grave, her eyes serious. She spoke with explicit precision. "No, you do not need a priest to perform anything. Because you are both *born of heaven*, you imbeciles. Your *souls* are heavenly matter. Follow the recipes, recite the rituals—in Latin. Call upon that spark inside of you and imbue the hardware—breath, saliva, or blood will do—and you're good to go."

Remi smiled. "*Exorcizo te, omnis spiritus immunde, in nomine Dei Patris omnipotentis, et in nomine Jesu Christi Filii ejusmodi, Domini et Judicis nostri, et in virtute Spiritus Sancti*, yadda yadda yadda."

"It's a beginning," Lily said, "but only a beginning. Not all surrogates are the same, and not all rites work on each. Sometimes it's hunt and peck."

I shot Remi a glance. "How do you know all that?"

"Studied Roman Catholicism," McCue replied, "along with a bunch of other religions. Doctorate, remember?"

"And you studied *exorcism*?"

He shrugged. "Was always kind of interested in that kind of thing. Rituals, rites. Maybe I was meant to, bein' as how we're heavenly matter supposed to battle evil." His smile crooked off to the side. "Hell if I know. But it might could come in handy, I guess, if we go runnin' into any demons."

"The Zoo," Lily said.

We looked at her blankly.

"The roadhouse," she clarified. "You know, that big building standing maybe thirty yards away?" She hitched a thumb in that direction. "It's haunted."

I stared at her. "*Haunted*?"

"Married couple, once owned the place. Benign spirits, mostly—supposedly scared some people by doing the typical ghosty things: moving stuff around, screwing with the power, changing the temperature, weird noises, popping up here and there. At least, those were the stories; who knows if they were true. But it *became* true when the hell vents cracked open. Suddenly there were reports of paranormal activity echoing exactly what the stories claimed."

"Wait," McCue said. "You're saying you don't know if these ghosts ever *actually* existed, but they exist *now*? How can ghosts do that?"

Lily looked at me expectantly, and I sighed deeply. "What Grandaddy described . . . if it's true that all the legends and stories are now real and among us—well, it could be rooted in thought-forms. Tulpas. What's imagined becomes real. Corporeal. And I can't believe I'm even saying this."

"Baudelaire," the cowboy murmured. "And what was it Grandaddy said about disbelief opening the door to demons?"

Lily nodded. "You must accept that these ghosts are now real, thanks to Lucifer. But now it's much worse, because demons are riding them. One person's been killed already, two weeks ago. Autopsy said a heart attack, so no one thought any different, but there are certain signs if you know what to look for."

"What signs?" I asked.

She flicked her gaze to Remi. "You've heard of the 'odor of sanctity,' have you not?"

"Sure. It's a pungent, flowery scent associated with the bodies of saints, particularly stigmata. Though I heard stories that some sick people, on the verge of death, reported smelling something strong and sweet."

Lily nodded. "Surrogates have a similar scent. It's not sulfur—that's too obvious, and they're not stupid, these demons—but a mix of resins and oils. The Egyptians called it *kapet*, the Greeks *kyphi*. Temple incense, mostly."

My brows shot up. "Demons smell like ancient Egyptian temples?"

"Why not?" she asked. "Why is the 'odor of sanctity' sweet, like orange blossoms or other flowers? And it isn't like demons naturally *reek* of it, though the scent intensifies significantly with death."

I huffed a dry laugh. "So, we go around sniffing people to find out who's a demon?"

"Pretty pervy," McCue observed. "Might could get in trouble for that."

Lily smiled briefly. "The woman earlier, the surrogate who attacked you, Gabriel. Did you smell anything?"

I shrugged. "Perfume." Two sets of eyes stared at me. "Oh. Yeah. Okay. Well, *shit*. Am I supposed to worry about every woman I get up close and personal with, now?"

"Can you remember her scent?" McCue asked. "Would you know it again?"

I thought back. My mind had not exactly been on *perfume* with her hands on portions of my anatomy. But yeah, I'd been aware of a scent. "I couldn't tell you what was in it."

Lily's torc glinted as she shifted. "Do the job right tonight, you'll know what it smells like. Go over there, flush out the demons, kill 'em. Don't worry about exorcising them; the bodies aren't possessed humans, aren't actual living human hosts, but *ghosts*. The humans are long dead. You only use exorcism if a living person has been possessed, because there's a host to save."

"Flush 'em out . . ." Remi echoed dryly. "Any suggestions how we do that?"

She sent us both a glance that was clearly amused. "Oh, I think that will take care of itself."

95

I was reminded of how she'd described us earlier: *newbies.* "Wait," I said. "Grandaddy said hell could track us now, because our *beacons* are turned on. Our souls? So we go after these things, and they know we're coming?"

And I recalled what the other woman had said to me. *"You lit it up last night. I felt it. And it shines so bright, it does. It's so very pretty. But now I'm going to extinguish it. I'm going to extinguish you."*

Lily said, "You can be proactive, or *reactive.* It's your choice. But yes, you are targets now. Anywhere you go where there are surrogates, they'll know you. Not all are strong enough to track you—there's a hierarchy among them as there is among the heavenly host—but all can sense you. You walk into a place where even a lesser surrogate has set up shop, made it a domicile, just as this roadhouse is, and that being will know you. But you'll learn to do the same, to sense a demon's presence."

I shook my head. "How the hell are we going to be able to do that?"

She folded her arms, leaned against the cabinets. "The way Jubal explained it to me is that you, Remi, can read people. At some point, with experience, you'll be able to recognize a host who's been possessed no matter how human it appears. *You,* Gabriel, are sensitive to places. Kind of a living Electromagnetic Field meter. In certain places you'll sense demonic presence, whether they're in human hosts or something else. But it takes time to learn. No one is *born* knowing everything, even with heaven's essence in you. You'll have to survive long enough to learn."

Yeah, a good goal, survival. I was up for that.

"So—tonight you'll go in after your first surrogates. Whether you live or die is up to you." Her tone sharpened from matter-of-factness to a hard precision. "But you need to realize this, to always remember this: if you die by normal means—and that's possible, because you wear human flesh—you go to heaven. But a heavenly soul that is extinguished by a demon goes to hell. Literally, *to hell*. Forever. No angelic rescue." Her green eyes were piercing. "And you really don't want to go there, because Dante got it right about all those circles and suffering. Trust me, it's no comedy, and it's certainly not divine."

"Dante emerged from hell," Remi pointed out, before I could. "Found paradise. Found God."

"And if we're made of heavenly matter—" I began, but a look in her eye made me stop. "No go, huh?"

"Jubal could tell you better than I."

"He's not here, and you're hedging," I accused her.

Lily shrugged. "I have my own agenda. I'm not an angel, remember. I'm not even a Christian." Her smile was faint, and oddly feral. "Remember the mythology, Gabe. All the various branches. Parse between them. You'll find your answers there."

McCue's tone was skeptical. "*If* you're the Morrigan."

"Do the job," she told him, unfazed by his observation. "Survive, come back to me, we'll talk further. If you die, well . . ." Again, that feral smile, ". . . then it doesn't matter, does it?"

I eyed her thoughtfully, realized we'd get no more out of her with this particular line of questioning, so I moved on. "We were in the Zoo last night, and I didn't sense anything."

"Did you try? The way Jubal always asked you to?"

I rolled my shoulders, sensing criticism beneath her tone. "It's not a habit, and there was no reason to."

"And you wouldn't have recognized it if you had; you're still

97

just a baby." She twitched her brows dismissively, mouth flat. "So, now you *try*. Become that EMF meter. Your grandfather started you, but it'll take time."

I remembered the day before upon the mountain, when I'd sensed the peace of the place, the slow beat of the earth's pulse.

I looked at McCue. "Since you read people—you get any kind of vibe off that woman? The demon?"

Remi cocked an eyebrow. "Other than she had the hots for you and was ready to jump your bones? Yeah, I noticed you two on the way out the door. 'Course that was before she decided to gut and strangle you, that is. Nope. Nada."

I considered that. "It might have been helpful if you had."

"What, you want to drag me around to bars where you go to pick up women so I can tell you if they intend to kill you? Not my idea of a good time, boy. Not for me, leastways. That's on you."

I frowned, looked at Lily. "Did *you* know what she was?"

Her eyes sparked. "Who, me? When I'm just an imaginary creature out of mythology?" But she relented. "Macha might have. Dogs are very good at sensing things, far better than humans. But me, no. I didn't know what she was until she tried to extinguish you. You might do better to ask if Jubal knew last night. He's a seraph. They know far more than the rest of us."

Just like that, Grandaddy was outed as something a little more important than an agent. But her words stung. "He'd warn me. He wouldn't throw me to the wolves like that."

She laughed at me. "I saw you, Gabriel. All that woman did tonight was give you a stare, a glint, a smile. After that it was all testosterone, boyo. No throwing was done at all, to wolves or otherwise, that you didn't do yourself." She gestured at the items spread out across the counter. "Take it. Guns, knives, ammo, herbs, water, oil—call it a starter kit. You'll add your own things to it along the way. Like I said, I'll resupply you when we're in the same vicinity—and there are others of us out there, too—but you'll need to find your own sources, learn how to do this for yourself. For one another."

I cast a glance at McCue. *For one another.* When we were as yet strangers. But the cowboy looked back steadily, briefly quirked brows and tilted his head slightly as if to say he was willing to wait and see.

Lily noted the exchange. "You are not the only soldiers in this fight," she declared. "There's a *world* out there in trouble, and neither I nor Jubal nor anyone else in this war can be in all places. Yes, your bright little heavenly beacons may—*may*— summon help in times of great strife, should you call on them to do so, but most times you'll have to pick up that shovel and dig yourselves out of whatever hole you're in. But then, you've been taught self-reliance. Whether you knew it or not, Jubal was training you. But so was life. Now—" She waggled beckoning fingers. "—come on into the living quarters, have some whiskey, kick back for a bit. In about four hours, couple of hours after closing time, you can head over and kill a pair of surrogates." She shrugged. "Or, well . . . die."

I shook my head. "We could just walk away. Call bullshit on everything, go back to our lives. Be normal."

"There is no more 'normal' for either of you." With a gesture, she led us out of the garage into elegant surroundings. "And have you ever walked away from a fight in your life, Gabriel Harlan?"

"Well, no. But I sure as hell don't go looking for them, either."

"Doesn't matter." Lily waved us to a seat upon the couch, the recliner. She poured whiskey into glasses, presented each of us with one. "Things are different, now. This rig is protected, but the minute you step outside it, that ends. They know you're here, probably knew it last night when you put on the rings and clasped hands, but I'm betting they held back because of that woman. She must outrank them."

McCue shook his head. "Quite a picture, ain't it? Demonic chain of command."

I, in the recliner and somewhat uneasy about the nearness of perch and crow—the bird was *huge*, with a mean eye and a nasty-looking beak—met Remi's eyes. The cowboy's expression was thoughtful.

Lily shrugged. "One hierarchy in heaven, another in hell. Balance. The two surrogates would have gone after you last night, unless someone of higher rank staked a claim. First dibs on Gabe because of *primogenitura*. You'd have been next, Remi."

I swore, ran a hand through loose hair. "So—you're saying *for sure* she's a demon?"

"I'd think so," Lily replied matter-of-factly. "Probably possesses a human host."

I thought about that. It made me exceptionally uncomfortable. Nothing about her had suggested she was anything but all human, entirely a woman, and a highly hot one at that. But . . . now major squick factor, yeah.

I shifted in the chair and looked at McCue with an undisguised appeal. "Listen, if you're good with seeing demons in people—you gotta let me know if one's hitting on me."

The cowboy's grin was slow. "Or if you're hitting on her?"

"*Yes*," I said fervently. "I mean, that is, if you feel it. Smell it. Whatever it is you do."

"I don't do anything yet," McCue said, eyes bright with humor.

"Because I don't want to fu—" I broke off, slewed a glance at Lily.

"I am familiar with the word," she said gravely. "And yes, it's entirely possible a surrogate might seduce in order to extinguish you. They've been known to do that kind of thing."

"Sooo, a succubus, in essence." I heaved a sigh. "Damn, *everything's* real, now? Succubi, incubi, sirens, kelpies, selkies . . ." I trailed off, because she was nodding. "Godzilla?"

"Probably not Godzilla," she conceded, "or King Kong. Not sure about a Transformer. But sure, Remi can get into his truck, drive away. You can get on your bike, *ride* away. But they'll follow you. They know you, now. You walked into their domicile, and you ignited your souls."

I remembered that moment. Remi McCue and I had clasped hands, clicked rings together at Grandaddy's behest—and now everything in my life, in *our* lives, was changed.

Lily Morrigan—*the* Morrigan?—drank whiskey, sat down upon the carpeted floor and crossed her legs, completely at ease. "It's not an easy life, but if you listen and learn—and rely on what you've been taught—you'll make out all right." The wolfhound folded down and settled, putting a massive head into Lily's lap. She stroked the wiry hair, gazed on us both out of bright green eyes set in fair, unblemished skin. "I know this is new—but you need to understand the risks. There's no going back. You can't do control-alt-delete. You are what you are. But what you need to remember is . . . *hell knows you're here.*"

CHAPTER EIGHT

F our hours later, under Lily Morrigan's sharp, bright eyes, I wanted to laugh out loud. But McCue was being very serious, and she equally so; I doubted they'd understand my humor.

We were gearing up like some kind of serious macho testosterone movie. Or, yeah, like the elegance of James Bond discovering what new tech Q had for him.

I grinned. Biker leather and cowboy denim. Elegance, my ass.

When it came to armaments, I opted for the long-barreled version of the Taurus Judge, preparing to load with the silver-jacketed .45 caliber rounds Lily explained had been washed in holy water, then dipped in oil of abramelin.

"Which recipe?" I asked dryly. "Samuel Mathers'? Aleister Crowley's?"

"The original," she answered. "Abraham the Jew's, as described in the Book of Abramelin. But there will be an extra ingredient in the mix just to give it a little kick: the breath of two souls born of heaven. So go on, boyos. Blow on the bullets."

McCue's head shot up. "Do what?"

I stared at her. "You're kidding, right?"

Lily didn't smile. "I don't joke about weapons of war."

After a moment's thoughtful hesitation, Remi took five bullets into the palm of his hand and blew gently upon them, looking to Lily for confirmation. I, desiring more of a flourish to make a point, picked up the bullets one at a time, huffed a brief breath at each, then loaded it into the chamber.

"Yes," Lily said, "you looked as silly as you thought you would. But it's cover your ass time, is it not?" She paused, took from a drawer a shoulder holster and a belt-mount. "Arizona is open carry. No one will give you a hard time. Gabe, you can go with the shoulder holster under your jacket. Remi, you're a Texas cowboy. Your belt will work."

After a moment's hesitation, I stripped out of my jacket, strapped myself into the shoulder holster, put my jacket back on.

I owned a Bowie, but felt most comfortable with the KA-BAR I habitually sheathed at my spine for a fast reach-around. The KA-BAR was a plain old steel knife, no silver involved, but it was comfortable and familiar, and tonight I wanted it within reach. Just having it on me offered a little ease in the midst of confusion, a mental anchor of sorts. At Lily's suggestion, I wiped the blade down quickly with holy oil.

Remi had opted for the Damascus Bowie, the Hibben trio of throwing knives, and the short-barreled Taurus. But when it came to the Remington shotguns, I recommended powdered-iron cartridges.

When McCue looked a question, I explained that folklore ghosts were most susceptible to iron. Which sounded stupid when I said it, but that's what legend and folklore claim. "Since we're doing the Cover Your Ass thing. Though I sure as shit never thought about using shotgun shells on ghosts. In stories, it's blades."

McCue seemed unfazed. "If it's folklore, it's your wheel-house," he said. "I'll recite the Latin, handle exorcisms, throw knives as necessary, shoot the hell out of whatever—hell, I'll *pray* over 'em, if that'll work . . . but I've never contemplated killing *ghosts* before, so if you've got a leg up, go for it."

"Well, iron and salt are used for dispersal of, or protection against, ghosts," I explained. "Supposedly to get rid of a ghost for good you have to destroy its source material, such as bones. Now, you *do* understand I've never actually done this before. Just studied it." I'd taught it, too, but didn't say that. "But I don't know jack about demons. Unless you're a priest, who does? It's not exactly normal."

Remi McCue grinned. "I've studied exorcisms recited in a dead language. You've read how to destroy *ghosts*. Oh, son, we are so far beyond the vicinity of normal that it ain't even funny."

I reflected that this was undoubtedly true. "So, Lily . . . we go in there, flush 'em out, then shoot 'em to back 'em off? How do we actually *kill* them?"

"These ghosts were humans, once," she replied. "You can kill a human by shooting it with anything, if you hit the right spot. What's true in life is true in death. So hit the same right spot. But regular ammunition won't work on a ghost or a sur-rogate."

I nodded. "Got it. Powdered iron to knock them off-stride, then silver bullets dipped in holy oil—"

"—and don't forget we breathed on 'em." McCue was grinning. "Breath of death, instead of breath of life. Kinda like it." He paused. "Bein' as they're demons, and all."

I shrugged. "So long as we don't have to kiss 'em, I'm game."

McCue nodded, looked at Lily. "Just to clarify—if we wing a ghost, we don't kill it. But we put a shot wherever it'll kill a human, we're good?"

"If it's a *human* ghost," Lily clarified. "And yes, you can disperse a ghost temporarily if you wing it, or even with less contact than that. One BB might do. But recall that these are *demons* in ghost form. It won't take long for either demon to reconstitute. The first time, they may respond as a real ghost would and dematerialize, because a ghost has sense memory of itself as a human, but that won't last. Demons can't be effective if they don't establish their own powerbase within the host as soon as possible. You can't just wound a demon in the form of ghost or spirit and keep driving it away. Once, maybe. After that, bet on them being very corporeal, very strong—and seriously pissed off. Call it paranormal adrenaline. That's when iron won't work."

McCue looked at me. "Silver bullet to heart or head."

I grinned. "Works for me." But amusement died. I met Lily's eyes. "Do they know we're coming?"

Lily stared right back. "I don't know."

After dark, the cowboy and I crossed the lot between Lily's RV and the roadhouse. The moon was nearly full, and the swath of stars above the city was astonishing in its clarity. The only artificial illumination came from the bug light over the back door.

—————

No alarms on this place," I noted quietly after we inspected the entire perimeter of the big log building and met out back once more. "Well, far as I can tell."

"So, we break a window and just two-step in there?" McCue asked in a low voice. "This is for shit, you realize. This is breaking and entering. We get arrested—how the hell do we explain anything?"

"Wanted to shoot some pool, maybe? Who can tell with drunk guys. Which is about the only cover story that might work." I attempted to peer in a window, but it was blocked by drapes. "You can tell 'em anything you want to, even the truth, but it won't get you very far. So the key is: *Don't get caught.*" I knelt at the door, set down the shotgun. Gestured Remi to bend down and kept my voice very low, almost a whisper. "You got that little flashlight Lily gave you? Shine it here, on the lock."

McCue, squatting, turned on the flashlight, bent down to aim it. Like me, he spoke barely above a whisper. You'd have to be kissing close to hear us. "What the hell are you doing— wait . . . are those—?" He didn't finish, just rose abruptly and grabbed my right arm, literally yanking me away from the building. "You've got *lockpicks?*"

I shrugged. "Well, if you don't have a key—these'll do."

It's difficult to sound scandalized in a strangled whisper, but he managed it. "You ride around on a motorcycle carrying lockpicks? Just how often do you do this sort of thing?"

"Breaking in, or attempting to kill ghosts hosting demons?" I grinned at his expression. "I know how to use them—" I'd

107

actually learned in prison, though I didn't tell him that, "—but I don't *carry* lockpicks, no. Or didn't until tonight. Lily slipped 'em to me. Now, come on. Let's get this done."

He followed me back the few steps to the door. "This is not what I signed on for."

I squatted again, motioning for him to aim the flashlight at the lock. "You've been a good boy all your life?"

"Damn right I have," McCue whispered back. "Well, except for that little fracas me and Luke got mixed up in at my high school graduation. But that didn't amount to much. Busted nose, a few teeth knocked out—not mine, you understand. I had some moves by then." He paused. "*Better* than Jagger."

I felt the tumblers shift and click. I removed the picks, set my hand on the doorknob and turned. Yup. Pushed open the door but didn't enter, just knelt there and zipped the pick kit closed, tucked it into a pocket. Then I picked up the shotgun and slowly rose.

McCue stepped close against the chinked log wall. "How often you used those suckers?" he whispered. "You do this regular—this breaking in? Does Grandaddy know?"

"If I tell you it makes you an accessory."

"I'm already an accessory on this break-in, asshat!"

I ignored the conversation. "You do know how to shoot, right?"

McCue's quiet tone was dry. "Guess we'll find out. Meanwhile, you sensing anything *surrogate-like* in there? Since you're a living EMF meter and all."

"I'm sensing a certain amount of cowboy bullshit. And anyway, she said it would take time. No, I don't get any kind of vibe, other than feeling pretty damn stupid about this whole thing." I pushed the door open with infinite care. "I think we should have asked Lily a lot more questions."

Remi leaned close again as he spoke. "You're the folklorist. Seem to know this shit."

"That doesn't make me a *ghost hunter.* Buster. What the hell ever."

"And I didn't get the feeling she was going to say much more other than telling us to come back *with* our shields—or on 'em. You know, all Spartan-like."

"You don't look too Spartan in that hat."

"Protective coloration," came the whispered reply. "Now, of the two of us, who's more likely to be taken for a drunk cowboy wandering around a cowboy bar after hours in the dark, should the cops come by—a guy who *is* a cowboy, or an ex-con biker dude? With lockpicks in his pocket. And guns, which he shouldn't rightly be carrying since he's an ex-con. And should we even be talking?"

"Why not?"

"Well, if ghosts—or demons—have working ears, we might could give ourselves away if we keep having long-winded conversations."

"No one could hear us from a foot away," I pointed out, well within that foot, "and if what Lily told us is true, they already know we're here and we could probably shout at the top of our lungs." I eased my way inside the door. Same door I'd exited a matter of hours before, in pursuit of the woman—who wasn't, as it turned out, actually a woman. And there came the squick factor again. I sought another topic immediately. "You know, some people believe Einstein proved ghosts exist."

McCue, trying to combine utter disbelief with keeping his

voice down, sounded strangled. "Einstein? Why are we talking about Einstein?"

"But I think it's bullshit."

"*Einstein* is bullshit, or these 'some people'?"

I shrugged. "We're made up of electrical energy. People, I mean. And Einstein said that when people die, that energy goes somewhere. Into the environment. That it can't be destroyed, only changed from one form to another."

"So, that's where the EMF meters come in. Or you. Sniffin' out that released electrical energy."

I took a few more steps inside. "That's the theory." Muted light at the back of the bar didn't illuminate much, but it kept the place from being pitch black. I advanced a few more steps.

McCue followed closely. "Mighty thin theory."

"That never stopped conspiracy theorists, or UFO whackjobs."

"You know, according to the Bible, there's no such thing as actual real ghosts. You die, you get judged, you go to heaven or hell. End of story. Which jibes with what Grandaddy said."

I shook my head. "He said a lot. What specifically do you mean?"

"I'll quote chapter and verse later, but the Bible says if there *are* ghosts hanging around, they're demons. That any paranormal activity, if evidence of it is found, is because demons are controlling it. But there are positive spirit beings. Angels." He paused. "I wonder . . ."

I put a hand on a pool table to spot myself, moved carefully around it. Cradled the shotgun in two hands again. "Wonder what?"

McCue was very close. "Do you suppose we give off any

kind of special electrical energy? You and me, I mean. Because of our beacons."

"What, you mean like Iron Man's power plant?"

"I wonder if we'd set off EMF meters. Or airport scanners. Or if an MRI or CT machine would pick up anything."

"Maybe we should go to Vegas," I said dryly, "see if we can take control of all the slot machines. Make all those little old ladies happy with their nickels."

"They might could give us a percentage," McCue agreed. "We'd be rich in no time, five cents a deposit. Now, what was it Lily said about these ghosts? Husband and wife?"

"She tripped at the top of the steps, fell down them and broke her neck," I explained. "Despondent husband killed himself a year or two later. If the impulse for these demons is to initially behave as the ghosts would, they'll hang around where they died."

"So we look for her on the stairs?"

"And for him in front of the fireplace, where he offed himself."

We moved through the pool tables, stepped out onto the main floor. In silence we waited, examining surroundings in low-level illumination.

I reflected that yes, one might term it "spooky." All kinds of dead animals with colored marble eyes and bared yellow teeth hung off the walls, crouched along the beams, inhabited corners. Antlers on mounted trophy heads stabbed the air.

I heard the clink of glass from the bar and jerked my head around.

No one was there.

Flames roared up in the fireplace where none had blazed before.

The chair before the fireplace rocked, with no one in it.

"Okay," McCue murmured, "this officially qualifies as weird."

"Or haunted."

"'Haunted' is weird." He paused. "You getting any kind of a *feeling* about this?"

I shook my head. "You're supposed to be the one who can sense demons. You getting anything?"

"Smells a little funny."

I opened my mouth to make a comment, but suddenly a woman stood before us, appearing from out of the dark. I stared in disbelief. Her head, the neck obviously broken, lay loosely on one shoulder, which grossed me out. But it didn't seem to bother her.

Then she grabbed Remi McCue and flung him across the room.

I heard the cut-off yelp from McCue, the crashing of body through tables and chairs. Then she was right on top of him, and in his hands was a shotgun, not good for close-in fighting. Even as he tried to raise it, the woman—*ghost? demon?*—chopped down hard at the barrel. It clattered out of his hands.

Definitely corporeal. Definitely *pissed*.

I yanked my revolver from the holster and fired a powdered iron shell. The woman disappeared—dematerialized?—but, dammit, in the middle of the melee I had not gotten off a chest or head shot. Winged her, maybe. Damn—I'd been right there, *right there*, and hadn't made the shot. Not the kill shot.

Or whatever it was when you destroyed a ghost. Or a demon. Or whatever. Ghosticide? Demonicide?

I moved rapidly to the wall, putting my back against it. Heart rate was high, and I released a long breath. "Lily is *so* going to give me much shit about all of this," I muttered, revolver cradled in both hands. "Hey, McCue?" I saw no reason to keep my voice down now; the female ghost clearly knew I was present. "Remi? Hey—cowboy!"

No answer.

Shit.

I waited a moment, listening hard. No more clinking of glasses at the bar, no more creak of the rocking chair, no more crackle of flames in the fireplace.

When no further attack seemed imminent, I opted to see if I could work my way across the roadhouse, discover if McCue had survived being flung across the room like a rag doll. Because I was certain Lily would give me more shit if the cowboy was actually dead.

Hell, Grandaddy might *murder* me if I'd got Remi killed.

But that was the last coherent thought I had, because every dead, stuffed, marble-eyed animal in the place *came alive*.

And all of them apparently had me on their menu.

CHAPTER NINE

Well, hell," I muttered.

I did a quick mental inventory of my personal armory. Five shots left in the shotgun, five in the Taurus; plus the Bowie and KA-BAR.

But—what the hell works on reanimated stuffed animals? That wasn't anything I'd ever read about. And could they actually see out of those fake-ass marble eyes?

Cougar. Bobcat. Lynx. Wolf. Some bristly pig-looking thing with nasty tusks. All prowled toward me from out of an almost lightless space, clearly able to see very well indeed out of their fake-ass eyes. They even *sounded* real.

They also sounded hungry.

"Hey, McCue! You alive over there?" Backup would be good. "Would an exorcism work on these things? Maybe knock the stuffing out of 'em?"

No answer. I began to wonder if maybe the cowboy truly was dead. The idea sent a curl of nausea through my belly.

Lily Morrigan had said a heavenly soul extinguished by a demon would not go to heaven.

And for some inexplicable reason—considering I didn't

truly know the man—that really, seriously, *significantly* pissed me off. Because if heaven was real, so was hell. It blind-sided me, the anger. And it fueled me.

I took out the cougar first, then the lynx, followed up with the bobcat, the wolf. The pig-thing took my last round.

I heard Lily's voice again, *'You've only got five shots, but if you can't put down something within five, maybe you deserve to be dead.'*

Yeah, well, that might be true if the target were just one thing, not *five* possessed animals—that were deceased, but somehow not.

"Bear!" shouted the cowboy, who was, hosanna and halle-lujah, not dead after all.

I swung around, reaching for the Bowie. I'd forgotten about the damn stuffed grizzly.

I thought about diving for the shotgun lying on the floor, but that meant I'd be going *to* the bear. The very large bear who could indeed see me out of its fake-ass eyes. Because it stared right at me.

Shit. I wasn't good at throwing knives. But I sure as hell wasn't going to *close* with the sucker. So I threw it.

And missed.

I was out of ammo, lacked the rifle, figured I'd miss with the KA-BAR, too. And time was just flat gone. So I grabbed up billiard balls already racked on the nearest table and began hurling them at the bear. I'd been a pitcher in high school; I nailed the sucker a few pretty good ones right in the face. Even broke out one of the eyes. But the bear kept coming.

"Duck!" McCue yelled.

I flung myself down as far from the bear as I could get in one frantic leap aside before dropping, automatically shielding my head. And then I heard a series of reports as Remi fired all five chambers from the revolver into the bear.

As the animal toppled, I shoved myself out of the path of destruction. The massive grizzly fell hard and heavy, face down. For one startled moment I was eye-to-eye with the dead—re-dead?—bear, and then I scrambled to my knees and scooped up the other shotgun. I tucked it under my arm between ribs and elbow, then dug into a jacket pocket for additional ammunition to reload the revolver.

"Mighty fine shootin,' there, Tex," I noted as McCue came cautiously forward to inspect the bear.

The cowboy looked around the field of battle. "Man, looks like we took out half a zoo."

I slid bullets into the revolver. "What's that pig-thing?"

"Javelina. With a 'j,' but pronounced as an 'h.' You know— just so you sound smart when you tell stories about this."

I was pretty damn sure I wasn't going to be telling any stories about the night stuffed animals came to life in a cowboy bar in Arizona. "Hava-what?"

"Javelina. Peccary. Not actually a pig. They inhabit Mexico, the Southwestern U.S." He gazed down at the pile of bristle and tusks, lips pursed as he nodded appreciation. "Males can mass over eighty pounds. Nasty suckers, they are. We got 'em in Texas, too."

I noticed he seemed a little shaky. "You okay?"

McCue nodded, ran a tentative hand through short dark hair at the back of his head and winced. "Caught me a good lick on the edge of a table, but it's too far from my heart to kill me." He glanced around. "Where's my hat? I feel naked."

I caught a glimpse of something behind the cowboy. *"Down!"*

I yelled, and as McCue dropped I fired the shotgun at the husband half of the ghost couple.

Who nonetheless managed to grab McCue around his throat as it went down, because I had pulled my shot upward, too worried about nailing McCue with the buckshot spread. I saw the spray of—goo?—burst from the male ghost's head as he—*it*—collapsed, but there was nothing about him that suggested he was dead. Well, dead again. And despite the fact the man—or ghost, or demon—was missing half his head on one side from the original shot that killed him, and a divot in the other side of his skull where my spread had struck him, the ghost-demon had both hands gripped around McCue's throat from behind, digging fingers in.

Corporeal, all right. Because even as he lay tangled on the floor with the ghost-demon, Remi was clearly being strangled.

"Are you really that stupid?" I walked up to place the muzzle of the Taurus against the oozing head. "It's a silver bullet dipped in holy oil, asshole, and from this range I don't miss."

And I fired.

The ghost-demon, which resembled nothing so much as a perfectly presentable, infinitely normal man missing part of his head, made an odd discordant noise like a deflating bagpipe, rippled head to foot, broke up as if pixelated, then collapsed into a pile of dust and grit.

McCue, who was clutching his throat as he lay on the floor, croaked, *"What the hell are you doing?"*

"Killing me a demon." I reached down a hand. "Come on."

"Jesus, man, I was right in front of it—you could have hit me! And you splattered its brains all over me!"

"*Ghost* brains," I reminded him. "Not real."

"They sure as hell *felt* real! A little *warning* next time. Holy Christ."

I was aware of an odor. Sickly sweet. Powerful. Jesus, but it stank. "It was a bullet, not buckshot. Went right through his head. Dude, you whine like this all the time?" I gestured with my outstretched hand. "Come on. Up from there."

McCue clamped onto my hand, allowed himself to be pulled up from the floor. He opened his mouth to say something more, and then I felt a flash of heat in my hand, startling enough that I jerked my hand away from McCue's and stared at it in alarm.

What the—?

McCue echoed me, and I glanced up to find a pair of very startled blue eyes fixed on my own.

I heard Grandaddy's voice again. *'That day when you offered to carry your brother's pain, begged me to lift it from him, to give it to you, I knew you were ready. And you consented. But you weren't sealed to Matthew that day, Gabriel. Because he isn't heaven-born. You were sealed to Remi.'*

It rose up like a tide, a slow but relentless drive of water to the shore, to break upon the land. And I knew in my bones.

This is what we were meant to do. It's literally what we were *bred* for.

The certainty was profound.

Remi said, "Right now I'm about as confused as a goat on Astro Turf. But—this is right, what we're doing. This is necessary."

In an accord bordering on elation, I grinned at him. "Let's go kill us another demon."

And then Remi's expression changed. I saw the revolver

come up, heard the click on an empty chamber; McCue had not reloaded in the aftermath of being jumped by the male ghost. Breathing had come first.

I twisted, wrenched myself aside as I brought my own gun up; saw the glint of something in reflected light: one flash, two, a third. A glitter of silver, the silence of steel as it cleaved the air.

One. Two. Three. A perfect, deadly progression of superb physical awareness, of perfect control. McCue's movements had been smooth and effortless.

The female ghost dropped. Three hilts stood out from her— *its?*—heart, like a tight bullet grouping.

And then the body, if it could be called a body, did the wheezing bagpipe rippling pixilation thing, collapsed into dust and grit, and the three throwing knives, falling, rattled against the floorboards, chimed steel-on-steel as they landed one atop the other.

That sweet smell again, almost overpowering. And ash. Charcoal. The astringency of *heat*. A trace of burned flesh. The stench of corruption, of putrefaction.

I held a revolver in one hand, cradled a shotgun in the crook of an elbow, felt like I'd run a four-minute mile in three. But the tide rose up in me again, bringing with it an awareness of accomplishment. Of an abiding satisfaction. A trace of something edging toward euphoria.

I grinned at Remi McCue. "Oorah! We just kicked us some evil ass!"

McCue bent, picked up his knives, safed them home in the tri-part sheath. Then he went back into the dimness, returned with his hat. His grin matched mine. "How about we light a shuck and clear out before the cops come? 'Cuz I'm not too sure how they'll take to a tale about shooting the stuffings—the *literal* stuffings, I mean—out of already-dead animals."

I tucked my revolver into the shoulder holster. Yup, bear, cougar, lynx, bobcat, a hava-pig-thing all down from their mounts and shot full of powdered iron and silver, sprawled across the floor amidst a scattering of pool balls, might cause some consternation among the authorities. I already had a rap sheet, but this? This was just plain damn weird.

I heard it in my head: *'Why, yes, Officer, we shot up all the dead, stuffed animals because they came back to life, and then we killed a pair of ghosts that were actually demons. Because Lucifer is coming and we're supposed to save the world.'*

Hell, I wouldn't go to jail for this. I'd go to a mental ward. "We gotta come up with a cover story," I murmured. "Maybe a whole boatload of them." I pushed the door open, stepped into the coolness of the night.

McCue came out behind me. "A great philosopher once said, *You may all go to hell, but I will go to Texas.* Seems an appropriate quote for demons, don't you think?"

I shook my head as I walked across the lot toward Lily Morrigan's big rig, shotgun cradled across my elbow. "No philosopher ever said that."

"Davy Crockett said that."

"Davy Crockett? Davy Crockett wasn't a philosopher!"

"He most certainly was. He also said, *Be always sure you are right—then go ahead.* Words to live by, son. Words to live by."

"I suppose you've got a country song for all of this, too?"

"Well, I might could sing the theme song to the Davy Crockett TV show—I've seen the whole thing on DVD—but there's also 'Angels Among Us,'" Remi replied promptly.

I thrust up a silencing hand. "Don't start. Do not start. And we're not angels. Grandaddy said so."

"Close enough. We're kissin' cousins."

I cast him a glance. "Actually, I'm more a fan of Camus. *Nobody realizes that some people expend tremendous energy merely to be normal.*"

McCue considered that for a moment. "Then I reckon the two of us are gonna be expending nine whole boatloads of energy from here on out just to *fake* normal."

I reached the steps of the rig first, glanced back over my shoulder. *"Only the guy who isn't rowing has time to rock the boat."*

"That Camus again?"

I pulled open the door. "Sartre."

"Well, if Lucifer plans to row the boat, we'll just have to rock the hell out of it." Remi paused, followed me up the steps. "Rock *him* the hell out of it and right back into the pit."

Lily Morrigan, as we entered, waited in the driver's seat. "Go put those shotguns in the back. We're leaving." She started the rig, gestured for us to hurry. "Too much noise," she said. "Scanner says the cops are on their way. We're moving down the road a bit."

"My truck!" Remi protested.

I was horrified. "My *bike!*"

"Tomorrow." She put the rig in gear, started to roll. "And don't worry about them tracing you through the plates; they'll have no idea you're with me in an RV campground, nor will they have any idea those vehicles are connected to what just happened. They'll think you guys got drunk and took Uber or Lyft home."

"Shit," I muttered; I did not want to leave my bike. I put out my hand to McCue. "Give me your gun. I'll put it up." I accepted the second shotgun from McCue, walked hastily back to the garage, found the right cabinet and hooks, safed the shotguns, latched the doors, went back to the front. Remi had hung his hat over the window valance, found a spot on the couch. I dropped into the armchair beside the crow's perch.

"How many shots?" Lily asked.

"For the demons?" I shared a puzzled glance with Remi. "Missed the first shot, sideswiped a head with a second, then took the guy-ghost out with a bullet straight through the skull."

Her gaze was level. "I heard more shots than that."

I was astonished. "You were counting? Seriously?"

She turned the rig north onto Route 66, the Mother Road. "Yes."

"Why?" Remi asked.

At this hour, the street was nearly devoid of vehicles. "Your grandfather asked me to."

I eyed the big crow, seeming unperturbed upon its perch as the RV jostled down the uneven paving. "Why would he do that?"

She was very clear. "He said Remi might at some point opt for knives, which are silent. He said you would go with the revolver, and do what needed doing in two shots. Well, I heard more than two shots."

"That's because every stuffed animal in the place came back to life," Remi protested, "and those damn ghosts, or demons, don't exactly hold still." He moved aside hastily as the big Wolf-hound bitch expressed a desire to join him on the couch. She didn't ask. She just—arrived.

I was annoyed. Yeah, he had missed the first shot. The

second had hit the target, but failed to put the ghost down. "Most of those shots were aimed at the animals. The stuffed animals. The stuffed *dead* animals. That you didn't warn us about." I paused. "Did you expect that to happen? Was that some kind of test?"

Lily laughed. "What you should expect is to expect anything. And if you want to talk philosophy, here's a saying for you. About the Irish. You might find it apropos." She lifted her voice, shaped the words with a lilt more pronounced than she'd had before.

> *"Be they kings, or poets, or farmers,*
> *They're a people of great worth,*
> *They keep company with the angels,*
> *And bring a bit of heaven here to earth."*

She grinned at us. "That's you, boyos. That's the pair o' you. A bit of heaven here on earth."

With great seriousness, Remi drawled, "I'm a Texas boy. Of course I'm a bit of heaven." Then he smiled real slow. "Or so the ladies tell me."

Lily laughed. "I don't doubt it!"

"Oh, Jesus." I rose, walked back toward the kitchen. "I need a drink."

The cowboy quirked his brows. "It's four o'clock."

I began opening cabinets. "That's close enough to five."

"In the morning!"

"That's close enough to five."

CHAPTER TEN

I did indeed pour myself whiskey, once I dug a bottle out of the kitchen cabinetry, even as Lily pulled into the RV campground site assigned to the massive rig. I was more than a little impressed as she wheeled the big motorhome through the narrow road hedged by huge pines, seemingly unfazed by the challenge.

I reflected then that I should probably say nothing whatsoever about being impressed, since she would, in all likelihood, consider it some kind of sexist comment, but I rode a motorcycle, after all, which was infinitely easier to park, so what did I know? I was pretty damn certain *I* couldn't handle the motorhome in close confines.

And I also reflected, with a weird twitch of disbelief, that the most impressive thing about the whole situation was that the woman driving the giant RV claimed to be *an ancient Irish goddess.*

Christ, and I'd thought it was culture shock when I went to prison.

The big RV swayed, and I decided it was easier to ride out the parking job from where I stood in the kitchen, rather than

falling over on my way back to the armchair, as she maneuvered the rig into the narrow site. So I clung to a cabinet, braced
myself with spread legs and loose knees; saw Remi's amused
eyes on me. But since the cowboy was currently pinned down
by the weight of half a huge dog, I wasn't certain McCue was
looking any more badass than I was.

So, we take out demons and undead dead animals, and we
fall down in motorhomes or get engulfed by snoring dogs.

Yeah. Badass, all right.

Lily parked, turned off the engine, opened the driver's door
and climbed down, out of the rig. I turned loose of the cabinet
and made my way back to the armchair.

"You want help hooking up?" Remi called.

"I do not!" Lily called back.

"Yes, ma'am," McCue said. "Not sure this gal would let me
stand anyhow." And he placed a hand on the wolfhound's
head, threaded fingers through wiry hair.

I heard the sounds of compartments being opened from
outside, rapping and banging, and shot Remi a glance. "What's
she doing?"

"Hooking up water, sewer, power," the cowboy answered
matter-of-factly. "You ever been in an RV before?"

"No."

McCue grinned. "It's not exactly rough camping. 'Specially
not a rig like this."

Lily came back in after a bit, cast us a quick smile, then
triggered toggle switches above the door. "Lap of luxury,"
she said.

And the motorhome, on the whine of hydraulics, *grew.*

"Damn," I muttered. When the sound shut off I realized the

RV was now twice as wide as it had been. "It's like a pregnant house. On wheels."

"Slideouts," Remi explained, which told me exactly nothing.

"Couch, dinette," Lily said. "Both convert to beds. You two can crash on those. Bedroom's mine, of course." She plucked the glass from my hand, downed what was left of my whiskey, gave me back the empty glass. "It's five o'clock," she said simply to my raised brows. Then she moved on through to the kitchen. "Coffee coming up. You two go clean those guns, oil up the knives. And from here on out, any time anything calls for oil, make it holy oil. Water?—holy water. Always. Leave nothing to chance."

I shot a glance at McCue. "Holy water go for showers, too?"

She was taking a coffeemaker out of a cabinet, pulling grounds out of the refrigerator. "Screws up the plumbing, pretty much, because of the salt in it. But, you know, you can always buy *bath* salts, exfoliate your heavenly skin so you'll be smooth and pretty for the demons. 'Course you'll need to bless it first."

McCue intoned, "*We humbly ask you, almighty God: be pleased in your faithful love to bless this salt you have created, for it was you who commanded the prophet Elisha to cast salt into water, that impure water might be purified.*" He paused. "Well, leastways, that's the beginning."

I clapped a spread hand over my face in disbelief. "Stop quoting!"

Lily laughed. "Havin' a hard time of it, are you, Gabe? Not quite reconciled to what you are? Here, let me help." She walked over with a bottle, poured more whiskey into my glass. To Remi's glance of disbelief, she said simply, "I'm Irish. What do you want?"

"Coffee," he answered pointedly.

She grinned. "Irish? Or straight?"

"I think I'll just go clean my weapons," Remi observed, but didn't immediately move. He pointed to the dog sprawled half across his lap. "Is she going to let me up?"

"*Faigh suas ó ann*," Lily said. "*Lig cinn an buachaill bocht.*" The wolfhound lifted her head, and from gold-brown eyes stared at Lily, who then said, "Yes, I mean it." And the dog rose up slowly, slithered off the couch, collapsed upon the floor.

McCue stared at her. "That first part wasn't Texan."

"I told her to let the poor boy up. More or less. So, now you're unencumbered by the terrible great dog." She waved a hand. "You're free to move about the cabin."

Remi got up, hesitated a moment as he touched the back of his head, proceeded on through the motorhome and into the garage.

I watched him go by. Blood. There was blood on the collar of his shirt, spotting down the back. I set down my glass with a thunk, followed McCue into the garage. "You're bleeding."

Remi unholstered his gun, placed it on the cabinet counter. "Like I said, I got up close and personal with a table."

"You didn't say you cut yourself."

McCue shrugged. Lily came through from the living quarters, carrying mugs of coffee. "Cream and sugar are up front," she said, then frowned at Remi. "What'd you do to yourself?"

He looked a little like a deer caught in the headlights. "I'm fine!"

"You're bleeding." She set the mugs down, tapped her hairline above her forehead. "Right there. Just now."

"Back of his head, too," I said. "Whacked his head on a table. I don't know what that is in front."

Lily stepped in close and caught a handful of McCue's shirt, holding him in place before he could back away. She pushed back his hair, uncovered a small wound. "That," she said, "looks like buckshot caught you." She turned her head to look at me.

And just like that, I was flung back years to the day I stupidly tricked my brother Matty into riding his bicycle down a hilly street while blindfolded.

When Grandaddy had said, *"Do you understand? If you do something stupid, if you do something wrong, there are always consequences. You might have killed your brother."*

It rose up in me abruptly, the same wave of fear and remorse and terrible sense of guilt that had overwhelmed me when my brother had been injured. Here. Now. Again. It wasn't Matty—and yet, oddly, it was.

I'd pulled my shot intentionally when the ghost had grabbed McCue, trying to keep the buckshot spread away from human flesh. But I'd gone into the fight with an unfamiliar gun, unfamiliar ammunition; had walked into the middle of a wholly unfamiliar kind of battlefield—and got bitten in the ass.

McCue, who'd been bitten a little worse, smiled crookedly. "Guess you might could use a little target practice." And then his smile faded. "Hey. Hey, it's just a joke. This ain't nothin,' trust me. What—are you squeamish? One of those badass studs who passes out at the sight of blood? Because you sure look like you're goin' to. You okay?"

No, I was not okay. I remembered with visceral clarity how

sick and frantic I felt when Matty had been injured, and how grateful I was when Grandaddy had lifted the pain from my brother and transferred it to me. Because pain didn't matter when it was my own. So long as it wasn't my brother's.

I could have killed Matty.

I could have killed Remi.

Lily grabbed a mug from the counter, pressed it into my hands. "There's whiskey in it," she said. "You look like you need it."

Grandaddy had said, "*Matthew was Remi's proxy. He represented the younger brother you needed to have, to trigger the drive to protect.*"

Well, if I was supposed to *protect* McCue, I'd done a piss-poor job of it.

"Can I take this from him?" I asked. "Grandaddy did it for me years ago—lifted it from my brother, gave it to me. Can we do that?"

"Jubal can," Lily answered. "I can't. Neither can you."

I stared hard at the cowboy a moment, cast a fleeting glance at Lily, then turned abruptly and headed toward the front of the motorhome.

I heard Remi ask a question. Lily said simply, "*Primogenitura.* But it's a process, a growing into it, and not a perfect one."

I brushed the scar in my eyebrow. Hell. It had been a process with *Matty,* but at least I'd figured that one out. I'd learned how to bring order to the chaos that was my brother. All I had to do was make it my *own* chaos.

Which was how I'd ended up in jail, by saving my brother and killing a man in the doing of it.

Not long after sunrise, I hoped to hitch my way to the Zoo, maybe a mile, mile-and-a-half down the road from the campground, but few vehicles were out so early Sunday morning. So I hoofed it. And was grateful beyond measure to discover, when I got to the big roadhouse, that my Harley was exactly where I'd left it. The only other vehicle in the parking lot was a bright silver extended cab Ford F-250 pickup bearing Texas license plates, parked over on the side between the roadhouse and a large pine. Remi's, I figured.

I picked up my helmet, donned it, pulled on gloves, threw a leg over the saddle, lifted the bike, started to tap up the kickstand, then paused.

Something. *Something.*

After a moment I let the bike settle, checked out the surroundings. Still felt twitchy. Finally I swung my leg back over, put down the helmet, and walked around to the rear of the building.

If the cops had come to check out reports of gunfire, they hadn't been concerned enough to mark the place off with crime scene tape. Maybe they'd chalked up everything to vandals. After all, the only things killed were dead animals, and ghosts.

Well. If dead things could be rekilled. Still wasn't clear on that.

I paused outside the back door, glanced around, saw no one. A hand on the knob found the door locked again, but that was no impediment. I wielded the lockpicks again, then stepped inside the bar and shut the door behind me.

I lacked the shotgun, but had collected the short-nosed Taurus revolver on my way out—silver bullets—the Bowie, and my KA-BAR.

The stuffed trophy animals were still dead, and they still lay where they'd fallen after being filled with consecrated silver and powdered iron. It was, my watch told me, around 6 a.m. Maybe the cops didn't care about bodies other than human; and obviously the owners either hadn't come at all, or had come and gone.

I walked quietly through the alcove hosting two pool tables. The balls I'd hurled at the bear remained scattered on the plank-wood floor. I moved past them, beyond the dead animals, onto the dance floor in the center of the roadhouse.

Up on the mountain, I'd sensed the deep peace of the environs, had recognized that the area was sacred to both the Navajo and the Hopi. But this place? A roadhouse? It was where people went for a vast variety of reasons, including simple enjoyment, but also to fill the otherwise empty hours.

How often had I done the same? Days on the bike eating up miles of interstate from sunrise to sunset, hours wasted in bars, a cuisine of crappy food. A come-down, my father told me, after all my promise. My mother had said no such thing, of course, but I saw the look in her eyes, the worry, the trace of disappointment. I'd missed none of what they felt, in their eyes and postures. They'd expected better of me. Matty was the one who'd worried them. And then . . . well, then their eldest had seemingly "gone bad," too, only worse.

I'd never told them the whole truth. And my brother? No, Matty never would. Matty just enjoyed the hell out of the fact that his older brother had rushed to his rescue yet again, had taken the fall; and then Matty Harlan just kept on *keeping on* the way he always had, knowing his big brother would always pull his fat out of the fire no matter what.

And now? Now that brother had been told he wasn't even human. Wasn't actually *related* to Matthew Harlan. Was related, instead, to Remi McCue. Who maybe, it occurred to me, was worth more than Matty.

Guilt flooded me. Where the hell had that come from? Matty was *blood*. Matty was my baby brother.

Wasn't he still, despite the whole heavenly matter bullshit?

Huh. Maybe not.

I stood in the center of the dance floor and let myself go quiet, the way I always did when Grandaddy asked me to. Remi had referred to me as a *sensitive*. Yeah, if you wanted to hang a name on it, even if it did sound a little wussy. I'd always gotten vibes from certain places, and then Grandaddy asking me what I felt, what I sensed . . . I'm more open to surroundings than most, yeah.

And here, now, early on a Sunday morning in a place where the night before McCue and I had killed two ghosts who'd become demons, and shot the hell out of reanimated dead animals—well, what did I sense *here*?

I closed my eyes. Let myself go very quiet, go inside myself. Invited the roadhouse to speak its own language.

Peace, upon the mountain. Safety. Here, there was joy, and noise: the sound of live country music; the crack of cue ball against solids and stripes; the shuffle, thump, and slide of boots against parquet; the clink and chime of glasses and bottles; laughter, the rare but not unheard-of bar fight. I smelled beer and hard liquor—this was most definitely not a wine bar—a trace of ancient tobacco predating no-smoking laws, raw wood, wood stain, lacquer and leather. Perfume and after-shave. Felt warmth upon my skin from the crush of bodies, the breath of cold and snow blowing in an opening door in the midst of winter; felt the stomp of snow-caked boots against matting and wood to free them of cold-caulked encumbrances. And heat when summer was upon the place.

And I sensed evil.

Not the place. Not the roadhouse. But something that had inhabited it. Not for long. But evil had entered. Benign ghosts, Lily had described the former owners. Doing no harm. Things moved around, a woman on the stairs or in a booth, a man in the rocking chair before the fire. No reports of trouble, merely some kind of *presence*. But what I felt now was something ma-lignant.

The bulk of it was gone. It was just a smear, a stain, the taste of, well, of *afterness*, for all that wasn't a word. Maybe it should be.

The afterness of evil.

A woman's voice said, "I need to talk to you."

CHAPTER ELEVEN

I spun, snaked my hand up beneath my jacket to pull the revolver, cradle it high in both hands. Beyond the raised gun I caught the quick impression of shape, of a woman: black hair, dark Asian eyes, hands lifted palm-up before me, as if to ward off bullets. But other than raised hands, nothing in her posture spoke of fear, aggression, or hesitance. It struck me that she merely wanted me to stay put.

"You can shoot if you like," she said, "but it won't harm me. Bullets can't. Nor can the knives you carry."

I sniffed surreptitiously. No discernable scent. "Well," I began warily, figuring the answer might be vital to my survival, "what *can* kill you?"

She blinked at me, then smiled. And laughed, showing good teeth. "Like I'll tell *you* that?"

I shrugged. "Had to ask."

"You can put the gun away."

Yeah, right. "I kinda like it right where it is."

"You can't hurt me with it."

"Call it my security blanket."

She smiled faintly. "Yeah, well, a blanket can't do anything to me, either."

Her black hair was chin-length and she wore bangs cut straight across her brow. Striking, if not pretty. And though she was clearly Asian, the epicanthic fold was not pronounced. Her tip-tilted eyes were so dark as to appear pupil-less, but the *impression* of pupils was there, even in poor light.

I stared at her, wondering if the gun maybe *would* hurt her—or if she might be telling the truth. Because I felt pretty damn vulnerable at the moment even with a gun and two knives on me.

The thing about shooting stances is, at some point you get tired of holding a revolver at the end of outstretched arms. I'd trained enough to be good at holding the stance a fair amount of time, but I was out of practice after eighteen months away from weapons.

But I wasn't about to lower my arms. "Who are you?"

"I'm Grigori."

I raised my brows. "Not a woman's name I've heard before."

"That's not my name," she said impatiently, "it's what I am. Grigori. A watcher. And I shouldn't even be here, because we're supposed to *watch*. But—much of that ended eons ago, when some of us fell." A gesture seemed to indicate she wanted to brush away anything nonessential. "You need to know, you and your soul-brother—you're not being given the whole story. It's not just good versus evil, heaven versus hell. There's far more to it than that. You need to know this. Because they'll try to use you, the fallen Grigori. The *other* Grigori. Some of them escaped from hell, too, when the demons climbed out amidst the earthquakes. Some are here on earth."

I stared at her, then finally lowered the gun. If she wanted to harm me, she'd have done it already. "What the hell are you talking about?"

"I'm talking about *hell*!" she snapped. "And heaven. It's not straightforward, any of it. The man you call Grandaddy's only given you half the story."

That lit a coal in my belly. "You're suggesting he's hiding information?"

"Every angel in heaven has an agenda," she said. "Every angel who is here on earth, and in hell. Lucifer is an archangel. He was God's favorite, which is part of the reason God was so upset by the betrayal. Do you believe it can't happen again? He fell, was cast out—so were others. Many of the Grigori—"

I interrupted. "Which you claim *you* are; so how do I know you're not playing me?"

"At this moment you and Remiel are innocents being set up for manipulation," she went on tensely, as if running out of time. "I'm not telling you which side to take. I'm just warning you not to accept everything at face value. Yes, the war has begun—but it's not just black and white. Everything is—"

I cut her off sharply. "—shades of gray? Okay, I get that. It's what life is. But given a choice between heaven and hell, how many people—other than the evil whackjobs—are going to opt for bad over good? Dark over light?"

She shook her head. "When most can make a choice, yes, they choose good—or at least the lesser evil. Happens all the time in politics. But I'm just saying there's a much larger picture than what's been painted for you."

I blinked at her, brows raised. Dryly, I said, "*Larger* than good versus evil? Larger than the End of Days and man's continuation upon the planet as we know it?"

"*Quality* of life," she said sharply. "It's not a question of euthanasia because life's gotten really crappy for a pet, or even a person. It's not a choice of whether survival is a desirable goal, but whether that survival, in the worst-case scenario, maintains even the smallest trace of hope. Because without hope, it's all despair. And that's deadly. That's what kills, in the long run. So *think*, Gabriel. What are you truly fighting for?"

So, she knew who I was. And as absurd as the words sounded, it's what Grandaddy had impressed upon me. "To save the world."

"And just which world is that?" she asked. "The one you know now, the one Lucifer desires, or the world that is merely collateral damage after the immoveable object hits the irresistible force? Rock and a hard place, Gabriel. Who *cares* whether the rock hits the hard place if nothing lies between to be harmed? Then it doesn't matter. So, the rock loses a chip or two, the hard place cracks a little . . . *it doesn't matter*. It only matters when there's *flesh* between the two, flesh that can bleed, can cry out, can die. Humans, Gabriel. Never lose sight of humanity. This world was made for them."

"You're saying heaven doesn't care about humanity?"

"I'm saying that it may become a case of the needs of the many outweigh the needs of the few. And humans are vastly fewer in number than are the inhabitants of heaven or hell. So, yeah, humans may wind up getting hammered."

In sheer incredulity I'd gotten stuck on her first sentence and missed everything else. "You're quoting *Mr. Spock?*"

"Or Jeremy Bentham," she said impatiently. "Philosopher, jurist, social reformer. '*It is the greatest good to the greatest number of people which is the measure of right and wrong.*'"

God, we were having Philosopher Wars. McCue would love it. "'The greatest number of *people*,' is what you said. That suggests it is about humanity."

"It was a human who said 'people.' Heaven may view it differently."

I stared at her. "Whose side are you on?"

"I'm *Grigori*," she emphasized. "Are you totally ignorant? I'm an angel! Of course I'm on the side of heaven."

I grunted in derision. "I'm supposed to buy that, after you've just announced that some of you joined Lucifer in hell, and that a fair number of heaven's inhabitants may not give a damn about humanity."

"They all give a damn," she snapped, "but a portion of humanity may simply get in the way. What part of 'collateral damage' do you not understand? Are you a total dipshitiot?"

"'Dip'—what?"

"Dipshit. Idiot. Dipshitiot."

The absurdity completely swamped me. I could find no words. None at all. In any language. In fact, the only thing I was physically, mentally, and emotionally capable of undertaking at that moment was to go prop myself up against the bar clutching a useless gun. Where I broke into long, slightly hysterical laughter.

Like a dipshitiot.

When I wiped the tears from my eyes, she was gone.

———

Okay, yeah, I could have reentered Lily Morrigan's rig with a little less drama, but the door really did get away from me as I yanked it open. It crashed against the side of the RV, and by then I was through it and standing in the entry way.

Remi, who apparently had dozed off on the couch, sat up swiftly even as Lily pulled a gun from somewhere, the crow flapped its wings and loosed a horrific sound lodged somewhere between a gargle and a horror film shriek, and the wolfhound leaped to her feet growling, peeling back her lips to display a fine set of highly intimidating teeth.

I sliced the air with the edge of a flattened hand. "Okay. My life over the last forty-eight hours has become something of a cosmic joke. I'm not even sure it's real anymore. I'm not even sure *you're* real. For all I know I got slammed by an 18-wheeler, and I'm lying in a hospital somewhere in a coma dreaming up this whole entire screwed-to-hell scenario—a scenario *about* hell!—or maybe I'm actually dead; or maybe somebody slipped me a roofie; or, for that matter, maybe Rod Serling is standing in the wings while they play the spooky damn *Twilight Zone* music; or maybe this is even the holodeck on the fucking *Enterprise* and I'm a token redshirt, but I've about had it. I got mysterious women coming out the wazoo: a she-demon trying to gut me or strangle me; one sitting *right here in front of me* who's playing Need To Know with Irish mythology as she arms me with magic guns, bullets, and *holy oil*, for Christ's sake; and some chick named Gregory informing me it's not just good versus evil anymore but humanity caught in the middle *between* the forces of good and evil and, as it turns out, heaven has a few angels with *agendas* and the needs of the many outweigh the needs of the few, and humans are outnumbered and are therefore *screwed all to hell.* Literally!"

I stopped then, because I was out of breath.

Remi, who'd been staring at me in alarm as I began, relaxed back into the couch and eyed me in something akin to compassion. "Could you have possibly fit any *more* movie and TV references into that?"

"*Yes.*"

Lily put the gun away, said something soothing to both the crow and the wolfhound, then fixed me with wide green eyes. "A woman named Gregory?"

I reached around, caught the door, pulled it closed. "Well, not exactly. What she said was Gri-*gor*-i. That she's an angel."

"A *Grigori*?" Remi asked in shock.

I eased between bird and dog to reach the armchair, dropped my ass into it. "You know what that means?"

"Watcher." Lily lowered herself to the floor to sit beside the wolfhound. "And also fallen angels."

"She said *some* are fallen. She said she wasn't. That not all are." I shrugged. "Though we don't know that she's telling the truth."

Remi rubbed a hand through short hair. "The ones who fell started out okay, here on earth. But they kind of screwed the pooch when they got a little up close and personal with womankind, and got cast out for good. Some believe that was one of the deciding factors for the Great Flood."

"Nephilim," Lily put in. She noted my blank expression. "You're not all that up on your Bible, are you?"

"Basics," I answered. "I was into folklore, not religion."

"The Grigori were sent here to be actual guardian angels," Remi said, "when humanity was still wearin' diapers. All kinds of conflicting stories exist, but in Judeo-Christian texts it says they started sharing knowledge not yet intended for human-kind: astrology, divination, herb lore, even magic. I can see where magic might could be a bit chancy, but I don't know why the first three were considered risks."

"Too much too soon," Lily put in. "You don't generally ask a toddler just learning to stand to go out and run a marathon."

"And?" I prompted.

"Nephilim," Remi said, repeating the word Lily had used. "They're the offspring of human women and angels. Grigori specifically." He paused. "Bad juju, according to some of the ancient texts, though others were kinder. But the upshot is, all those watcher-angels who dared to sleep with human women got cast down from their places, and the kids, all male, were considered genetic no-nos."

"So God, being pissed off with a lot of things by then," Lily went on, "including his rebellious son, Lucifer, from whom He took back the car keys and tossed out of the house, decided it was time for a do-over. But he didn't want to wipe out all of mankind, so he sent Uriel to Noah."

"You should know the next part," Remi noted. "About Noah. It's kind of famous."

I shot him stink-eye. "What concerns me is that she said Grandaddy hadn't told us the whole story." Now I looked at Lily. "Why would she say such a thing? Why would she suggest humanity might get caught in the crossfire and end up collateral damage?"

"Because humanity might," Lily replied. "He didn't lie to

you, Jubal didn't. It *is* about Good versus Evil, Heaven versus Hell. But if you want a metaphor, look at traffic lights." She shrugged when we both stared at her. "What falls between red and green?"

We exchanged blank glances, then chorused dutifully, "Yellow."

"And what happens when a light turns yellow at a very busy intersection when everyone's in a hurry?"

"Drivers step on the gas," Remi answered promptly.

I, who had experienced several near-misses on the bike, added, "And cars often collide."

Lily nodded. "Humanity is the yellow light."

"Then what are we?" I demanded. "In the metaphor, I mean. Since we're not demons *or* angels *or* humans."

Lily laughed. "You're the *traffic cops*, boyos! For when all the lights fail."

After contemplating that a moment, Remi said, "Well, that just tickles me plumb to death."

And I, whose annoyance and adrenaline had run out at pretty much the same time on a wave of weariness—we'd been up for something like thirty-six hours, plus hiked a mountain and killed shit—slid down deep in the chair and stretched out my legs. Planted an elbow on the chair arm and propped up my head against a hand. Around a yawn, I said, "At least they're hot."

Lily was not following. "What's hot?"

I waved my hand in an indistinct gesture. "You three. Legion, Lily, and Greg." I allowed my eyes to drift closed.

"Well, I've only seen two of the three ladies," Remi said, "but I'll agree with you on those counts. Yup. Pretty as twelve acres of pregnant red hogs."

For a moment I assumed I'd heard that wrong because I was just on the verge of a coma. But no. I hadn't.

My eyes snapped open. "Did you seriously just compare women to *hogs*? Do you even *know* how many women would have your 'nads for that?"

Remi quirked a brow. "It's just an old Texas saying. I didn't make it up."

I looked at Lily to gauge her reaction.

She smiled, lifted one shoulder in a casual shrug, said, "If all the boyo wants are hogs in his bed, that's one way to make sure of it."

A slow but distinct parade of considerations crossed Remi's face. Finally he said, "I might could retire that one."

"Uh-huh," I agreed pointedly; preferring, in the interests of male solidarity, that Remi survive.

He said, rather mournfully, "But to a man who loves bacon—"

Lily advised, "Shut up, Remi."

"Yes, ma'am."

Smart man.

CHAPTER TWELVE

With the dinette transformed to a bed—McCue took the pull-out sofa bed—I slept hard for several hours, rousing only when the scent of coffee permeated my senses. I discovered Remi up and pouring mugs full; Lily, the cowboy said, had taken the dog for a walk.

I crawled out of the sleeping bag Lily'd thrown at me, staggered my way to the bathroom, staggered back out and accepted the mug Remi offered. After drinking half of it, the staggers went away, and I felt alert again. It was verging on afternoon, but it felt like morning.

"You drink this much booze all the time?" McCue asked in an idleness underscored with—something. "I mean, God knows I party now and then, and I can hold my beer, but you been hitting the hard stuff."

"Three days," I murmured, rubbing my forehead.

It baffled him. "Three days what?"

"Three days of drinking after eighteen months with no booze," I explained. "I think I may be forgiven."

His eyes went blank, and I knew what he was thinking.

"I'm not on the wagon," I said. "Not working the program.

145

Best explanation: the wagon got stolen and locked in someone's barn." I stretched, cracked my spine.

"If you say so." Remi swallowed coffee. "Can you run me down to my truck in a bit? I feel lost without my wheels."

That's right, his truck was still at the Zoo Club. "Sure." I wandered into the garage, squatted at the cabinetry, began pulling open drawers.

Guns, ammunition, knives, flasks, bottles of a clear liquid and something oily, myriad tins and packets of herbs, bags of silver shot, boxes of bullets and cartridges, a loose substance that smelled like iron, an array of equipment used for making bullets and filling shotgun cartridges, knife sharpening stones, polishing cloths, chamois. In the deepest drawer was a stack of multi-sized bowls made of wood, brass, silver, steel, iron, and heavy glass, some carved with glyphs, some markedly plain. Small tripods, bowl rings with legs, clear glass containers of various liquid substances including something the dark, rich red of aged blood.

I found, too, a drawer containing sharpened stakes and crucifixes.

"You gotta be shitting me . . ." I took out one of the stakes, examined it. It was perhaps eighteen inches long, of a gnarled, striped wood, smooth, polished to a sheen akin to glass. It was twisted, with silver set throughout. The wood felt silky in my hands, and warm. Almost alive. Carved into the butt end was a Christian cross.

Remi had followed me. Now he leaned a shoulder against the wall, threw most of his weight to one leg, crossed a booted ankle over the other casually, cradled a mug in one palm. "A week ago, I was at a rodeo. Rode me a saddle bronc, bareback bronc, even a bull. Made it to the buzzer on the broncs, but that big old bull threw me off like I was a fly perched atop his back. He swatted me good. There I was in the dirt, and that old boy ducked his head and tried to hook me. I saw that horn comin' down from above, comin' *right at me*, and I thought: I'll die, or I won't, but I'll know one way or another in under two seconds."

I looked up at him. McCue's face was pensive, but his eyes strangely calm, considering he was talking about nearly being *gored by a bull*. "Yeah?"

"Clown distracted him, another got me on my feet, and I jumped up on the fence as that old bull headed through the alleyway. It wasn't but ten minutes later, just as I picked up my gear bag, that Grandaddy called. Said I was *needed*, summoned me here. But he didn't say why, and I didn't ask. He trained me just to answer whatever he suggested."

I nodded. "Didn't tell me anything, either, just that he wanted to meet me here. I was up in Oregon. I've always done what the man asked of me, never even asked 'how high' when he suggested I jump. Just did it. But had I known about *this* . . . I don't know. Not sure I'd have come." I ran a hand through long hair, pushed it off my face. "Hard to wrap my head around, you know? But I remember things—things he said when I was growing up. They made no sense then, but . . ." I let it trail off, because I still wasn't sure what I thought of anything, of anything at all to do with angels, demons, Lucifer, the End of Days, and any other crazy thing Grandaddy had alluded to.

"And now they do," Remi finished. "Make sense, I mean. It's the craziest damn thing I've ever heard, what he told us the other night. They oughta lock me up for even thinkin' it might be real."

147

I knew what was coming. "But."

"But," Remi agreed. "Then I stand right here and look at what's in those drawers and cabinets, and I remember what we did last night. What we killed. Or whatever it was we did to those—things. And right now that piece of wood you're holding might could be something meant to kill vampires, if all the folktales are true." He smiled, drank down some of his coffee. "That's your wheelhouse. So—*are* they true, those stories? We going all Buffy the Vampire Slayer on their sparkly little undead asses?"

I dropped the stake back into the drawer, closed it and rose. "Hell if I know. But something tells me we're going to find out. Because beacon or no beacon, *something's* happening. Grandaddy sure as hell seemed to sprout wings out there on that mountain. Then there's our own personal Irish goddess, a demon in a hot chick's body, and a third chick warning me that you and I are being set up by celestial beings with ulterior motives. Not exactly Charlie and his angels." Skewed humor bubbled up. "Hell, with Grandaddy in the mix, in this case Charlie *is* an angel."

After a moment, Remi's tone changed. "I heard what Grandaddy said about your parents. But you've got a brother, right?"

I thought about my parents, who I hadn't seen for eighteen months—my cop father not being inclined to visit a son in prison, and backed up by my mother—and my brother, home for Sunday dinner, whom I'd floored with a single punch the day before I left to answer Grandaddy's summons.

And while in prison I thought about having a normal life to go back to, but I didn't, really. Just a bike and the open road. Matty would know why, because it was his fault my normal life was over. It always was his fault. But now he wouldn't have me to pull his ass out of the fire.

I hitched one shoulder in a half-shrug. "Yeah, I've got a brother. Let's leave it at that."

McCue was very quiet for a long moment. "I've got a daughter. She's two. But she lives with her mother, who's got a new beau, and I don't hardly get to see her. Maybe twice a year, if I'm lucky." He grimaced. "I guess now I won't even have that."

He straightened, pushed off the wall, headed swiftly back toward the living quarters while I stared after him.

Remi left his hat behind when I ran him down to the Zoo Club on the motorcycle. When the bike rumbled its way into the gravel-and-cinder lot, we discovered a police SUV parked next to Remi's silver pickup. I felt a familiar pinch of apprehension in my gut, even though it was wholly illogical; I was out of prison by some arcane maneuvering of a celestial being, so I didn't think that was the issue. Probably someone suspected the truck had been abandoned, since it had been parked between the tree and building for well over twelve hours. I goosed the throttle enough to roll the bike slowly toward the truck to drop off Remi.

An officer stood at the driver's door, hands cupped around his eyes to peer into the interior. As I halted the bike nearby, I felt Remi unwind himself from behind me, the shift of weight off the bike; felt the brief clap upon my shoulder that spoke of thanks. I intended to pull out again, but something made me pause. Something made me turn off the engine, remove my helmet, and wait.

"Officer!" Remi called, raising a hand as he walked beyond the patrol SUV toward the driver's side of his truck. "Sorry about that. I got a little liquored up last night, and this feller—" he hooked a thumbed over his shoulder in my direction, "—kept my drunk ass off the streets. I do apologize. I'll get that outta here right quick."

The officer straightened, turned to McCue with a smile, took a few steps away from the driver's door. He was young and fit in a dark navy uniform, with a peak-crowned, round-brimmed trooper's hat, and a spray of freckles across his face. "Sure thing. But can I see license and registration, just to make sure everything's in order?"

"'Course." Remi unlocked the truck and pulled registration info out of it, then handed it and license to the cop, who accepted them with thanks but didn't even glance at them.

In the same friendly tone, as he looked across the truck bed at me, he said, "You lit 'em up nice and bright two days ago inside this building. I think all of us within a five hundred square mile radius felt it. Now you're broadcasting loud and clear."

I felt a wash of ice down my spine as I realized the magnitude of our stupidity. Over two days we had been warned multiple times by multiple people, and yet here we were, both exposed with no weapons that might work against this kind of enemy. We'd left everything at the motorhome. Hell, Lily didn't even know where we were.

Newbies, indeed. Dipshitiots.

Swearing prodigiously, I dropped my helmet even as I threw a leg over the bike and pushed upright onto both feet, reaching back for the KA-BAR at my spine as I took three long running steps toward the truck. Remi vaulted up into the cab and dove for the open glovebox.

The surrogate in a cop's body, meanwhile, just smiled at us benignly, even as I paused at the back of the truck with the knife gripped in my hand while Remi dug a revolver from the glovebox.

I exchanged a glance with McCue, and saw the same question in the cowboy's eyes. *What the hell do we do now?*

"Broad daylight, here, where anyone can see you," observed the demon, "and just what are you boys planning to do? Kill a cop? Because you're not currently packing what can kill *me*. It's the host who'll die. Besides—" he spread his hands in a non-threatening gesture, "—right now I'm just saying hello to the new kids on the block."

The cop stood several long paces away from the open truck door, where Remi had placed himself behind the wheel with his torso turned outward and two hands steadying the revolver. He flicked another quick, questioning glance at me, and I felt a sense of helplessness well up along with anger.

"That was quite an auspicious beginning last night, taking out two of us," the demon continued, "particularly for rookies. You are to be commended. But don't get too cocky; those were just rank-and-filers. Lesser demons. Cannon fodder, as it turns out. Now, my paygrade's higher, and if you boys want to take a few shots at me, cut me with that KA-BAR, you go right ahead. A report on a certain silver Texas truck has already been called in. My host ends up dead or wounded? It's not me who'll suffer."

"Then what the hell do you want?" I asked. "We just going to stand out here all morning monologuing like in a bad TV show?"

The young cop still looked friendly and cheerful, lacking the alpha aggressiveness of some law enforcement officers even if he did rest the heel of his hand upon the holstered gun. "Well, actually I was here as cleanup detail. While those two ghosts didn't leave any bodies, per se, you did cut the connection between the hosts and their cohabitants. That means there are the remains of two of my brethren still inside that building. They're dead, as humans reckon such things, but there are *remains*, just as with human bodies. We look after our own." He shrugged. "Everyone comes home."

Remi, still tucked up in the open truck cab with the gun in his hands, sounded scandalized. "Home to *hell*?"

Which did strike me as a rather odd thing, now that I thought about it. Did hell view its demons as soldiers? Were there rituals and rules?

"Or Hades, bottomless pit, underworld, the *habitation of fallen angels* . . ." the cop went on, then waved a dismissive hand. "It doesn't really matter what name you hang on it. It's still just home to us, and the sooner I get those two back there, the sooner they'll be reconstituted. So no, I'm not here for you; I don't have the time. There'll be others along directly who feel a little differently. In the meantime, have a nice day. Oh, and— happy birthday. Welcome to the war."

I saw a pixilation in the air, the displacement of delineated image, now all jagged and broken up. A sudden blast of grit-laden air at my face made me duck aside and thrust a warding hand into the air, but too late to prevent the wash of irritation in my eyes. I smelled the rich, cloying stench, tasted it as I swore and wiped involuntary tears away from my cheeks with the back of my hand.

When my eyes cleared, I saw the cop had disappeared. "Where the hell did he go?"

Remi slid out of the truck and dropped to the ground, holding the gun down along one thigh. "He said he was here for the *remains*. I'm betting he's inside the building collecting what's left of those demons."

"Yeah, well . . . now what?"

"We take him out," McCue replied, heading for the roadhouse. "Ain't that what we're for? Besides, he's got my license and registration. Come on, son, let's go in after him before he grabs up those remains, takes 'em to hell, and they get . . . what'd he say—reconstituted? Yeah. That."

In two jogging strides I caught up. "Take him out with what, Tex? You can't use your six-shooter on a cop, now, can you?"

"I could," McCue offered, moving swiftly. "Or you could, since you're the one so handy with a gun. You could shoot him in the leg."

I was astonished. "Shoot him in the leg? What the hell for?"

"I reckon a demon would rather have a host that wasn't ventilated," Remi answered. "We might could maybe drive out the demon that way."

"Oh yeah—and then when the cop realizes I *shot* him, he'll thank me? I don't think so. Because how do we know if the guy will realize his body was borrowed by a demon? I'm not shooting him!"

"Well, it was just an idea," McCue said. "But I got a better one anyway. Let's go throw Latin at that sucker instead."

CHAPTER THIRTEEN

t was a half-assed plan, but I couldn't think of a better one. We really couldn't shoot or stab the host. I mean, did the cop even know he was being, what—ridden? Possessed? Would he be sane once we exorcized the demon? Hell, would he even be *alive?*

Grandaddy had said the learning curve was steep. Lily'd said we'd pick up details as we went along. Of course, that was supposing we *survived* long enough to learn anything at all.

"You go around back," McCue suggested. "Pick that lock if it needs doing. I'll try the front door."

We moved stride for stride toward the building, then split up. I headed around back, wondering if there was any way I might distract the surrogate if I beat Remi inside. I didn't know the Latin for the rite. Hell, I didn't even know if exorcism actually *worked*.

The surrogate could have killed us, I suspected. He hadn't. I wanted to know why. I mean, as a cop he could have shot us both, I suppose, then crafted a story after the fact, but that would draw a lot of attention from police department to reporters and prevent him from collecting the remains of the surrogates Remi and I had killed. For some reason that seemed to matter a great deal. *Everyone comes home*, he'd said.

Home to hell for reconstitution? Then sent back into the field to find more hosts?

Around back, I pulled open the screen door quietly, then closed a hand around the knob. Tried it. It turned, the tongue-latch gave, and I eased the door open.

Remi was already inside. Remi was *chanting*.

I moved swiftly through the pool tables and found the cow-boy standing in the middle of the dance floor as he let the Latin of the *Rituale Romanum* roll from his tongue. I heard nothing of Texas in it, just smooth vowels and consonants, an easy familiarity with the cadences and inflections.

Before him, on hands and knees, the cop was vomiting. But it wasn't food or liquid he was bringing up. Wasn't yellow-frothed bile. Neither was it smoke, nor light. It was gout after gout of something black and shiny, glinting in the light.

No, not something. Actual *things*.

Things that were *alive*.

I stopped dead, appalled. From the cop's wide-open mouth, from his nose, his ears, poured streams of black, glittering cara-paces. Like an army of ants on the march, the beetle-like things clustered upon the floor, then moved en masse in my direction.

McCue cut off his ritual long enough to yell at me. "Get some water! Throw salt in it! Spit in it! Then pour it all over those suckers!" And went right back to chanting.

Okay. Water and salt I could do. Spit, too; half-assed holy water, since I didn't know the blessing, but Lily had pointed out we were ourselves a kind of blessing—hence, the spit, as with breathing on the bullets—so maybe it would work.

I rounded the bar, grabbed a pitcher, filled it at the sink, dumped salt into it and basically hocked a loogie of saliva into the pitcher.

I swung back around the bar, saw the river of—holy shit, were those *cockroaches?*—flowing toward the back door. I sucked in a breath, stepped right into the middle of that river, and began sloshing salt- and saliva-laden water over the roaches. Beneath my boots, they crunched. And once the makeshift holy water hit them, they burned.

Carapaces cracked open like popcorn. Each gave up a spark. And they *stank*.

I swore, took a couple of long staggering steps away, then stood staring at the field of roaches turning into crispy critters. The stench was acrid and eye-watering. I thrust an elbow across my mouth and coughed into it, knuckled involuntary tears away.

McCue was no longer chanting. He coughed too, spat, then knelt beside the sprawled body of the young cop and placed fingers against his neck. After a moment he nodded, then carefully rolled the guy over onto his back. "Pulse is steady, so's his breathing. Far as I can tell, he'll do."

Yeah, well, maybe physically. But otherwise?

I surveyed the field of the fallen. Little curled-up, crispified bodies. The stink was fading, but I still tasted it. Acrid, metallic.

I leaned forward, spat. Wiped my mouth against the back of my hand. "Maybe we ought to add Roach Motels to the armory."

Remi, now standing, was shoving a booted foot this way and that, as if gathering dirt together. "I don't get it. There aren't any *other* roaches, or roach remains, from those two we killed here last night, right in this room. What the hell was this demon coming back for?"

I went over, saw he'd boot-scraped together a pile of something. I had a vague memory of the two ghosts, once they'd ceased their weird deflating bagpipe noises and shimmering, basically collapsing into exactly what McCue had scraped together.

I cast a glance over my shoulder at the carpet of burned little roach corpses, then squatted to take a closer look at Remi's pile. Ash. Dust. Some sparkling grit, like obsidian. "I don't get it, either."

The woman's voice said, "That's because they were ghosts, not possessed humans."

She startled me enough that as I lurched up I overbalanced and landed right on my ass. Lily Morrigan, standing just inside the main door, gave me a long look, then shook her head in resignation.

"That matters?" McCue asked.

Her green eyes were bright. "It does."

I pressed myself up off the floor with a one-armed thrust. "Why? I mean, ghosts aren't *real*. I mean, not *real* real."

"Are they not?" She lifted her chin. "I'm an ancient Celtic goddess, and *I* am real. Now, come along. The young boyo will be awakening soon. He'll be confused, but he's still a cop. Best we be elsewhere to avoid awkward questions."

McCue indicated the swath of burned roaches with an outflung hand. "Can't another demon come along and gather up the remains? Take 'em back to hell and bring 'em back to life?"

Lily shook her head. The neck torc gleamed. "*Rituale Romanum*, holy water imbued with heavenly essence, and salt. No demon of this paygrade's coming back from that. Same with the ghost remains. They were lesser demons." She tilted her head. "Now, come. I hitched here; I'll catch a ride with Remi, and we'll go back to the rig. Time for debriefing."

Debriefing consisted of Lily interrogating us. What had we said; what had the surrogate in the host's body said; what was our original plan of action; how had we carried it out, and how closely did our actions align with the plan for the evening, this whacking of two ghost-demons, and so on and so forth. I was bored within five minutes, and let Remi do most of the talking.

The crow, upon the perch, rotated its head and fixed me with a bright and beady eye. I noted the powerful beak— throughout history, they pecked eyes out of dead and dying bodies, did crows and ravens—and shifted slightly backward in the armchair.

I rubbed the pad of one thumb against the leather upholstery. "Look. We did what you wanted. We took out those surrogates in ghost form, killed off the reanimated stuffed animals, and exorcised a demon out of a human who'd been possessed. We *saved* him, right? So what more do you want? Didn't we pass your tests?"

"Barely," Lily said, from the driver's seat turned backward. McCue was behind the dinette table. The wolfhound lay close by. "You were sloppy last night, then walked into a situation this morning without a single weapon to aid you."

"We got it *done*," I declared.

She flicked a glance at McCue. "Did you?"

He'd hooked his hat over the window valance, scrubbed a hand through short dark hair. "End result, yeah."

"And what might you have done differently?"

He shrugged. "Thrown Latin at him sooner? Before he went into the building?"

Lily leaned forward. Her legs were planted, thighs spread, and she rested her forearms atop them, hands dangling. "Do again what you did today," she said, "and you'll end up dead."

The wolfhound rose. She shook herself off from head to toe, then turned toward Remi and glowered at him across the dinette table.

So, okay. We had the Morrigan mad at us, and her sisters equally pissed.

I stroked loose hair behind one ear. "Just exactly how long are we to do all this surrogate-killing shit? What's our tour of duty?"

Lily said, "Until the job is done."

"And how long is that supposed to take?"

Her tone was bland. "How long do you suppose ending the run-up to Armageddon *should* take?"

"Overnight would be preferable," I told her pointedly.

"Well, those odds aren't exactly good," Remi observed. He looked at Lily. "You got a Bible on hand?"

She rose. "Which flavor?"

"King James, or New King James."

"Why does it matter?" I asked, as Lily walked past us to the cabinetry.

Remi shrugged. "Scholars say both the King James versions are closest to the original texts. Ninety-eight percent. Other versions are a little more casual about the vocabulary." McCue took the volume Lily handed him as she returned to the big driver's seat. "Okay, let me look something up. I think it's Mark . . ." Remi paged through rapidly, murmuring to himself about days and hours.

I frowned. "What are you looking for?"

"Here." He planted his index finger against the page. "It's Mark 13:32. *'But about that day or hour no one knows, not even the angels in heaven, nor the Son, but only the Father.'* So it looks to me like the angels have no idea how long this might last. Just God."

"Huh." I scratched an eyebrow. "What is it you say, 'might could'? Well, it might could be helpful if God let us in on that intel."

"Signs," Lily put in. "War, for one."

Remi quoted, "'*Nation shall rise against nation, and kingdom against kingdom.'*"

Her eyes were bright. "I'm not the only one here. I have sisters other than Nemain and Macha. Co-workers, you might say, in the art of war. Athena. Kali. Bellona. Enyo—and no, not Enya, the Irish singer; I've heard that joke already. Ifri. Neith." She shrugged. "Many of us have come. Male gods, too."

"So . . ." I thought about it a moment. "If you're saying all the gods and goddesses of war are here . . ." But I broke off and clapped hands to my skull, squeezed my eyes shut. "No. No. I'm reverting back to the theory that I'm in a coma somewhere and this is all a hallucination."

"False prophets," McCue added. "Fake news, maybe?"

"But not all of it's fake," I said between gritted teeth. "The news."

"Politicians," he went on. "Religious leaders. Misleading the elect."

I opened my eyes. "Okay, so now you're saying some religious leaders predicting *the Apocalypse* are false prophets? I mean, how does that even make sense? If we're on the cusp of it, according to Grandaddy and other angels, then aren't the false prophets telling the truth?"

Remi shrugged. "I reckon it depends on what they're sayin,' and how they're sayin' it."

"Moral decay," Lily said. "Another of the signs."

I couldn't help myself. "Cats and dogs living together."

"Yes, my kind are here," Lily said. "We are here, but not all of us are working with the angels. Many are on the other side."

"Why?" I asked. "I mean, what brought you here from—wherever it was you were?" I caught Remi's eye, shook my head in disbelief before turning back to Lily. "What would induce gods and goddesses to pop out of some kind of alternate universe, the whole space/time continuum thing, to join this battle between good and evil?"

She shrugged. "We're being paid."

It took half a minute to process that and then I was astounded. "So, what, you're saying *gods and goddesses* are mercenaries? Seriously?"

"In a manner of speaking."

"Then what the hell are they paying you with?"

Lily smiled. "War."

I wanted to growl in frustration. "But the goal is to *stop* the war."

"The goal is to stop the end of the world," she pointed out. "We're using war to do it."

"But why are some of you on one side, while others are backing the devil?"

"War," she repeated. "Are you totally ignorant? There must be *opposing sides.*"

I let that insult slide. "Besides war," I said, "what do you get out of it?"

Her pupils spread. They were still round, unlike those of the cat-eyed demon chick, but it was unsettling nonetheless.

"To be *known* again," she said; and her tone suddenly deepened. "To be in the world again. We are far more than words on a page or on a computer screen. *People worshipped us.*"

The crow mantled, shifted on the perch. I eyed it uneasily. It eyed me back. Hackles rose on the wolfhound's spine.

Holy shit.

"But this isn't heaven," Remi said.

I blinked, the moment broken, and looked at him blankly. "What?"

"The battle is to take place in heaven. Listen up—'*And there was war in heaven: Michael and his angels fought against the dragon; and the dragon fought and his angels.'*"

Lily had a quote of her own: " '*On earth as it is in heaven.*'"

Well, hell.

I looked at the woman who called herself the Morrigan. "Goddess of Battles, is it?" I asked. "*Prove it.*"

The sleeve tattoos on her bare arms writhed. "All right," she said; apparently she'd been waiting for it. "*Agus mar sin beidh mé. Téigh abhaile liomsa.*"

And the world whited out.

CHAPTER FOURTEEN

I woke up to the whistle of the wind, face-down, conspicuously asprawl, in grass wet with heavy dew. For a moment I was horribly disoriented, as if rousing up from a four-day bender: pounding head, mangled brain, dicey belly, shivers inside and out—and then the fragmented pieces began to coalesce.

I opened my eyes. Peered at what I could see of the world. Grass. Tall. Brown. Dead.

I lay there a long moment, putting together the concussion protocol: name, birthday, date, mother's maiden name, the whole password recovery bullshit. Except, well, no capital letter, number, or an oddball grammatical symbol, apparently not understood by computer coders. Were they just *unaware* of the ampersand, caret, and tilde? Okay. Yeah. Me. Among the living.

I dragged my elbows to my ribcage, took a queasy breath, pushed partially upright. Ducked my head and remained bowed down, elbows planted, skull clutched in my hands and ass stuck up in the air.

After a long moment of even longer dire mutterings, I pulled my knees under my belly, rocked backward, and pushed myself into a seated position, more or less, butt planted, and boot heels, knees bent upright. I was dew-soaked head to toe, hair loose, tangled, soggy. I wiped vaguely at my face to clear it.

My hand came away red.

Not dew. Blood.

Wet head to foot with *blood*.

The breath gusted out of me, followed immediately by the F-bomb. And three more, raspy and slurred save for the hard *k* at the end, as I shoved myself upward, stood unsteadily.

My t-shirt, beneath the open leather jacket, was wet and chill against my torso. I pulled it away from skin, felt at flesh, did a mental inventory, but other than a headache nothing hurt. Nothing suggested any part of me was bleeding at all, let alone enough to wet hair and clothing. I let the tee slop back.

The wind yet blew, whispering now. Otherwise the quiet was almost uncanny. No birds at all, no insects. Just—silence. Save for the breeze and the rustle of tall grass.

I smelled blood. I reeked of it, as did everything around me. And it's a sharp, metallic taste, like copper, or iron, with a thick, throat-cloying fug. I pulled the loose flaps of my jacket aside, rattling metal buckles and studs. Noted that my black leather pants were smeared from belt to ankle.

I scrubbed the back of a hand against a cheek, though probably all I did was rearrange blood. My gag reflex engaged, then eased before I hurled, though bile burned partway up my esophagus. With effort I swallowed it back down, then finally took a good look around.

I wasn't alone. Thousands of men were present. Before me, behind me, beside me. All lay sprawled upon the battlefield in

attitudes of death: prone, supine, some limbs reaching sky-
ward, others twisted, or hacked away. Eyes closed. Eyes open.
Mouths agape in frozen grimaces, or features utterly slack.
Long hair, braided hair, subtle plaid trousers and tunics of
earth-born colors. Torcs glinted, as did brooches and wristlets.
The wind caught at cloaks, fluttered cloth.

I drew in a very deep breath, then blew it out hard. The sky
above was a hazy blue, the sun muted. Still no sound beyond
the wind and the sibilance of waving grass.

No man moved, or moaned. No man cried out. No man
gave any evidence of being alive. Empty of blood, what had
been warriors were nothing now but sacks of flesh shaped like
men, fallen helter-skelter across the plain.

I began walking, stumbling, because there was nothing else
to do. And as I walked, a slow, turgid urgency rose up.

Remi McCue. The cowboy. I needed to find him; and that
need set a band around my chest, squeezed my ribs and or-
gans. Was he dead? Alive? Had the Morrigan also brought him
here to this field of death? That they were Celts, I knew; she
was a Celtic goddess, and this was her home. Was McCue, like
me, surrounded by bodies? Or was *he* a body?

I walked the plain, squelched through soil turned to mud
because of all the blood. Felt the whip of grass against motorcycle leathers. No loom-woven, woolen trousers and tunic for
me, no cloak, no torcs or brooches. I was as I had been in Lily's
motorhome, in leathers, a t-shirt, and motorcycle boots.

Except for, well, the blood all down my front.

Shit. Shitshitshit. Where the hell was McCue?

I could search for days, pull bodies aside, tip sprawled forms
over, and not find him, not amid so many. So I stopped where

I was, cupped hands around my mouth and shouted for the cowboy.

No answer. Nothing. Only the rush of wind across the plain.

The quiet was just *wrong*. This was a battlefield. Dead lay everywhere. There should be carrion birds plucking out eyes, flapping wings, shrieking warning to others to stay away from claimed human prizes. And insects buzzing, chirping, rattling, humming on noisy wings.

Then came sound. A voice, shouting my name.

I spun quickly, saw a man in the distance. He was mostly indistinct, but I could see the unmistakable outline of a cowboy hat.

Relief was palpable. I flung an arm upright, swung it back and forth, then shouted his name and broke into a jog even as he came on.

When he was close enough, I saw that he hadn't escaped the carnage. His clothing was soaked and richly red, and his hands and face were smeared. Twins in survival, we two: men who did not belong here.

Remi halted. I saw a bloody handprint against the cream of his hat. He eyed me up and down, registering my condition.

"Not mine," I said. "You?"

The tension in his body eased. "Mine, neither." He took off his hat, rubbed a forearm through matted hair, and left another hand print upon the pale felt, though this one was lighter, smudged. "Well, hell. I reckon we got us our answer. She's the real deal, all right. Let's just hope she sends us back when she's done making her point." His eyes fixed on mine as he put his hat back on. "Guess she took it personal when you asked her to prove it."

I stretched out arms from my sides, let them slap back

down. "Do you blame me? I mean, come on! This whole thing is unfuckingbelieveable."

He smiled a little. "That's right, you believe you're in a coma somewhere and hallucinating. So my question to you would be: Why the hell am *I* in it?"

I swore, raked a spread-fingered hand through damp hair. Grimaced because it was blood, nothing so benign as rain or dew. "Hell if I know. But what I *do* want to know is where Lily is. I'd like to take a shower, change clothes, you know? Get rid of all the blood, knock back a couple of drinks."

His brows ran up. "You always drink so much?"

I scowled at him. "Give me a break. Making up for lost time. It'll pass."

He nodded thoughtfully. "Might could do with a drink myself, seein' as how we got, what, translocated?"

I felt helpless, which made me surly. "Let's just say Scotty didn't beam us here. But I'd like to figure out how to get back. Because unless Grandaddy means for us to hunt demons in *Roman-occupied Britain*, we've got no angelic mission here."

Remi looked across the field of the dead. The look on his tanned face was pensive. The wind rippled his denim shirt, snatched at the points of his collar. "Which battle do you suppose this was?"

I stared at him in surprise. We'd been taken through time, and he wanted to know what battlefield we were smack in the middle of? "Why does it have to be a *specific* battle?"

His gaze came around to mine. Something bright sparked briefly in his eyes, and then he smiled faintly. "Just trying to figure out where—and *when*—we are. So we know what comes next. I'm thinkin' it might could be important."

Well, there was that. Hands on hips, I turned in a full circle. Still no carrion birds, no insects. Still just the wind hissing through the grass.

Finally I shook my head and met his eyes. "Could be one of many battles. The Celtic tribes were always killing one another."

He shrugged. "Seems like a lot of men for mere tribal squabbles."

Okay, yeah. McCue was right. I looked around again, saw the narrow plain was bounded by trees on two sides, and the distant uncertain darkness that suggested trees behind us. I turned in a circle, then gave up. "Yeah, no, I've got no idea where *or* when—"

But I wasn't allowed to finish, because suddenly Lily was standing six feet away. The wolfhound was at her left side, and the crow flapped and soared idly in the air. Piercings and torc glinted in the sunlight, and the red shock of her hair was bright under the sky. The remarkably fine bones of her face stood up beneath pale skin.

"Look again," she said. "Are all of the dead, men? Are all of the dead, Celts?"

Remi stared at her a moment, then moved hastily to several bodies. Two he turned over, then straightened, turned, and looked once again at Lily. His face was taut. "Okay," he said; and there was no lazy drawl in it, only tension. "Women, too. Is that what you want us to see?"

Lily's smile was luminous. Otherworldly. She looked beyond—or *through*—me.

I swung around abruptly, following her line of sight, saw the field shift before me. I blinked my eyes wide. Men, yes, but now also women, as McCue had noted. The body count abruptly increased.

"Holy shit," Remi said.

"Look again," Lily repeated. *"Feuch dè bha, faic dè tha. See what there was, see what there is."*

McCue and I glanced at one another, then did her bidding.

Now *chariots*, where there had been none. Unhitched, up-ended, broken, wheels missing, and the scattered bulks of slain horses.

Ten, maybe fifteen paces away from me, a Roman soldier, complete with armor of leather and metal strips, the iconic helmet with cheek-guards and upright plume. But only *one* Roman. All the other bodies I could see, male and female, were Celts.

I closed my eyes, burrowed inside myself to find the part that *sensed*, as Grandaddy had called it. Beneath the sun of a younger earth I let it come to me, the knowledge. Heard the clatter of shields, of javelins; the wet slop of Roman gladii against wool-wrapped flesh. And the war cries, the screams of horses, the shouts of men, the ululations of women who wanted nothing more than to throw off the Roman yoke.

I opened my eyes. I knew.

"Boudicca," I said grimly. "Her final battle against Gaius Suetonius Paulinus, 60 or 61 Common Era." I gestured, indicating three directions. "Narrow plain hemmed by trees, and a forested gorge behind, cradling the Roman formations. No Britons could sneak up, or lay ambushes. It could only be a frontal attack. And it was disastrous."

"Why disastrous?" Lily asked, watching me closely.

I gazed across the plain. *"Eighty thousand* Britons died, with maybe, and *only,* four hundred Roman soldiers lost."

"Jesus," McCue murmured.

"I was there," Lily said simply, "as I am here. At war, I am always present. And this *is* a war, boyos, never doubt it. Apocalypse, Armageddon, End of Days, Ragnarok . . . call it what you wish. This war is the end of all, unless it is *won.*"

The Morrigan, Goddess of Battles, stood before us clad in knee-torn jeans, a tank top, bare feet. The multi-colored spirals and angles of her sleeve tattoos writhed upon her forearms, as if alive. Her eyes were vastly bright.

She smiled faintly at McCue. "Those cowboy boots of yours aren't precisely ruby slippers, but I'll wager if you tap the heels together three times, we'll go home." She paused; the wolfhound yawned prodigiously. "Well, to what *you* boys know as home."

Remi blinked at her, looked at me with brows raised.

I shrugged; who the hell knew? *I* sure didn't.

So he gave it a try. Three taps of his boot heels, and the world once again whited out.

CHAPTER FIFTEEN

I came to my senses much as I had in Roman Britain, save there was no blood in my hair, on my face, or a blood-glued t-shirt stuck to my torso. Nor was I lying face-down upon the ground. I was however, sprawled partly upright and wholly inelegantly in the motorhome recliner, arms hanging over the sides, legs outstretched loosely, and my ass nearly off the edge of the seat.

I was so close to landing on the floor that I flailed without anything approaching coordination, grabbed hold of the chair arms and shoved myself upright, which wasn't necessarily the best idea in the world for my innards, though it took precedence over doing an ass-plant on the floor. No, what this abrupt movement did was set my head to aching and my belly to churning. Bile—or something more—once again climbed my esophagus; and once again I swallowed it down. Then closed my eyes tightly, pressed a hand across my eyes, and cradled either side of my skull with thumb and fingers.

All I could manage was a tight-throated rasp. "Can we *not* do that again? Jesus Christ. That's not how they do it on TV and in movies, the whole—" I waved a hand in an indistinct circle,

173

"—scrambling the atoms thing. It never appears to be *painful*, you know? Nobody ever hurls."

"You challenged Lily to prove something," a deep voice said. "That's a very foolish thing."

My eyes snapped open. I registered McCue across from me, clean again, hat bearing no bloody hand prints, forearms resting on the dinette table, but looking tight around the mouth. He squinted at me, then poked a finger in the air to direct my gaze elsewhere.

Oh. "Hey, Grandaddy."

He stood tall and solid in the aisle, shoulders thrown back in his frock coat, silver-white hair flowing to shoulders. He was patently displeased.

"Well, what the hell did you expect us to do?" I disliked my defensive tone at once. Better to be a little belligerent, under the circumstances. "Just *believe* some tatted-out chick in a red Mohawk and piercings who claims she's a Celtic goddess?"

"I *am* a Celtic goddess," Lily stated. "Do you require another trip to a battlefield? Perhaps the American Civil War?"

It was Remi's turn to speak, and he sounded no more pleased than I as he looked at Grandaddy. He seemed relaxed as he leaned back against the dinette cushions, but the flesh at the corners of his eyes was lined. "You piled our plates high. Might could explain a *little* more, don't you think?"

Grandaddy's blue eyes weren't unkind, but certainly serious. "No man—even one born of heavenly matter—who is raised as a human can take everything in at once. It's not like sticking a flash drive in your USB port and downloading, since you don't *have* USB ports."

I muttered, "The number 42. And Johnny Mnemonic."

Grandaddy looked perplexed, and McCue just gazed at me blankly.

I waved my hand again. "You know—Life, the Universe, and Everything. Could be cool if it *was* just downloaded, you know? Into our heads."

Remi looked at Lily, who was seated on the floor with a wolfhound head in her lap. The rest of the dog lay stretched out behind her. "Did he order scrambled eggs for brains during that trip back?"

"It can be disorienting," Lily replied, "but I think this is just Gabe."

"Just me," I agreed, then clasped hands behind my head and cracked my neck. "So, Grandaddy, we don't know everything there is to know about angels and demons and gods and goddesses and monsters and all kinds of shit that goes bump in the night, and even the kitchen sink being thrown at us, for that matter. Oh, wait—can a sink be haunted? Hey, maybe you've got a textbook for all this bullcrap. That would help. I'm a pretty fast reader."

Grandaddy didn't crack a smile. "You'll be given information as circumstances require it, as time goes on. At this point, it's for you both to find out what you can do, how to do it, and how to back one another up."

"Hey, *he's* the one got me translocated," Remi protested. "I was just fine with believing she's a fictional character out of fictional Irish folklore, no questions asked." He flicked a wary glance at Lily, then looked at me with accusation in his eyes. "I don't call that 'zactly backing me up."

"How the hell did I know she could actually *do* it?" I threw back. "But now we know, and we can proceed accordingly." I looked up at Grandaddy looming in the aisle. "Is there any-thing in particular that brought you back here? Like, it's time to provide more of this angelic intel we'll need?"

"Not intel," he said. "An assignment. Time to clean out the rat's nest. Clear the domicile."

Remi shot a frown at Lily. "You used that word before. 'Do-micile.' Beyond someone's house, what's it mean?"

"Demons *move in*," Grandaddy said, before Lily could speak. "It may be into a body—or, now, into creatures from legend and folklore—or into a *place*. If it's the latter, they set up shop, make it a home. That's what they did at the cowboy bar. Two took on host bodies, made them corporeal, and damn near killed you both."

"'Host ghosts'?" I suggested. "Naw—'ghost hosts' sounds better. So, what about them?"

"The ghosts were owners of the roadhouse. Or rather, the *ghosts* of the owners, right?" McCue seemed to be picking his way through a minefield, apparently unwilling to just blurt things out the way I did. So much for having *my* back. "So the surrogates, in ghost-form, legally—and spiritually?—now own the bar. And they made it a domicile?"

"We killed them," I pointed out. "Or disappeared them. Or whatever it was we did to their demonic little asses." I shot a glance at McCue, was inspired. "All they were was *dust in the wind* when we were done with them."

"Don't start up with Kansas," Remi suggested, "or I'll be singin' country music again."

"Oh, God. No. I'll even beg." I started to cross forefingers in a warding sign, but Grandaddy's big hand came down and closed upon mine, damn near crushing my fingers.

176

"No," he said; it was enough to stop me cold. "Do no such thing!"

I sat frozen in place. So did Remi, and Lily. Grandaddy was bent low to capture my hands with their linked fingers, now folded down. Behind his shoulders I saw the shimmering pixilation, the prism, the pressure, the impression of wings.

"This is *real*," Grandaddy said; there was neither kindness nor patience in it. "Do you not understand? *Everything* is real! Would you place a *warding sign* on him? To consign him elsewhere, to damn him, when he is your greatest support?"

Holy shit. I swallowed tautly, coughed a little. "Uh—no?"

His hand did not release my own. My fingers protested. "*Think*, Gabriel. You studied folklore. Legends. History. Remi knows how cultures believe, how they worship. You are neither of you stupid, but *foolish*, oh yes. Now, grasp this. As I told you explicitly, but let me say again: Everything you've read of legends, fairy tales, folklore, mythology, even Bible stories, *is now made real*."

In the sudden absence of speech, I heard the wolfhound's heavy breathing. She slept hard with her head in Lily's lap, twitching and damn near snoring. Not exactly goddess material.

Okay. Okay. Lily Morrigan, *the* Morrigan, had proved herself real.

I drew in a deep breath, nodded, and Grandaddy released my hands. I shook them out, rubbed knuckles, plowed on. "So, we also took out that other demon. The one in the cop. He said the others were lesser demons, and his paygrade was higher." I debated saying the next thing, said it anyway because it was true. "We still took him out."

Grandaddy straightened and gazed down upon us. I decided

then and there we should never sit in the man's presence again, unless *he* was sitting. The man, as seraph, was downright intimidating.

He could be dryly, and subtly amused, could Grandaddy. I'd seen both. But he was neither at this moment. "Your mission tonight is to go back to the Zoo Club. Eat, drink, dance, shoot pool—it's immaterial. Merely be there. And wait."

I was wary. "Wait for what?"

"For the surrogates, of course."

Remi went wide-eyed. "*More* demons?"

"Oh, shit," I muttered, remembering. "That demon chick knew we were there. She said she felt it when we clasped rings and lit our heavenly asses right up."

Remi sighed deeply, rubbed a hand through his unhatted hair, then absently attempted to finger-comb it back into order. "That cop demon said something, too. That we'd be hunted."

"You are now prey," Grandaddy said, "but also predators. Tonight you'll be bait. And any who come to you, any and all, who attempt to snatch the lions down from the heights, are to be destroyed. The bait shall bite, and clear the domicile." He paused. "You have an hour before you go. Make use of it."

I chewed my bottom lip for a long moment, turning things over in my mind. Then looked at Lily. "You got a whisk broom and dust pan? You know, for demon remains?"

"Stop," Grandaddy said sharply. "Gabriel, *stop* this. You must understand—"

It exploded from me as I shoved myself to my feet and stood but two feet away from him. "I *do* understand! How could I not? I was *raised* to handle guns, *raised* to understand folklore and legends, *raised* to—or imbued *with*—this primogeniture bullshit, and a useless ability to *sense* places. Holy shit, Grandaddy, I was just at Boudicca's final battlefield! I *tasted* death there. Heard it. Smelled it. And it reeked. It *stank*. Blood, bowel, urine: men, women, and horses . . . yes, I get it! I *get* that a stranger is now bonded to me; I *get* that I have a holy GPS unit in me; I *get* that you want me to destroy surrogates . . . but I was raised a human and I'm scared shitless. What makes you think I can do this?"

The syllables were exquisitely clear. "You killed a man."

My knees literally went weak. I locked them rigid and held my place. I felt hollow, a little sick, and hyperaware of McCue's sharp, startled attention. Limbs prickled, like cold sand running out. "And I went to prison for it."

Grandaddy's face was terrible. "*Who do you think sent you there?*"

CHAPTER SIXTEEN

I stared at the man I loved more than my own father. Felt tears gather in my eyes. Literally felt sick to my stomach.

Thought: How could—? Why did—? But couldn't finish either question, aloud or in my head.

"Yes," Grandaddy said, knowing exactly what I couldn't bear to ask. "Yes, I arranged it. I didn't force it, but I *manipulated* certain things, I nudged, made sure various details were in place so the goal would be reached as it was intended. Yes, the man is dead; yes, you killed him; yes, you went to prison. Because all that was necessary."

I stared at him, still in disbelief. "It was *necessary* for me to kill a man? *Necessary* to go to prison?"

"It was."

"Why?" I was now able to ask it. "Why on earth would you do such a thing? Why was it *'necessary'*?"

His tone was unrelenting. "Because you must be strong. Because you must understand. There will be hardships. Challenges. Things you wish not to do. Times when you are helpless, perhaps even a prisoner. You will be required to kill, Gabriel, and you must not hesitate."

Okay, creepy cult leader talk. "But—"

He cut me off. "When a man comes at you with a gun in his hand, it's possible he's not a man at all, but hosting a surrogate. Until Remi can tell demons from humans at distance, you must be prepared. No, we do not advocate killing possessed humans—always do your best to save them—but there will be occasions when killing surrogate *and* host is best for the greater good."

My breath ran choppy from my lungs. I stopped seeing Grandaddy, saw instead the Asian woman, the Grigori, warning me that not all angels were on the same page. That some had an agenda, and humans could very well be collateral damage.

I swallowed hard, refocused. It was Granddaddy before me again. I cleared my throat, looked at McCue. "You ever kill anyone?"

His face was tense, eyes unblinking. I couldn't read his expression. "No."

Grandaddy said, "It was not required of him. You are the alpha, Gabriel."

I did not look away from McCue. His opinion mattered. "*Could* you kill someone? Someone who looks like a human?"

I saw a shift in his blue eyes, some unnamable emotion. "I don't know."

I weighed him, as best I could; he was a stranger to me, whatever he was intended to become at some point. *Sealed* to me.

I looked at our mutual whatever-he-was, who had never been a stranger but now was both less and more of a man—a man?—than I'd known. "You said he'd be my backup."

Grandaddy didn't hesitate. "Yes."

I shot a glance at Remi, then just plowed on through. "Well, in this war you've thrown us into, what good is he if he can't kill a demon wearing a host body?"

Remi sat abruptly upright. He was not pleased. "I saved your ass the other night when the ghost—the *demon*—had ahold of you. And the bear. Remember the bear? And I exorcized the surrogate from the cop's body so the cop, the host, is still alive. Hell, boy, I'm not sure you'd have survived had I not pinned the host to one place and spouted Latin at him. And it was *me* who had to tell you what to do: water, salt, spit. You want backup? Start there. Seems to me you've had plenty." He flicked a glance at Grandaddy. "But he's the alpha, is he?"

"Give him time, Remi. You *might could* be surprised."

"Okay." I was exhausted all of a sudden, dropped down into the armchair. "Yeah, okay; you're right. But I'm just not understanding why Grandaddy—or whatever he is to us, being as we're all cut from the same heavenly cloth—felt it was necessary to *set me up* so I'd kill a guy." I remembered the moment I'd pulled the trigger, the shock on the man's face as the bullet struck; and from my brother the whoop of exultation, of relief, the cheers of victory, as if he were an athlete who'd scored.

Scored—because a man had died.

Grandaddy's tone lost its edge. "You killed that man to save your brother. It's what you've done all of your life, made Matthew's problems your own. And he knows it; he knew it then, that night." I stared hard at the floor beneath my boots, thumbed the back of one hand over and over again in a nervous gesture. "He has abused your trust countless times, Gabriel. But Remi will not. Remi is not your brother. He is *more* than brother. And when the time comes, he will always save you."

I leaned forward, slid elbows down my thighs. Kept on rubbing the back of one hand. "Hell, Grandaddy—I don't even know if I *can* shoot a demon wearing a human host. I didn't exactly enjoy killing that guy, regardless of what he was. And prison?" I straightened up again. "Prison cost me time, a job, a girlfriend, my self-respect, and it lost me my father, basically. He didn't mince any words when he told me what he thought of me. He'd already raised one son he couldn't respect, in Matty. And then . . . then it was my turn. You'd think a cop could understand that the shooting was justified. But he threw me under the bus. Hell, he told the judge he should throw the book at me!" I couldn't help the bitterness. "Some support *that* was. Some backup, huh?"

"And now you are out," Grandaddy said. "You are free, according to the law, and accountable only to me. You made sacrifices, yes. But now you are needed, and your particular skillset is required. Yours and Remi's."

I looked at the cowboy, caught a level stare unlike any I'd seen from him before. I needed confirmation he felt as lost as I did. "This is all kinds of fucked up."

Before Remi could say anything to indicate agreement or repudiation, Granddaddy stepped in. "That's what the End of Days *means*, Gabriel. And now it's up to us—you two, me, Lily, all the other angels and our allies—to *un*fuck it."

R emi and I drove to the roadhouse in his truck, fully armed, revolvers loaded with what I dubbed magic bullets, plus knives bathed in breath and holy oil. Remi said not a word on the way, probably, like me, contemplating what the hell was about to happen and what we were supposed to do about it. He didn't say anything even when we pulled into the parking lot. McCue shut off the engine, but made no move to get out. I stayed put, too.

Early evening, but the sun was down. Monday was not a party night such as Friday and Saturday, but going by the parking lot a fair crowd was there nonetheless. Even as we sat in the truck, staring through the windshield, another pickup pulled in. Two Native American men climbed out, headed toward the door. A Toyota Forerunner turned off the highway; when parked, it disgorged a couple of college-age boys dressed cowboy style, and one thin, blonde girl probably not old enough to drink. Then a minivan arrived, and two middle-aged white women got out, settling purse straps over shoulders and moving close together for confidence as they walked toward the entrance. Too old for soccer moms; and anyway, soccer moms would be home with their families at this time of night, instead of at a roadhouse on a Monday night. I'd never played soccer, myself.

Finally I broke the silence. "What do you suppose the staff thought when they found those animals lying all over the floor? Especially the bear."

"Vandals."

"What about a field of crispified roaches and the remains of two ghosts who were possessed by demons?"

"I reckon that likely did not cross their minds," Remi replied. "Whose mind *would* it cross? Three days ago, I was just a cowboy on a West Texas ranch who likes—*liked*—to rodeo on weekends."

I stared out the windshield and said nothing. McCue now knew what I'd been and where.

He drew in a deep breath, blew it out on a gust. "How's this going to go?"

I didn't avoid it or beat around the bush. "*Should* it go? Seriously. What's to keep us from splitting up and leaving? You've got a daughter—go back home to her. Me, I'll just . . . I don't know, have you drop me off at a biker bar. I can hustle pool for some bucks, hook up with someone who'll help me collect my Harley from the campground without alerting Grandaddy or Lily." Well, I hoped.

McCue didn't look at me, just stared out the windshield with both hands hooked loosely over the top of the steering wheel. The big neon Zoo Club sign illuminated him in profile. Cheekbone, the shine of an eye. Gaze fixed on the building. A glint of silver from his ring.

It made me look down at my own hand, see an identical ring on my finger. What the hell were we doing?

"I remember," he said, "when you tried to walk out the other night, and Grandaddy sat you back down."

I kept my tone level. "Grandaddy's not here."

"Yeah, well, maybe his *angelic powers* can still reach this far."

I chopped a sharp laugh. "If they can, why doesn't he take care of this domicile clearing operation on his own?"

"Because *we're* supposed to." McCue turned his head, looked at me. "Get it?—this is a test. And I reckon it's as much about taking hard advice as it is about taking out a demon."

I rubbed at my forehead to stall, then met his eyes. "And if it's in a human host?" Remi said nothing, and I knew what he was thinking. "*Yes*, I killed a guy. I had no choice, not if I was going to save my brother's life. But I don't go around shooting people."

McCue's tone was on the dry side. "Not what I was going to suggest. Was gonna say, what's to stop us from escorting our surrogate outside into the dark and exorcising him? Just like we did with the cop."

Relief washed through me, that he didn't after all consider me eager to shoot humans hosting demons. Exorcism seemed like a very pro-active, healthy, positive approach. "So, do we steal a pitcher of water, throw salt and spit into it, sneak it outside when we do our escorting?"

Remi said, dryly, "I figure a glass might be a little more inconspicuous. There's salt and pepper on the tables, we'll ask for water, and then, well, one of us can spit into it."

It was automatic, as if I were with Matty. "*I* did it the last time."

McCue's expression was deadpan. "Guess that means I can't do me a little snuff. Who knows if tobacco might mess up the holy water."

I stared at him. "You chew tobacco?"

"No, no, you don't *chew* what I use," Remi replied. "That'd get you sick right quick. It's powdered, just sits in the mouth between the lower lip and gum . . ." Then he grinned at me. "Greenhorns, I'm tellin' ya. Fall for the stereotype every time. Come on, then. Let's go visit us a bar and see what turns up."

I grabbed the door handle. "And if nothing does?"

"Grandaddy seemed pretty certain-sure about it. I'm betting he knows something."

I elbowed open the door, climbed out, shut it. "So, how's this going to go?"

Remi exited the truck, shut and locked it, then glanced at

me across the hood. "I already asked *you* that. Figure it's up to you to call the shots. You're the alpha, right?" And he strode off.

After a hesitation, I stretched my legs and caught up, heard him humming. Heard *what* he was humming. "Is that what I think it is?"

He ignored the question and sang a couple of lines.

Yes, it *was* what I thought it was. "You're not old enough for that song, and neither am I."

He broke off to comment. "But you know what it is, don't you?"

Well. Yes. "Oldies station. Don't judge: sometimes it's all I could get."

He didn't alter his relaxed, loose-limbed stroll across the parking lot. Maybe it's the boots that make cowboys amble so slow and easy, or what *looks* like slow and easy. "I figure this demon-baiting is something of a gamble, isn't it?"

Okay, I knew what was coming. Or something like it. "Here we go."

And he said, in his slow Texas drawl, "I just found myself in the mood for a little Kenny Rogers. This being a gamble, and all."

I squinted up at the stars as we climbed the steps to the entrance. "Let's just hope we don't do any *folding* tonight. Of ourselves, I mean."

CHAPTER SEVENTEEN

I t felt odd being back inside a roadhouse that over the past three days had hosted a hot demon chick, two demons doubling as ghosts, a Grigori—oh man, gotta ask Grandaddy about that—a Celtic goddess, stuffed dead animals that had come to life, a possessed cop, and a seraph.

And, well, *us*.

The animals were all back in their original spots, including the bear, though I noted if you looked hard enough you could see a broken-out eye. And judging by the customers wandering around the place, there'd been some vacuuming up of demon remains. Which amused me; how ignominious was that? Sucked into a vacuum bag, then thrown out with the trash.

Actually, come to think of it, fitting.

Remi led the way to the same alcove we'd inhabited when Grandaddy laid down the law about the end of the world and what we were and what it was we were intended to do. Both of us automatically spun the chairs so the backs were angled against the wall and we could watch the customers as well as one another.

We'd managed quick showers and fresh clothing before

heading out. Once again, I wore biker leathers and boots, and McCue his cowboy duds from head to toe. And again I stuck out, though the clientele did not appear to be as full-bore cowboy as Friday and Saturday nights. Naturally Remi fit right in. A pretty waitress came by, gave us menus, took a drink order—water included—as McCue picked up the salt shaker and gave it an appraising once-over. Then he studied the ring on his forefinger.

"Looks a little weird, huh?" I asked. "Two guys wearing matching rings."

He got it after a moment of blankness. His smile was crooked. "I suspect no one'll think we're married. We're too similar. Brothers, maybe, and a family crest."

I didn't think we were *that* similar, though yes, one might assume we were relatives of some kind. Same dark hair, though mine was past my shoulders and his was cut short; bone structure and overall build that echoed one another despite slight height and weight differences; but he was tanned while I still bore the jailhouse pallor. Plus our eyes did not match, with Remi's a clear blue, mine mid-brown.

"Genetically speaking," I said, "I'm not sure it can happen."

He looked at me, frowning faintly. "What can't happen?"

"Blue eyes. Brown eyes. Siblings."

McCue smiled. "Missed out on Mendelian genetics, did you? Yeah, it can happen. Has to do with dominant and recessive genes. But anyway, I don't imagine it applies to us, bein' as how we're not, you know, *human*."

It kinda creeped me out, thinking about that again. I mean, I'd heard and seen much over the last couple of days that persuaded me the world was not, after all, completely as I had viewed it, but *born of heavenly essence?*

The waitress stopped by and set down a pitcher of beer and two mugs along with a glass of water for each of us. Remi actually tipped his hat to her in thanks. She smiled, asked if we'd had a chance to look at the menus.

No, we had not, but pretty much every restaurant served burgers and fries, and both of us asked for that. McCue very clearly specified mustard and waited for her to confirm she would bring it.

As she collected the menus and walked away, I asked, "You got a thing for mustard?"

Remi drank down a third of his beer, then nodded at me. "You ever notice how everyone brings ketchup, or it's sitting on the table already, but you have to *ask* for mustard?"

I blinked at him. "That would be a 'no.' I have not spent any time at all noticing things about mustard."

"Well, pay attention," McCue directed. "Happens all the time. And then usually the server forgets to bring the mustard, and your burger goes cold while you wait for it. Or you have to ask for it again."

I mulled that over a moment. "I never really put much thought into it."

Remi said, with deep gravity, "Mustard is the forgotten condiment."

I lifted my mug, contemplated him over the rim a moment. "We have to carry salt around with us these days. Should we add packets of mustard to our supplies?"

He smiled his slow smile—I suspected many ladies fell for

it—then picked up the salt shaker and tipped it over the surface of his water glass, tapped the butt end with the other hand. White granules poured out and clouded the water.

I grinned. "Don't forget to spit."

"You know," he said, "you'd think blood would be better. I mean, there's iron in blood. More protection for us, more threat to surrogates."

"Well, you can't really go around cutting into your hand or arm to spill blood into your water glass without alarming people, despite what they do on TV," I explained. "And anyway, the hand has more nerves and pain receptors that many other areas on the human body."

"So spit it is," Remi murmured, and lifted the salted water glass to his mouth to attempt the business at hand without grossing anyone out.

I drank beer as he set down the prepared glass and pushed it up against the wall for protection. It wasn't much to look at, but the pitcher of salt and saliva I'd poured over all those cockroaches exiting the cop's body had sure done a number on them. I wasn't sure I'd ever forget the sound of carapaces popping, and the stench.

"So Lucifer has a thing for cockroaches," I mused.

"Makes sense," McCue said. "I think they're something like three hundred million years old."

"And I'll bet they were disgusting even then." I paused. "Do we even know how old Lucifer is?"

"Depends on who you ask."

"If he's really old, maybe he'll tire easily. I mean, maybe he has a bad prostate by now, has to piss sixteen times a night. That would interfere with ending the world."

McCue eyed me over the rim of his mug. "You're talking about an archangel. *Do* they piss?"

"I'll ask Grandaddy next time we see him."

The waitress arrived then bearing plates of burgers, fries, and a bottle of ketchup. She set everything down with a flourish, then asked if she could get us anything else.

Remi said very politely, "Mustard, please." And shot me a look as she hurried off.

"The forgotten condiment," I noted. "It's very sad. Adding it to the armory might not be such a bad idea. Along with Roach Motels." I blopped ketchup onto my burger along with salt, rearranged ingredients and stuck the bun on top, then poured ketchup over the fries. "Do you think Lily will be open to that?"

Remi, still waiting for his mustard, watched me bite into the burger. "I'm not sure we could convince her or Grandaddy that mustard is a ward against evil, but we can give it a try." He waited a moment, then asked, "You sensing anything? And by that, I mean *sensing*."

I swallowed burger, washed it down with beer. "I know what you mean. And no, but then I haven't really tried. And back at you: you sensing any demons around?"

After a moment he said, "Maybe we should both do our respective things and see what turns up."

I paused before taking another bite of burger. "Can we finish eating first? I mean, Grandaddy didn't prohibit us from eating. In fact, he said we could even shoot pool. So let's eat, finish our beers, then do our respective things."

"I can't," Remi said. "I don't have any mustard."

I stared at him over the burger clenched in my hands, then

carefully set it down. I pushed my chair back, rose, glanced around, spotted the bottle, took two long steps to another table and liberated the bottle of mustard from the inhabitants. "Sorry," I said. "Popeye needs his spinach."

Of course by the time I turned back to our table the server had brought the bottle Remi requested and now we had two.

McCue was squirting mustard onto his hamburger. "You should give that back to those folk. It's the polite thing to do."

"I'm keeping it," I told him. "I'll put it in one of the cabinets with the guns, holy oil, holy water, knives, ammo, even the stakes meant to kill vampires."

McCue bestowed a lazy smile. "That'll do."

I went back to my fries, burger, and beer.

Once done eating, with plates collected and mugs refilled, we stared at one another. McCue said, "Do you sense anything?"

"I haven't started yet. You?"

"Me neither."

I thought it over. "Maybe we ought to walk through the crowd, see what we feel. Meet back here."

Remi pushed away from the table, grabbed the homemade holy water, headed around the busy dance floor. No live music tonight, thank God, just a juke box. I could hear myself think.

I wandered back toward the pool tables, remembering the blonde demon chick. It was not an entirely welcome recollection, since she'd come close to doing both a hand-job *and* trying to kill me almost simultaneously. Talk about mixed messages.

I hung out by the tables, trying to sense something. Anything. And for the first time since being released from prison, all of ten days ago, I felt vastly uncomfortable having people behind me. The hairs twitched on the back of my neck and my shoulders itched.

I reached under my jacket to the butt of the gun, then realized I couldn't exactly pull it out if the demon showed. Or a knife, either. Arizona was open carry, but I assumed drawing a gun in a dancehall full of people would not be well-received. It might even get me shot, if there were any wannabe heroes.

Remi was right: we needed to grab the host body and take him—or her—outside into the dark. Hell, if you had to say *surrogate* instead of *demon* in a room full of people who might overhear, you couldn't exactly shoot or knife the host in the middle of a bar.

But I had an idea a demon might not feel the same reluctance. I didn't know what one could do to us. The woman had tried to gut, then strangle me. So maybe demons had to use human means to kill us.

I went to a wall and placed my back against it to ease the itch, then unfocused from the surroundings and tried to feel out the heart of the place. But I heard the clack of balls, the jukebox, laughter and loud voices, which made it difficult to concentrate. When Grandaddy had asked me to sense stuff, it had been outdoors in quiet places, such as on the mountain looming over the roadhouse, and when I walked through this place the night the Grigori showed up.

I wondered if there would be bleed-over, if I did get a sense of demonic presence. Two demon-inhabited ghosts, and a cop. Could I cancel those out and track down the new threat?

195

I went inside myself. Eased my breathing, tried to relax my whole body. Slowly let the surrounding environment fade out.

"Hey dude, you okay?"

Vision focused again. Standing before me was one of the college-aged boys I'd seen in the parking lot. Red hair, blue eyes, freckles, boots, and a big buckle. He looked honestly concerned.

"What?" I asked.

"You okay? I mean, you look like you're about to blow chunks."

Well, that was an illuminating image. And then it crossed my mind to wonder if this kid might be whoever—or *what*ever—we were supposed to 'clear' tonight.

And could Remi sense him, if he was? That would be awesome. But a quick darting glance told me McCue wasn't handy, nor the glass of holy water. Maybe I could use the Vulcan nerve pinch or something, get him outside, and do the exorcism.

I decided to go for it, hoping I might see something in his face, his eyes. "You a surrogate?"

He was baffled; but then a demon would know how to use the host's expressions and movements. "A—what?"

"You here because it's a domicile?"

He blinked. "I'm here because it's a bar."

I scowled at him. This was going nowhere fast. "Don't you have school tomorrow?"

His brows knit. "It's summer."

Well, there's that. "Okay, then don't you have to work to-morrow?"

His eyes were wide and concerned, but not necessarily with me. He took one step backward. "Dude, you're not my father, you know? And I just meant you looked like you were going to puke, so I was going to get you a chair. 'Scuse me for caring."

A demon could be polite. The cop had been. They wouldn't necessarily *look* like they served Lucifer.

I remembered how the eyes of the blonde demon had shifted, with pupils elongating into something resembling a cat. I was tempted to ask the kid if he could do that, but it would undoubtedly sound completely off the wall and thus draw even more attention. And what we didn't need was attention once we found the surrogate.

So, to put the kid's mind at ease, I told him I was not about to blow chunks so his shoes were safe, and thanked him for thinking to get me a chair. He nodded a little, then wandered off. I wandered off, too, looking for Remi.

He found me before I found him. He was still carrying around the full glass of cloudy holy water. "Any luck?"

He shook his head. "I'm smelling cologne and perfume, booze, and I know what everyone at the bar is drinking, and that apparently the steak here is mighty fine, but nothing more than that. You?"

"That I look like I'm going to blow chunks when I'm trying to sense something."

His eyebrows shot up. "You what?"

An idea occurred. "Come with me."

"Where?"

"Just follow me."

He obliged, and I led him to the pool tables. I glanced around, then told him to lean his back against the wall nearby and close his eyes.

"What the hell—?"

"Just do it. I want to try something."

Remi rolled his eyes after squinting wariness at me, then leaned against the wall.

"Take your hat off," I directed. "And mess up your hair."

"Do *what*?"

"Take your hat off, mess up your hair, then lean against the wall and look like you're going to hurl. Or pass out."

"Look—"

"Just *do* it," I said urgently. "I want to try something."

McCue drew in a very long breath, let it go slowly, took off his hat and set it on the nearest table.

I looked at it, then back at him. "It's upside down."

He ran a hair through his hair, ruffling it. "Yup."

"Why is your hat upside down? Is it a cowboy thing?"

"If you set your hat down flat, you can warp the brim. You know these hats are steamed into a specific shape. So if there's nothing to hang 'em on, you rest them on the table upside down."

"I did not know that," I replied. "Are you telling me cowboys in the Old West set their hats upside down?"

"No. Hell, them boys used to tote water in 'em sometimes. That's where the term *ten-gallon hat* came from, for a hat with a tall crown."

"So it *is* a cowboy thing."

"It's a cowboy thing." He paused. "My hair good enough for you?"

I gave it a look-see. He had a cowlick that stuck up in back, now that he'd mussed his hair. "You'll do. Now lean against the wall and look like you're sick."

"You gonna tell me what this is about?"

"Look, there's a guy—probably a college kid—who walked up to me, said he was checking on me because, according to him, I looked like I was about to 'blow chunks,' and he wondered if I wanted a chair."

McCue considered that a moment. "Well, that was downright neighborly," he observed, no more taken with this explanation than others, "but it could just have been a nice kid looking after a stranger. We do that in Texas."

"It could," I conceded, "in which case you'll be able to tell. But I've still got a hunch. Since you're supposed to *sense* things in people, I thought I'd send him over here."

"Why don't I just walk over by him?"

"Because he noticed me."

"You're a long-haired, leather-clad biker in a cowboy dancehall," he pointed out. "Of course he noticed you."

"What if it was more than that?"

"You mean, that he's the surrogate?"

"As you would say, he *'might could'* be."

Remi shifted against the wall. "Okay. Let's get her done."

The kid was shooting pool against his friend, whom I looked over, too. Watching them was the thin blonde girl who I believed was too young to drink, but she had a beer in her hands, probably bought by one of the boys. None of them was looking at me. None of them was looking at Remi.

I dug a ten dollar bill out of a pocket, walked slowly up to the table and laid it out on the top rail. "I'll play winner."

Both boys paused and looked at me in surprise. The redhead recognized me; the other, a sandy-haired boy, did not, but now he paid attention. "We're not playing for money."

"Why not?"

They exchanged a glance. "It's just for fun," the red-head told me. "We play for who buys the pitcher of beer."

"I lose, I'll buy you two pitchers."

They were clearly uneasy. The blonde girl came up, gave me a big smile. "I'll buy you a pitcher."

"I don't think you can buy *you* a pitcher," I said, and saw her face fall. "So you boys go ahead and finish your game, and I'll play winner."

The sandy-haired kid was so nervous he scratched on his next turn. Well, that worked for me. "You rack," I told the red-head.

He nodded, began pulling billiard balls from the pockets and collecting them at the foot rail to move them into a rough triangle with his forearms. Then the rack went down.

I walked over to him, like I was inspecting his rack as he rolled the balls inside it. "Hey," I said. "That guy look sick to you?"

He brought his head up. "Who—?" And then he followed my line of sight.

I'll admit it, Remi was doing a good job. He mostly leaned against his left shoulder, hunched a little, the water glass dangling from the rim in his right hand.

"Bad food?" I asked. "Or too much booze." I clapped the kid on the shoulder. "Look, you were thoughtful enough to check on me . . . how 'bout you see if he's okay. I'll just wait here."

The kid nodded, went unerringly to McCue. I couldn't hear the conversation over the sound of balls clacking and voices, plus now someone was speaking into a microphone in the main room, but I did see Remi nod at the kid, wipe a hand across his face as he straightened up, grabbed his hat, and wandered off just a shade wobbly on his boots.

The kid came back. "He said he had two shots of tequila too fast. He's gonna go outside, get some air."

McCue had headed toward the main room and the entrance, which wasn't the plan. It was the *back* door we wanted to use if we came across the surrogate. And I needed to know what he thought.

I looked beyond the kid, gave a low whistle. "Shit," I said, "I just saw one hot chick . . . dude, gotta check that out." I scooped up the ten dollar bill. "You mind?"

He'd barely said no before I headed off to work my way through the crowd. No more dancing. A mic was in the center of the parquet dance floor, and a couple of guitars were on stands close by. I crossed in front of the guy talking into the mic, but I wasn't paying any attention to what he said.

I found Remi waiting back at our table. I dropped into the chair, raised brows in a question.

"I got nothin'," Remi said. "He could be Lucifer himself, for all I know, but I didn't get any vibe off him. Offered to get me a chair."

"I wonder if that's code."

McCue stared at me. "Code for what? That he's a good kid? Some just are, you know. *I* was a good kid."

I sighed, turned back to gaze across the main room. The bar stools were full, and everyone had swiveled to face the dance floor. The man behind the mic announced they were ready, and called a woman forward.

It became abundantly clear, as a woman walked out of the crowd and stood behind the mic—I was pretty sure it was one of the middle-aged non-soccer moms—what was going on.

Remi read my stricken expression. "You didn't see the sign? Open Mic Night."

"In a *cowboy* bar!"

"Yeah. So?"

"They'll be singing country music!"

He gave me a long, assessing examination. "Probably," he agreed. Clearly, he thought I was pretty stupid.

"And butchering it." I paused. "Not that country music isn't already pretty butchered."

He set down the glass and drank beer, which now was room temperature. "So, what do we do now?"

"I don't know. Leave?"

"You want to risk Grandaddy's heavenly wrath?"

I turned my mug around and around on the table, watching it glumly.

The woman did indeed sing a country song, something about trashing a cheating boyfriend's pretty little souped-up 4-wheel-drive, which I thought was a weird way to describe a pickup. Pretty? (Of *course* it was a song about a truck.) The crowd rather raucously joined in on the chorus. I debated stuffing fingers into my ears, but decided I was badly outnumbered by country fans, and I'd do better to keep my mouth shut and mind my manners.

Remi abruptly sat bolt upright in his chair. "Listen, all we want to do inside is ID the surrogate, right? Then get him—or her—*out*side where we can do the deed in private."

"Well, yeah. That was the plan."

"So you get up—take the water with you—and wander through the crowd. Look for someone starting to choke, like maybe cockroaches are going to start spilling out of him."

"I thought they had to be dead for that to happen. Kind of obvious, don't you think? And people do cough just to cough."

He ignored me. "Make your way to him, threaten to spill the holy water over him, and escort him toward the back door. Can you whistle? I mean, like hailing a cab?"

"Yeah."

"So start checking people out."

Still struck me as lame. "What are *you* going to do?"

"I got an idea. Just look hard for someone acting funny. Don't pay attention to me."

And McCue walked away, making a beeline toward the man who had called the woman to the mic.

Oh, shit. I was pretty sure I knew what was coming.

Sure enough, Remi stepped up to the mic. He nodded his head around at the crowd as if thanking them in advance. The applause was tepid at best; likely the singers were regulars, and McCue definitely wasn't.

As he introduced himself, his voice was diffident, though the drawl was a little stronger. "I am a stranger in town, out of West Texas and headin' down to Phoenix. I hope ya'll don't mind if I sing somethin' for you. It was my nana's favorite song. Probably some of you know it, too, if you're church-going folk. Christmas services, at least. I know it's not what you usually hear performed in a roadhouse, but today would have been her ninety-fourth birthday. I hope ya'll will give me a listen."

Church-going folk?

"Schubert's 'Ave Maria,'" Remi announced earnestly, as he removed his hat. "Give glory to God." Then he drew in a deep breath, smiled shakily, nodded nervously—all an act—and opened his mouth.

Yeah, I'd heard him sing before. Just snatches, but I knew he had a pretty good voice. This was a little more than pretty good. But why now? Why that?

Oh.

Tune the same, still in Latin, but different lyrics. The guy was *singing* the exorcism rite.

Clever bastard.

But I didn't listen for more, because I was on the move with a glass of makeshift holy water in my hand.

CHAPTER EIGHTEEN

It's not easy looking for someone beginning to vomit cock-roaches in the middle of a roadhouse. I mean, it would be pretty damn obvious, but I assumed there was a step before the roaches actually put in an appearance. Remi'd specified someone just beginning to choke. And that's even tougher, be-cause any number of people might start coughing or choking for all kinds of reasons. People just do that sometimes, without being demons.

So I threaded my way through tables, walked the length of the bar, paused now and then to take a closer look around.

Pretty much everyone's attention was on Remi, except for those shooting pool. Because patrons were fixed on the perfor-mance, I could look into faces more easily. "Ave Maria" is sung in Latin, which is probably why Remi picked it, but I did notice a few people exchanging puzzled glances.

Well, it's true that the exorcism rite sounds nothing at all like the song celebrating the Lord's mother.

I saw nothing in the main room, heard nothing suspicious. Then I headed back toward the pool tables, where I found that someone *was* coughing. It was one of the college kids, the sandy-haired guy, not the red-head who'd come to check first on me, then Remi.

He paused, thumped himself on the chest and said something about beer going down the wrong way, began coughing again. The red-head looked suitably concerned, and the blonde girl was not present.

Okay, Remi had not covered what to do if the surrogate had *friends*. Maybe all of them were demons. Grandaddy had not specified number. I'd ask about that next time, if we survived *this* time.

I made my way to the table, put down the same ten dollar bill, called the next game—then with feigned concern looked at the kid who was coughing. "Hey, dude, you gonna be okay?"

It came out hoarse, and oddly suppressed. "Yeah. Fine." Then he clamped a hand over his mouth like he was about to puke.

I rounded the table, stepped close. "You need some help?"

Now he shook his head.

I closed a hand around his upper arm, as if I meant to help steady him. Then I leaned close and said, very quietly, "There's holy water in this glass. I'm suggesting we step outside so no one gets grossed out by the sudden appearance of a river of roaches spilling from various orifices, and have a conversation."

Then I whistled, piercing and clear.

In the kid's eyes was speculation, as if he were evaluating me and what I might do, or maybe daring me. Then, clearing his throat, he looked at the red-head, hovering to make sure his friend was okay. "Hey Rick, I'm going to go outside for a minute, get some fresh air. You go ahead and rerack 'em, okay?"

After a moment of doubt, Rick apparently saw something

that put him at ease. He shrugged, nodded, bent over the table with his back to us. Remi arrived—I heard someone else singing in the background. He paused briefly after giving the surrogate a hard look, then walked right on by and out the back door so it wouldn't look suspicious with *two* of us escorting the kid out. I clamped down a little harder on his arm and guided him toward the door. If he tried anything at all, I'd dump the holy water over his head, get him outside, and let Remi turn him into really ugly bugs.

The kid had stopped coughing, maybe because Remi wasn't singing the rite anymore. He'd have to start it over once we were outside, though probably without the 'Ave Maria' performance.

As we stepped out the back door, I pressed the glass firmly against the surrogate's back. A little water slopped out as we navigated the big step down, splashed the back of his shirt and soaked through. He hissed in pain, and the fabric began smoking.

Yup, we had the right guy.

Remi was standing beneath the big overhead bug light, which painted him slightly jaundiced. His face was tense, eyes very serious. "You took this host without permission. Now it's time to leave."

And he opened his mouth and began the Latin.

Nothing happened. The kid didn't cough, didn't choke. He just stood there in the spill of illumination, and smiled at Remi. "I hate to break it to you rookies, but I'm not a surrogate. I faked it."

Didn't believe him for a minute. "Uh-huh. And when the holy water hit you, it hurt," I pointed out, "and your shirt smoked and now has a hole in it." I stuck a finger through that hole, poked the surrogate's back. "See there?"

And out of the darkness came the blonde girl. "Angels can manipulate such things when it's needful. And we judged it was."

I stared at her. Shit. "So, *not* college kids, or a girl too young to be drinking."

Remi took an assessing look at her. "Well, aren't you half as big as a minute."

"I'm Candy," she continued; perhaps she didn't speak Texan, "and I'm older than dirt." She indicated the sandy-haired kid. "That's Dick, and that—" she gestured with her chin, "—is Rick." The red-head opened the screen door and exited.

My brows shot up. "Rick, Dick, and Candy?" I snickered. "What, you double as porn stars?"

"Well, our angelic names are difficult to pronounce." Red-headed Rick was matter-of-fact. "So we'd be explaining all the time to humans how we came by them, which is inconvenient. Easier this way."

Remi and I stared at one another, trying to figure out what the hell we were supposed to do now. I raised my brows in a question, and he shrugged back. Dick—the sandy-haired guy—removed his arm from my loosened grip. He smiled at Remi. "Singing the rite was genius. I admit, we weren't expecting that."

"This was a *test*," McCue said, sounding tense.

Candy replied, "We cleared the domicile earlier, but you still should have *sensed* something. Surrogates leave an essence for a while after they die."

Now Rick. None of them sounded like kids anymore. "Remiel, you were intended to find us by sensing our presence, to recognize all of us as angels, not surrogates, the way you did up on the mountain with the old man. You didn't."

Dick said, "And you, Gabriel, should have been able to sense that the roadhouse had been cleared, was no longer a domicile. You didn't."

It pinched; in fact, it reminded me of when Grandaddy was disappointed in me, but I didn't let it show. Just looked at Remi. "Guess we flunked."

He was frowning a little, attention distant, clearly thinking something over. Finally he refocused and said, "*Prove* you're angels. Isn't Lucifer the Great Deceiver? You could well be surrogates just playing us. Or playing *with* us."

I remember what Grandaddy had done up on the mountain. His wings had never been corporeal, nor did they exactly look feathered. All we'd seen was an impression in the air, a pale, pixelated image rising from his shoulder blades.

"Show us your wings," I challenged. "All three of you."

"No." Candy looked straight at Remi. "What do you *sense?*"

I heard the frustration in his tone. "You already said I failed in there. I don't sense anything yet, other than occasional hunches. And none of them have ever been about surrogates *or* angels. I don't have visions, I can't get any kind of read on people other than the normal kind of stuff, like expressions, tone, body language. Just like everyone else."

She tilted her head a little. "Try again. Try *now.*"

Apparently he did, and apparently this time he truly did sense something. I saw the stunned expression in his eyes, on his face as his mouth opened. He took two steps backward, then stopped himself. "Holy crap . . ."

Rick was amused. "Holy, yes, but not even remotely connected to crap, thank you very much."

"What did you feel?" I asked McCue sharply, because he looked like he might pass out.

He tried to speak, failed, closed his mouth, then tried again. "It's—impossible to explain. There just aren't any words."

"Not in human language, no," Candy agreed. "But in ours, yes. And it will become yours, too." She paused, engaged Remi's eyes. "In which language was the Bible written?"

He shook his head. "It wasn't a single language. Plus there's a difference between Old and New Testaments. Old Testament was primarily archaic Hebrew, though Ezra and Daniel wrote parts in old Aramaic. New Testament was Koine Greek."

Yup, handy to have a Biblical scholar on the team.

"Do you speak it?" she asked.

Remi made the *maybe/maybe just a little* gesture with one flattened hand, tipping it back and forth. "I looked up some translations for my doctorate."

"Eno no qyomto w hayo."

He smiled faintly. "Gave me an easy one, huh? *'I am the resurrection and the life.'"*

Rick said, "Learn it." He looked at me. "And you need to learn Latin. Aramaic can come later. In the meantime, Remiel will be able to translate for you. You'll have dictionaries and phrase books."

I quirked a brow at him. "What's wrong with English?"

"There are texts and concepts that can't be encompassed by English," he explained. "Surrogates read and understand English, plus their own language. They don't know Aramaic."

I was skeptical. "Wouldn't Lucifer? I mean, he was an arch-angel."

Rick shook his head. "Archangels speak an older form. No surrogate can possibly understand it."

"No grade school for demons?" I asked.

"Their brains are not wired to understand or to learn it."

I remained skeptical. "But humans are?"

Simultaneously, all three declared with impatient vehemence, *"You're not human."*

Oh yeah. Forgot about that part. "Okay, Latin's first on my to-do list. I'll learn Aramaic from Remi."

His tone was dry. *"I* have to learn it first."

I looked at the angels. "Can't you—I don't know—download Aramaic into his brain, or something?"

"We could," Candy replied, "but it would kill him."

"Pass," Remi said, predictably.

I sighed. "Now what?"

Dick said, "You will go back inside. Remiel will choose a person and try to pick up something of his or her feelings, while you, Gabriel, should concentrate on getting a sense of what was the domicile. You will need to know it."

I frowned. "I thought you said you cleared it out."

"You need to *see* it," he said. "Go behind the facade. You need to feel it, bone-deep. Every time you go someplace new, Remi will try to track surrogates, while you will sort out whether it's a domicile, or simply a place."

Candy said, with deadpan humor, "There is much for you to learn, but learn it you will."

I was incredulous. "A Yoda joke from an *angel?"*

211

"Of course," she replied brightly. "We get every first-run movie in heaven before anyone else does. Perks of the job."

"Huh." I thought about it. "That would be cool."

"Too," she elaborated, "it's a good way for angels intended to take a human host to learn something about humans first."

Remi and I looked at one another, brows raised. McCue said, "Ya'll do know movies aren't real, right?"

"But they provide insights nonetheless," she explained. "Now, go inside. Do your thing."

"Wait," I said sharply. "You're possessing the hosts, right? Yet Grandaddy said you didn't."

Rick said, "We borrow, from time to time. But where demons eat out the brain over time, we leave the hosts intact—and healthier than before—when we depart."

Eat out the brain? Holy Jesus.

CHAPTER NINETEEN

As commanded, Remi and I went back inside. Our table in the meantime had been appropriated by a couple helping themselves to what was left of our pitcher of beer.

Rude, dude. But I had a mission, and it didn't include arguing over booze and a table. At least, not this time.

McCue gave me a pointed sidelong look and a slight tilt of his hat—well, head—which I took to mean he was going to park himself close by and try to get a read on either the guy or the girl.

I went to the bar and planted my ass on a stool. Ordered a beer, hunched over it slightly upon its arrival, registered that the bartender was black and big, but didn't pay more attention than that. Mirrors along the bar back provided a view of the room behind me.

Unfortunately, Open Mic Night continued. As I sat in silence nursing my beer, on the verge of trying to *go behind the façade*, whatever the hell that meant, I heard portions of various songs, all country. Some singers butchered them, which made me wince and want to plug my ears, but I figured that was not a good idea in a place full of locals and regulars; others were passable, despite their poor choice of genre; and a couple were actually pretty good. One chick sang about a chick named Jolene begging someone not to take her man, a guy performed a raucous number about friends in low places, and two rough-voiced men sang a duet about mama not letting her babies grow up to be cowboys.

I wondered if Remi knew about that one. Probably he wouldn't like it. His mama *had* let him grow up to be a cowboy.

Okay. Time to try my thing.

It had been easy on the mountain to reach out, to let a sense of the place come to me. As then, I saw brief flashes of color around the edges of my vision, but this time red, which symbolizes passion, blood, and war. Not happy about that, though it didn't surprise me.

The red was superseded by something that felt—well . . . green. I sensed a flow of health, renewal, vigor, which made sense for a place cleared by angels. But the feelings were fleeting, leaving me trying harder to get a sense of the bar. Before, alone in the building, I had "remembered" feelings I'd never experienced. It was the *place* that exuded memories, but only in snatches. There was nothing I could latch onto, because the moment I tried, blankness washed over any sense of color, of place, of memory. The roadhouse felt weirdly empty despite the customers.

That is, until someone started caterwauling the high-pitched chorus of The Police's "Roxanne," which was considerably better than a country song, but the screech that came out of the guy's mouth was ear-shattering.

I winced in involuntary reaction, noticed the bartender was smiling as he came toward me. Now I paid attention. Big black guy, really big, probably six-four and maybe two hundred forty, fifty pounds. His head was clean-shaven, his voice deep. A black t-shirt was stretched over the bulk of muscular chest, shoulders, and arms. Looked like he could be a former NFL player.

"Yes, he is not one of our better singers, but he enjoys it and is a good man, so he is forgiven." The bartender had an accent, one with which I was not familiar. But he didn't sound disapproving, nor did his expression show any kind of hostility. "May I present another beer?"

Several nights before, a demon in the guise of a hot chick had tried to kill me. A Grigori showed up to warn me the war might relegate humans to collateral damage. A surrogate inhabited a cop. And tonight angels had actually chastised us. All four experiences made me wary of people in general, especially in the roadhouse. The back of my neck twitched again.

And asked if he could *present* another beer. Not normal phraseology for a bar. I shot him a searching appraisal. Angel? Demon? Grigori? Nephilim? A god? Just a human pouring booze?

He noted my assessment. "It was only a question," he said mildly. "There is no need for you to be biker threatening."

Biker threatening? Me? To him?

But if anyone else took it that way . . . well, I was in a bar full of locals and cowboys. "No," I said hastily, "no, man, sorry. Just—thinking about something. Bad memory." I placed a ten on the bar as tip, hoping to soothe him, slipped off the stool and headed over to where Remi ought to be.

He saw me coming, walked to meet me just off the dance floor. "You get anything?"

215

"Green." His brows inched up. "I think it means this is a safe place, now. Cleared of threat, or surrogate presence. But it wasn't clear, wasn't like the sense of a place I usually get." I checked his expression then smiled benignly. "Too much country music."

He eyed me. "You gotta get over that prejudice, son."

"Why?"

"It's just not a healthy thing."

I ignored that. "*You* get anything?"

"Yup." He was solemn. "The guy is thinking about bed sports later, and the girl is thinking about a favorite TV show she's missing."

"Really?"

"No."

I gave him the side-eye. "Seriously, did you sense anything?"

"Caught traces here and there, but not anything like the angels want. I think what we're doing is boot camp."

Interesting. "So none of this counts?"

"Oh, I reckon *all* of it counts. And I also expect we could be killed if we take a major misstep; there's no urgency, no incentive otherwise. I caught a good lick when that ghost threw me into a table."

I was visited by the image of Remi being actually, actively licked, which left me grossed out, and I attempted to mentally bleach my brain immediately. "So Grandaddy basically started grooming us for this job back when we were little kids. Now we're being challenged to show what we know."

Remi nodded. "To show what we know *and* whether we can do the job without getting ourselves killed. It's a GRE test for grad school. We get in, or we don't."

It was a startling concept. "You think they'll *kill* us if we don't pass?"

Remi shook his head. "I reckon they won't have to. I *reckon* a surrogate will take care of that for them. At any rate, how 'bout we go back to Lily's rig? We could—"

And he stopped dead, looked startled, a little tense; but a moment later it was like his hackles went down. He smiled, eyes going warm, as he looked beyond me. I turned, and there was Grandaddy.

I was a little uneasy about having him at my back. The last time we'd been together, he'd announced that it was his doing I'd gone to prison.

Remi said, damn near breathless, "So *that's* what it is!" At my frown of incomprehension, he explained. "I felt him. Almost like a vibration in the air. But—it's not like it was outside. It's—" he groped for words, "—just *bigger.*" He looked at Grandaddy. "I never felt it before, when you came a'visiting."

Grandaddy nodded. "We angels can shield ourselves. I dropped my shield just now so that nothing blocked you."

I stared at him. "What, like a Romulan cloaking device?"

He ignored me. "Remi, did you sense anything of the angels here earlier?"

"No, sir. At least, not until the girl did the shield thing."

Grandaddy nodded. "At some point it won't matter; you'll be able to tell when an angel is in the building."

Said I, "Well, I thought Dick—or Rick?—was a surrogate. But I didn't feel anything. I was just—suspicious."

Grandaddy declared, "Suspicion, when your gifts are yet too young to function properly, is healthy, and a sound safeguard."

"When *will* our gifts start functioning?"

"When they do."

Well, that was helpful.

Grandaddy smiled at my annoyance. "Now, you boys come with me. There is someone you should meet."

Remi and I followed him across the main room, threading our way through tables, and the someone turned out to be the big bartender. He saw us coming and I caught a glimpse of teeth as he presented Grandaddy with a smile.

"Is it time?" he asked.

"It's time."

He nodded. "Drinks?"

"Oh, I think it best," Grandaddy agreed. "Your best single malt, and best tequila; I'll have a Guinness."

I studied the bartender. "That was a joke, then, wasn't it? The crack about me being 'biker threatening.'"

He smiled again as he poured two fingers' worth of single malt, slid the tumbler across the bar toward me. "Not precisely so. I imagine others would indeed find you 'biker threatening,' on occasion. But you are no threat to me."

His accent was fascinating, and the clarity of his speech in a resonant voice. "I imagine not," I agreed. "I don't imagine *anyone* is a threat to you."

He poured tequila for Remi, then the dark beer for Grandaddy. "That is true."

I looked at Grandaddy. "How do you drink that shi—stuff. It's like motor oil. Used."

He smiled benignly and ignored me. "Now, raise your glasses and toast this man, for he is like none you have ever met."

"Angel?" Remi asked.

"No, indeed," the bartender said. "And I thank you for your courtesy."

Grandaddy, McCue and I clinked glasses, then we each took a swallow. The Scotch went down smooth. Our grandfather—or whatever the hell he was—said, "He's an Orisha."

The big guy nodded. "I am Aganju. Our pantheon is ancient." His dark eyes slid in Remi's direction. "But even you, with your doctorate, won't know me, or the others. We are forgotten."

McCue looked right back at him. "You said pantheon. The word refers to a collection of gods."

"And so it does." The big man smiled. "Orishas are of Africa."

"Huh," I said thoughtfully. "What's an Orisha?"

"A god."

"A *god?*"

He nodded, going solemn. "I am Aganju, warrior king, and lord of volcanoes and deserts. This place is my responsibility, you see. The volcano behind us, though it sleeps, and all the others; and the desert surrounding us."

"This is a desert?" I asked skeptically. "There are pine trees all over."

Grandaddy said, "It's what known as 'high desert,' here. But go two hours south toward Phoenix, and you will see a true desert."

Remi sounded thoughtful. "The Morrigan and an Orisha."

Aganju nodded. "Many of us are here, those made for war. We have been freed from banishment. Men long ago stopped believing in Orishas. But now they shall worship again."

I remembered Lily's impassioned speech about wanting the

219

same. Apparently this was a regular thing for old gods and god-desses, this needing to be worshipped.

"Finish your drinks," Grandaddy said. "We're going upstairs."

Remi and I exchanged puzzled glances, then knocked back what was left in our glasses, put them on the bar, and followed Grandaddy to a dark area against the wall. There was a stair-way, and while not truly hidden, neither was it obvious. Just—out of the way. I guess the one the woman fell down and broke her neck, thus becoming a ghost.

And I guess Aganju's presence explained why there'd been no questions about demon roach remains. But where the heck had he been when that was going down?

Oh yeah. A test. He could have been watching, for all I knew.

The staircase was narrow, with steep risers. As we climbed after Grandaddy, it became clear that Open Mic Night was over. The jukebox was playing again, and a thread of music followed us up.

At the top landing, Grandaddy led us down a hall, indicat-ing various open doorways. "Common room. Kitchen. One bathroom, two bedrooms." He stepped across the threshold into one of the bedrooms, and we followed. Smallish, but with a bed, a dresser, closet, desk. The north and west walls were constructed of large-diameter chinked logs, the others paneled in flat, grainy wood.

"Okaaay." I frowned. "What are we doing here?"

Grandaddy said, "This apartment is where you'll live. You can't stay with Lily, as she has her own missions and cannot always be here. For now, your territory is Arizona, so this will be both headquarters and home. And when you are ready, you will be responsible for all of the Southwest. No rent, no mortgage; free food and drink, if you choose to eat downstairs. TV. Wi-Fi."

It was muffled, but now and then, depending on volume, the jukebox downstairs was audible.

Oh, hell no.

I shook my head. "How about not here? How about a motel, or a rental house? I can live in a motel, no sweat. It's still better than a cell."

"Here," Grandaddy said.

I said with no little urgency, "I'd really rather not."

Remi was frowning at me. "What's wrong with here? Nice bedrooms, a kitchen . . . free room and board."

I glared at him and said with great clarity, "It's a cowboy bar!"

He didn't get it. "Yeah. So?"

In a strangled tone, I said, "They play *country music!*"

Grandaddy sounded inordinately cheerful. "Every night but Sunday, when the place is closed. Live music Friday and Saturday nights, Open Mic Mondays."

McCue, the bastard, was laughing at me. "Guess you'll be learning plenty of good ol' country songs, then. And maybe a little respect."

"I don't think so." I appealed to Grandaddy. "Please say you're joking."

He was amused but adamant. "Here."

I took two steps to the bed and dropped ass, planted elbows on thighs and leaned forward to grasp my head in disbelief and despair. "Shit. Shitshit*shit*. Just kill me now."

CHAPTER TWENTY

Grandaddy took his leave. Remi wandered off to tour the place while I sulked on the bed. He came back and said, "There's beer in the fridge." He offered a bottle. "Drown your sorrows."

I took the bottle but didn't crack the top. I just kind of stared at it in a daze. "It's too much."

"What, the beer?"

"No. *Everything.* Angels, gods, that Grigori chick—"

Remi interrupted. "To be accurate, the Grigori are angels, too. So are Nephilim, though admittedly they're also half human."

I began again, this time poking thumb and fingers into the air one by one to enumerate. "Angels. *Other* angels. Demons. Gods. Goddesses. What the hell else?"

"Creatures out of folklore. History. And, I guess, literature, from what Grandaddy said."

Now I opened the beer and downed half of it in two huge swallows. I looked at McCue in silence, then drank the rest of the beer. "If an African *god* works here, how come surrogates managed to establish a—what did they call it? Domicile?—without being killed off by this Aganju? I mean, he appears to be working for our side."

Time for more pointed questions. Remi smiled slow as honey. "Well, let's go downstairs and ask him."

I rose, set down the empty bottle. "He is a very large man."

"Big as all hell and half of Texas."

Colorful, but true.

We trooped downstairs into music, laughter, raised voices, the clack of billiard balls, which reminded me of the angelic trio, Rick, Dick, and Candy, who *did* have names like porn stars no matter what they said.

"How the hell are we supposed to live here?" I complained to Remi, who descended ahead of me. "Country music or no country music, the place is loud. And we're supposed to sleep above all this racket?"

He stepped off the final step and threw a comment over his shoulder. "I reckon you'll get used to it."

"No, I don't think so."

"You got used to prison, didn't you? A man can adjust to anything."

Well, that shut me down. I followed him to the bar in disgruntled silence.

Remi and I found two stools at the very end of the long slab of bar counter and sat down. Aganju was in the middle of a discussion with one of the patrons, an ancient, weathered cowboy who was going on and on about something. Aganju just listened and nodded, spoke a time or two, though I couldn't hear what was said.

"He an angel?" I asked.

"He's a god."

"No, not him. The old man."

"Well, if he is, he's got his cloaking device up and running."

I roll-tapped my fingertips against the bartop repeatedly, impatient. And eventually Aganju came down to us.

Before he could ask what he could get us, like any normal bartender would do who wasn't a god, I wasted no time. "Why was it you didn't clear this place of surrogates?"

"Ah." He nodded, as if he'd expected the question. "That requires angels. It is of opposites, you see. Black and white, good and bad. Angels and demons. I am not of your heaven."

"Well, then why are you here? You said you are an African warrior-king-god."

"And so I am. My day will come, and I shall wade through blood. But it is not the time."

Wading through blood, huh? Not exactly on my bucket list. "So, why are you here rather than in Africa?"

His teeth appeared again. "The war here will be of greater consequence than the petty coups of Africa. And nowhere else boasts six hundred volcanoes."

It was startling. "Six *hundred*?"

In his deep voice, he said, "Now they answer to me."

Holy shit.

Aganju continued. "Yes, I may kill demons. It is only the domiciles that are not in my purview."

I considered him. "Do you, what—smite them?"

He looked a little surprised. "Oh, no. That is for angels. I have a sword, you see. I take heads."

"Ah. Like the Highlander, movie and TV versions? Do you have Quickenings?"

The big man smiled. "I do kill them quickly."

"No, that's—" But I waved it off. "So, where is it?"

"My sword? It is here."

"You mean, beneath the bar? Like a baseball bat or a shotgun?"

Remi shifted on the stool next to me. "Are you done yet with your interrogation? You wanted to know why he didn't clear this place, and he's answered."

But I wasn't satisfied. "Could you have helped us with the ghost-demons? With the demon-cop?"

Aganju was solemn. "These things are for you to do."

That figured.

He added, "I go up upon the mountain when I am not here."

It was McCue's turn to question him, if with a little more decorum than I. "And what do you do up upon the mountain?"

His teeth shone pearlescent against dark skin. "I sing to her, and worship. But she sleeps, so she says nothing. I hope to wake her soon, and the others."

After a moment of arrested silence, Remi got there before I did. He straightened abruptly on his stool, tight as a bowstring. "Hold up. If you mean you want it to come back to life and erupt, you'll kill people, destroy the town." His sweeping gesture encompassed the bar. "These people right here. That old man you were talking to."

Aganju was unperturbed. "Such a thing will destroy demons, stop the Lucifer, and save the world. This is a good thing, is it not? To be victorious?"

McCue just stared at him, apparently struck dumb by the realization that Aganju was a bloodthirsty son of a bitch.

"Victory is good," I agreed after a moment, "but not at the cost of all these people."

"Men die. That is war."

Remi's tone was pointed. "And women and children."

Aganju said, with a weird sort of serenity, "That is the cost of war. We must all bear it."

Neither I nor McCue spoke as the big man went to another customer, but I could sense the cowboy's tension echoing my own. I was reminded yet again of the Asian woman, the Grigori, warning me that not all angels were on the same page, that humans would die.

And this guy, this Aganju, wanted to wake an extinct volcano.

Had Grandaddy brought Aganju and other gods of war to the here and now merely to serve a purpose without regard for the risk to humanity?

That made me uneasy. *Very* uneasy.

The Grigori had told me, *At this moment you and Remiel are innocents being set up for manipulation.*

"They'll do anything," I said, and felt a chill. "Everyone involved in this. Anything at all."

"It's Lucifer himself," Remi said. "It's the End of Days. Yes, I think they'll do anything, because *every*thing's at stake."

I gave him a sidelong glance. "And us?"

He stared down the length of bar at the African Orisha. "I have a feeling we'll probably do anything the angels tell us to."

Well, hell. "I would suggest, with all gravity, that we are well and truly fucked."

Aganju came back to us, set down a tumbler of scotch for me, tequila for Remi. "On the house. As all drinks and food are, for you. Call me Ganji; it is easier. And we shall be seeing a great deal of one another."

Oh, joy.

"And yes, you are." His gaze was unblinking as he stared at us both. He was certainly the kind of man who'd intimidate others easily—big, black, shaven skull—but that wasn't what he intended at the moment despite his size. He was perfectly matter-of-fact.

I was wary. "We are what?"

"Fucked."

Remi and I waited till Ganji was serving other patrons before we looked at one another. When we did, McCue's expression was a mixture of resolution and concern.

He said, "He's dark as the devil's riding boots—and I ain't talking about the color of his skin."

CHAPTER TWENTY-ONE

We departed the roadhouse after that, keeping our silence. I'd mentioned to Remi that if we *had* to stay at the Zoo, we ought to collect our clothing from the motel, and my bike from Lily's rig. So we climbed into his truck and headed north.

"Six hundred volcanoes," I pondered aloud. "I had no idea Arizona was so active back in the day. Or that this area had pine trees, for that matter, instead of big-ass cactus. Still doesn't look like a desert to me, high or low."

He didn't say anything until we turned onto the motel parking lot, and then he sounded subdued. "I don't like it. Not at all. But, like I said, we may have no choice 'cept to do what they tell us to. And what happens down the road? Grandaddy said we weren't angels *yet*. Suggests that if we live long enough, we might could sprout us some wings."

That was not a happy thought. "And we've got no idea how long this war is supposed to last, or what happens if Lucifer *does* get out of hell."

"I think that's what Lily and Ganji are for," he said, "and any others tied to this mess. Demons are the target now, but if

Lucifer goes bustin' out, I reckon the angels and all these gods and goddesses will unite to destroy him."

I mulled that over a moment. "Cannon fodder. That's what we are."

"Canaries in the coal mine."

I muttered a curse, unlatched the truck door and shoved it open. McCue did the same on his side, and together we walked to our respective rooms.

I had very little to collect beyond toiletries. When saddlebags are the only option for carrying stuff, you limit what goes into them. I had a pair of jeans, tactical BDU pants, a few tees, couple of Henley shirts, underwear. My world on a bike.

I'd done eighteen months in prison. Throughout, the bike was parked at my parents' house. When I went to collect it, my father—ex-military, current cop—gave me a piece of his mind about what a big disappointment I was, and did I know how embarrassing it was for him to deal with questions at his station about his imprisoned son?

I'd been a little busy trying to survive inside, so no, I really didn't spend any time thinking about my father's disappointment and embarrassment.

My mother visited a couple of times. He did not.

R emi and I met back at the truck and headed up the road to the RV campground. As we arrived at Lily's rig, I was astonished all over again by how large it was. Multiple *rooms* that slid out from the chassis, and that garage. I wondered how often anyone was banged up enough to use the cot, the medical equipment in the back end. I wondered, too, how much Lily knew about field medicine. She was in the business of war, not in saving lives.

Lily wasn't there—and then she was. She walked out of the trees with the wolfhound at her side. I heard the crow overhead.

It was dark because the campground was studded with massive pines that blocked much of the moon, but she had exterior lighting on the big motorhome. Her face was shadowed, then it came clear as she walked out of darkness into the sphere of light. I noticed again how the sleeve tattoos seemed to move on her arms.

"Have you seen the apartment?" She climbed the steps and swung open the door. She held it there, then stepped aside so the crow could fly in. The wolfhound followed, and Lily gestured for us to climb in behind her. "We'll hope it brings you better luck than the last two of you."

That grabbed my attention in a hurry. I stopped short just inside the doorway. "Last two? *What* last two?"

"The two boys before you," Lily replied. "Did you think you were the first, then?"

Remi poked at me to suggest I move, which I did, then he stepped in, removed his hat and hung it over a window valance. "Okay, so we're not the first. What happened to our predecessors?"

Lily's eyes were bright. "They were killed by demons, so no heaven for them. Now, shall I pour you some Irish whiskey?"

At the roadhouse, we'd consumed most of a pitcher of beer and a couple of tumblers apiece of tequila and scotch, so we both refused. "I thought you said this all began with the hell vents opening," I reminded her. "The earthquakes, and so on. That's only been a matter of a few months."

"It doesn't take so long to die, now, does it?"

I wanted to raise a salient point as comeback, but a wave of weariness reminded me I was way overdue for a decent night's rest. Besides, I didn't want to think too much about those two guys who died before us. I pushed back the sleeve of my jacket to check my watch, noted it was almost two. Last call, back at the Zoo.

Remi felt as I did. "We need sleep."

I nodded. "You know, it's going to be difficult for us to rest with all that racket going on. Hard to sleep, hard to stay sharp." I tried to turn it into a joke. "Maybe the reason the other two guys died was for lack of sleep."

Lily walked into the garage, came back with a small zippered duffle that she dropped on the floor by the door, and two sawed-off shotguns. Her tone was matter-of-fact. "They died because they were stupid. They enjoyed success for a while, but got cocky. They were torn into pieces by a demon, then eaten. Raw." Her smile was odd, like the death amused her. Well, maybe it did; she was a creature of war. "This is why you both have come to be here. Your predecessors died in the line of duty. Horribly. So there's a lesson for you: Lead with humility."

Remi and I exchanged a glance. In his eyes I saw the decision made not to get cocky, and he probably saw it in mine. Getting torn to pieces was, well, kinda undesirable.

Lily poured herself whiskey but did not immediately take a seat. She stood by the cabinetry, and the interior illumination highlighted the red of her Mohawk, painting her eyes greener than ever. It glinted off her piercings, off her arm cuffs.

With nothing else immediate to say, I mentioned we had met Aganju.

Her smile went wide. "And what was your impression?"

Remi resorted to a Texas-ism again. "Big as a Brahma bull."

I had no scale for that, so I asked. "How big *is* a Brahma bull?"

"Between eighteen and twenty-four hundred pounds."

I was stunned. "A *cow?*"

"Bull."

My disbelief was manifest. "And you *ride* those things?"

McCue nodded. "Bulls and broncs."

I reassessed him. He was tanned, and his hands were callused. A couple of shallow squint lines at the corners of his eyes suggested a fair amount of sun and good humor. Good-looking son of a bitch; and I say that because we do resemble one another.

I'd known him four days. It felt like four months. Still much to learn about him, but I was far more comfortable than I had been. I barely knew him, but trusted him. And trust had absented itself from my feelings during my trial. If that trust was an effect of *primogenitura*, it might come in handy. Grandaddy had said McCue would have my back, and I'd have his. It felt right.

So, there was biker tough, ex-con tough . . . and, apparently, cowboy tough.

I looked at Lily again. "Ganji is a very imposing man. God. King. Whatever."

"He sings to volcanoes," Remi added.

Lily nodded. "He can sing them to life."

McCue looked doubtful. "This one is extinct, not dormant."

"Doesn't matter. All wake to him."

"Okay, we don't really need the singing and waking," I said. "We'd prefer he didn't do that, actually."

She disapproved and apparently thought we were terribly naïve. "If Lucifer climbs his way out of hell, there will be worse than volcanoes and lava fields. Would you have everyone on earth die of spontaneous combustion?"

Remi cocked his head. "Dying is dying, ain't it? Means don't matter."

Lily studied him a moment, then said, "Just don't make Ganji angry."

Well, yeah. Okay. A good goal. He looked badass all on his own, but as a god who could raise volcanoes? Yeah, let's keep him friendly. I attempted a casual tone, but had the feeling she saw right through me. "So, you know one another? You and Ganji?"

Her smile and the bright snap in her eyes suggested she knew exactly what I was asking. "We all of us know one another, now that we are aware again, and here. The angels made it so."

"That's another thing," I said, "you speak with an Irish accent—"

"I'm Irish."

"—and he speaks with what I assume is an African accent—"

"Igbo."

"Ee—okay. But Gaelic is nothing like—Igbo. You're ancient. Yet you both speak English."

Lily was highly amused. "I'm speaking Gaelic."

Remi stared at her, frowning, and alert as if he were listening for subtleties. "It don't sound anything like Gaelic. Trust me."

Lily smiled. Once one looked past the tattoos, the piercings, the Mohawk to the woman beneath—she was striking in an almost eerie sort of way.

She said, "He speaks Igbo to you. We don't speak in English, we speak in our own languages. But English is how you *hear* it, as does anyone we speak with. Angels—and others born of heaven—know all languages on Earth."

"But we *don't* know," I told her. "I don't speak any foreign language."

"I speak Spanish," Remi said, "and, well, Latin. But we're hearing nothing like either."

She nodded; apparently this topic was expected. "You will. When you're older. For now, you will understand the language of those you work with directly. When you become angels, all languages will be yours."

Huh. Heavenly Rosetta Stone, maybe? "About that," I began, again attempting to sound casual, "Just when does this—promotion—happen?"

Lily was amused, but not blind to my play for information. "That is for Jubal to tell you—but he probably won't. Angels are secretive."

"No shit," I muttered.

She opened a drawer, retrieved a slip of paper. "Now it's time for you to leave. Take the bag—it's your starter kit—and return to the Zoo Club. Settle your things. Then go to this website."

I frowned. "What web—wait, we have a computer?"

"In the common room." She held out the paper.

The URL was foreign to me, except for the triple W. I handed it to Remi who took it, frowned over it, was clearly comprehending no more than I had.

"Wupatki," she said.

"Woo what?" My natural inclination was to think of the term *woo-woo*, denoting crackpot New Age followers and UFOlogists.

She spelled it, letter by letter. Oh, it was *wu* as in woo, *pat* as in pot, and a *kee*. Which told me absolutely nothing. "What's a Wupatki?" I'd never heard of a Wupatki in folklore. Some kind of monster?

"Not *a* Wupatki," Lily clarified. "It's a place. A National Park. Indian ruins. Where there is a barghest." She enunciated clearly. "A black shuck."

"Legends," I said tightly. "Real, now? All of them?"

Lily nodded. "Mythology, tall tales, fictional villains: all *alive*. The surrogates are riding them."

Remi looked perplexed. "What's a barghest? What's the legend?"

Lily's tone was sharp. "It's not a legend, it's a demon. Gabe will fill you in on the folklore. Now, go home. Type in the URL. The site is deep web, and you will find what you need to know there." Her smile was wide, showing small white teeth. "You must kill it, this black shuck demon."

Okay—or, well, maybe not okay. I'd go along for now, but I was curious. "What's it doing?"

"What demons do," she replied. "And in that form, it's shredding humans. Tearing out throats. Adults, but also children."

I hadn't looked at a newspaper for days, or watched TV. Remi's stunned expression suggested the same. If people were being killed by a beast, surely there would be coverage. We needed to check it out.

Lily's tone was level. "You must kill it tonight when the moon is full."

Now my brows ran up. "What, like a werewolf? That's not in any of the legends."

"The full moon has nothing to do with the demon in barghest form." She looked at me, then at Remi. "It has to do with how, in the night, you're going to *see* well enough to kill it. Now—*go*."

So go we did.

CHAPTER TWENTY-TWO

The Zoo's parking lot was empty; last call had come and gone, which meant it was after two in the morning. After a prison regimen with lights out at ten p.m., all the action and revelations were catching up to me.

We parked bike and truck around back. I unhooked my saddlebags; Remi climbed out of his truck with the bag Lily had given us as well as a larger duffle. He'd put the two shotguns in the gun rack across the truck's back window, safed below a handsome long gun stripped of bells and whistles. Winchester 1873, a model based on the original made *in* 1873, known as "The Gun that Won the West."

I tried the back door and found it unlocked. Not a particularly safe thing, but then I imagined a god could strike down—or, in Ganji's case, behead—anyone who came looking to steal stuff. Or maybe wake the volcano and lava the thief to death.

As we entered and thumped across the wooden floor in motorcycle and cowboy boots, supersized Ganji, who currently was not out singing volcanoes to life but rather incongruously washing glasses at the sink, greeted us with a smile.

He pushed a manila envelope across the bar. "Something came for you."

My brows ran up. "I thought with the domicile cleared—I think that's the terminology—no one knows we're here except for Grandaddy, Lily, and you."

He put his finger on the envelope. "*Gabriel* and *Remiel*. Are there more of you with the same names?"

Remi said in a dry tone, "You might could actually open it and find out."

I walked to the bar, dropped my saddlebags on a stool, took up the envelope. Remi put his duffels down as well and leaned slightly toward me to view the envelope as I tore it open.

A single sheet of 8.5 by 11 paper. Just plain old paper. I tilted it so Remi could read it, too. The brief message was formed of letters cut from newsprint, magazines, all in different fonts, different colors. Just like ransom notes in the movies. But this was not a ransom note.

Five words changed everything: *'I know who you are.'*

"What the hell?" Remi reached out, took the paper from me. "No signature, no name at all, not even in cut-out letters."

Ganji said, "Demons know you are here."

I shook my head. "Like I said upstream—the domicile is cleared. We killed the demons in ghost form, and Remi exorcized the one in the cop. Then I burned up the bastard's cockroaches."

Ganji's eyes were knowing. "What of the woman whose arm you broke that first night, the one who sought to strangle you? What of the Grigori?"

So, he knew about those instances. God grapevine? Or: "Lily told you."

Ganji nodded. "She told me, yes, but would not have spoken of it to anyone else other than your grandfather. And the domicile was cleared. No demons are here, nor will they be."

"Huh," I said. "So, they can't just gang up on us when we step outside? We're safe here, even if our blinking neon beacons are transmitting?"

"You are safe *here*," Ganji clarified, "and the clearing affords some protection immediately outside this building. But they know you are here, and they have access to you elsewhere. And since you are to seek them out, you must be vigilant."

Vigilant. Yeah. "They could just lay in wait for us. Watch, and wait for us to leave."

Ganji's tone was dry. "Vigilance." He drew two mugs of draft beer, set them on the bar, implicit invitation. Apparently a god didn't care if he was breaking the law by serving after last call. "When you, Gabriel, can discern a domicile, and you, Remiel, can discern a demon before it strikes, you will find it easier to survive."

"And when is that supposed to happen?" I asked. "Tomorrow? A week from now? A month? It probably would help us with the whole vigilance thing."

"It happens when it happens, as all things do."

"Not very helpful," I muttered, and Ganji laughed.

Remi's turn. "And what exactly is 'clearing a domicile'? Clear it how?"

"I do not know how," he answered, "only that it must be done by angels—or those born of heaven—after a demon's death, or the place might be renewed as domicile." His smile was slight, but a spark lit up his eyes. "Not very helpful."

I looked at the sheet of paper with its simple but discomfiting statement. "I'm assuming you didn't see who brought this."

"I did not. It was in the mailbox."

With no address or stamp on the envelope, it meant whoever it was had brought it personally to the Zoo. Which suggested that yes, other demons knew exactly where we were.

"Well, shit." I cracked an involuntary yawn, then sighed. "I'm going upstairs. I'm beat." I grabbed the beer with a nod of thanks to Ganji, grabbed my saddlebags, then headed toward the stairs. Remi was right behind me.

Grandaddy had shown us the bedroom on the right. I poked my head in the one across the hall, saw it was identical, said, "I'll take the other."

Remi didn't care. Just walked in and dropped his duffle on the bed, put Lily's bag on the desk. I went into the opposite room.

Now that it was mine, I took a closer look at the room's decor. All was rustic, made out of lodgepole pine. The woven bedspread and desk chair's upholstered seat seemed to be some kind of Native American design, but not like the omnipresent Pendleton patterns back home.

Dresser, and closet. I needed neither, though I guess I could throw my two pairs of pants, handful of shirts, and underwear into a drawer. I had lived so long in prison clothing with no true possessions that it felt odd to look back on my life before and remember things I'd owned. I'd discovered I didn't need any of them. But I missed my books.

Missed, too, the girl who'd broken off our engagement after I was charged with manslaughter. Around eight months after I went to prison, a brief letter arrived with interesting news: *I got married. His name is Paul.*

Now I stripped off my jacket, threw it over the chair, and

was in the midst of downing my beer when Remi appeared in the open door, tapped the jamb with one hand. "You need to come see this."

"No, man. I just want to crash. If we're going demon-killing tomorrow night, I need some rest. It can wait until morning."

"First of all, it's demon-killing *tonight*, since it's past midnight; and no, it can't wait."

He looked deadly serious. I heaved a sigh, nodded, followed. He led me into what Grandaddy had indicated was the common room.

Four-seater table in the middle. A computer on the desk. Floor to ceiling shelving jammed with books. A brown leather nailhead couch, and against the wall a flatscreen TV in a modest entertainment console.

"I input that URL." Remi gestured toward the computer. "Take a look."

Crime scene photos. Autopsy photos. Two adults—male and female—and two children maybe eight, nine, boy and girl.

Newspapers do not print graphic crime scene photos, and definitely not autopsy photos. Lily had said the site was deep web, not accessible to others. We, Remi and I specifically, were meant to see these.

The throats were torn out so badly that pearly neck vertebrae were visible in the mess of shredded flesh. The children were the worst because they had smaller necks. Long stripes, looking like claw marks, also scored all four bodies.

I said all I could manage. Nothing else sufficed. "Holy *fuck*."

Then I stood up, turned, took three steps away. Stopped and stood there feeling nauseated. I sucked air in, then blew noisy breaths out repeatedly.

Christ, if we could stop things like *this*, the "deployment" was worth it.

Remi's tone was subdued. "I tried to access other sites. Facebook, Twitter, Dallas Cowboys homepage, etc. Page errors all over the place. The only website comin' up is this one."

I returned to the chair beside Remi's. Abruptly, with neither of us touching the keys, the computer ditched the photos and posted a one-word message: *Table.*

"Table?" I found it utterly baffling. "What?"

Then another sentence replaced the first word: *Phones preloaded with pertinent numbers.*

I turned around and looked at the table. Two cell phones were lined up with precision, side by side. A tag on one said *'Gabriel,'* the other *'Remiel.'*

And next to them, credit cards. Black, with a silver pentagram and our names stamped in silver.

More words showed up on the monitor: *Phones will not dial other numbers. Cards not for frivolous expenditures.*

I needed some levity in the midst of serious shit. "So, what constitutes a—" I made elaborate air quotes "—*frivolous expenditure* when we're trying to save the world?"

Remi picked up his phone, studied it. I grabbed mine, turned it on, pulled up Contacts, found four names and numbers: Remi, Grandaddy, Lily, Ganji.

"Check out the back," McCue suggested.

I did. Impressed into the black case was the same design as on our rings, and on the credit cards: silver pentagram. I turned the phone back over, looked at the front of the bezel and screen. "No brand."

Remi nodded. "Maybe iAngel?"

I selected McCue's name, pressed a fingertip against the screen. Sure enough, his phone rang. Or, rather, it emitted a series of five tones.

"Oh, come on!" Now I was getting aggravated. "That's from *Close Encounters of the Third Kind*."

Remi looked thoughtful. "Maybe those aliens were actually angels."

I scoffed. "No angels we've seen look anything like those Roswell rejects aboard the Mother Ship."

Remi's face went very still for a moment, eyes distant. "What if the humans who got on the ship were intended to be angel hosts?"

"It was a *movie*! With actors. It didn't happen. It wasn't real!"

"It might could be," McCue said. "What if Steven Spielberg was hosting an angel when he made the film?"

And then he grinned.

I called him a vulgar name, turned on my heel and stomped back to my bedroom—but not before I picked up my credit card—where I closed the door firmly. Maybe he'd get the message.

Steven Spielberg—an angel? My ass.

CHAPTER TWENTY-THREE

I woke up to someone knocking on my door. Sunlight poured through the windows. I found my phone—my normal phone, the one that *did* dial other numbers—and saw it was 8:00 a.m.

I did not feel refreshed. I needed more sleep. I bellowed, "*What?*"

Remi's voice sounded odd. "You need to come see this."

Summoned by computer yet again. Muttering about rude awakenings, I found my leather bike pants, pulled on a fresh t-shirt, and opened the door.

Remi was not there. Barefoot, I padded down the short hall to the common room and found him sitting at the computer.

"What?" I repeated. "More cryptic statements?"

He was hatless, but dressed. Still all cowboy. "Exactly the opposite. Everything's normal. I can reach all kinds of webpages."

I massaged one eye socket, then ran a splay-fingered hand through loose hair. "And last night you couldn't."

"Last night I couldn't."

"Well, can you reach the site we saw before? The photos, stuff about the phones?"

"Page error."

I grabbed a chair from the table, dragged it across wooden floorboards, sat down just off Remi's right shoulder so I could see the monitor. "Now what?"

"Found a website for the place we're heading."

"Woo pot?"

"Wupatki. Look." He typed it into the search field, then clicked on a link. It brought up a page hosting a large photo of a substantial pile of rocks.

But a pile of sunset-colored stone, shaped kind of like squashed bricks, and organized one atop another to make walls, windows, doorways. It reminded me a little of castle ruins. "Native Americans lived there?"

"Anasazi and Sinagua. Built the pueblo in the twelfth and thirteenth centuries. And I think we ought to head out there now in the daylight, so we can scope out the place before we go lookin' for a demon wearing the shape of a—" he paused, gave me a sidelong glance, "—whatever the hell a barghest or black shuck is." Another pause. "What *is* a barghest or black shuck?"

"Also Hairy Jack, Padfoot, Churchyard Beast, Hateful Thing. Among other names."

McCue sounded annoyed and repeated himself with excessive clarity. "What *is* it?"

"It," I said, "is a dog."

"A dog? We're hunting a *dog?*"

His reaction didn't surprise me. "You know *The Hound of the Baskervilles*, by Arthur Conan Doyle? Features Sherlock Holmes?"

Remi nodded. "Never read it, though."

"The book's about a fearsome, ferocious beast believed to be straight out of hell. Tons of legends about it from all over England, which inspired Conan Doyle. Basically it's a harbinger of death, though some legends say different." I stretched, cracked my spine. "Mostly it haunts places, doesn't actively kill people."

"It is *now*," Remi put in. "Adults *and* kids."

Yeah. So it was. Subdued, I went on. "Best known name is plain old 'black dog.' Mostly it haunts places and *wasn't* particularly known for killing people, though obviously that's changed." I thought about the photos. Thought about the kids. Felt sick all over again.

"So we're gonna hunt us a dog."

"No, we're gonna hunt us a demon." I pushed the chair back and rose, shoved it into place at the table. "I need a quick shower, a little food." I looked him over. Neatly pressed clothes and different from the day before. "You good to go?"

"Already showered. There's coffee made," he said, "and eggs, sausage, hash browns. Also cereal. I had Wheaties."

"Breakfast of champions. Or also, I guess, breakfast of demon hunters." I left McCue reading about Wupatki, headed to the kitchen still barefoot. Boots could wait on coffee.

Coffee. Stuff of the gods.

But not of Ganji, I hoped, or it might taste like lava and ash.

We hit a minor glitch when it came time to head out to Wupatki. Remi had assumed we'd ride together in his truck. I said no way.

I told him, "I like the freedom of a bike on the open road."

His look was quizzical. "You're wearing leathers, a full coverage helmet, gloves, and boots. It's like armor. What it's *not* like is feeling the wind in your hair. And if you really want that, I can lower my windows."

"You have a horse, I think you told me."

Remi, frowning at the apparent non sequitur, nodded.

"*That's* not like riding in a truck, either," I pointed out. "And when on horseback, don't you feel different?"

Apparently he'd never considered that. After the brief parade of thoughts visible on his face, he arrived at an understanding and climbed up into his truck as I threw a leg over my bike.

Wearing my armor, as Remi described it, *was* an encumbrance. Zooming down the interstate in shirt, jeans, without gloves or helmet, was far more freeing than doing it all geared up. But bodies bounce when they come off bikes at high speed, and when head meets road it usually results in death or a persistent vegetative state. I wanted neither, thank you very much. Around towns at much reduced speeds, yeah, I might go without the whole shebang, but the interstate could be a vicious beast.

We headed north on Highway 89 about twelve miles, turned off at the sign for Wupatki and something called Sunset Crater.

Sunset Crater turned out to be a massive blackish purple-red cinder cone left over from an eruption. With my mind on Indian ruins, not on a mountain of cinders, I didn't much give it attention as I rode toward Wupatki—that is, until something reached out and grabbed me.

Not a person. Not a demon. A *feeling*.

Wrongness.

Evil.

I braked, rolled my bike onto the shoulder, stopped. The road was crowded by pines, firs, juniper, and wild grasses. Patches of cinders broke free of the soil, of the deadfall of limbs and leaves. The remains of jagged, broken lava flows had turned much of the area to black, blistered rivers of volcanic stone, intercut with trees. Trees and grasses also climbed most flanks of the crater.

Like an ice cube dropped down my back, I was abruptly chilled. I heard thin, high-pitched screaming.

Remi, too, had pulled over. He drove up beside me, dropped his windows, leaned low toward the passenger door to speak out the window. "What's up?"

I did not want words. I waved him into silence, concentrating on what I had felt. Climbed off my bike, took two long steps toward the huge cinder cone, then stopped short and blinked heavily, because it felt like my eyes weren't behaving properly.

The colors that crowded my vision were black and red. And I sensed a thrumming buried deep. Saw flashes of fire, of lava, of an undulation in the earth. Heard again the screaming.

Remi, out of his truck, came up beside me. His tone was low, and infinitely quiet. "What do you feel?"

I worked my shoulders, trying to shed the chill lodged in my spine. "Did you hear anything?"

"Sure," he said. "Rabbit. Maybe more than one. Probably a mountain lion. They hunt this whole area. You ever hear a rabbit die?"

I shook my head.

"They scream. Sounds like a human baby."

251

I thought again of the dead children and their dead parents. Neither were babies. But they were too young to die, and no one deserved to be torn apart by a demon in the guise of a massive dog.

"Do you sense anything?" I was tense, unsettled. "Any kind of—a human host? A surrogate?"

McCue shook his head. "But I suppose in dog form it could wander back and forth between the ruins and the crater. They're only about fifteen miles apart. I checked the papers, news sites—there've been no reports of anyone being killed *here*. Just at the ruins."

"And what do the papers and news sites say about it?"

"Mostly, they believe it's a mountain lion. Maybe a bear. They've gone looking, even on horseback, but found nothing. A few whackjobs claim it's extraterrestrials." He grinned. "That a space ship crashed and caused the crater in the cinder cone when it buried itself, and if the government would just allow people to hike up the cone to the crater on top, evidence would be found."

"So you can't hike the cone?"

"Nope. What I read said it used to be allowed, but it was breaking down the ecological integrity of the area, so it's closed off to the public now."

Anger surfaced. "I want this son of a bitch."

Remi said, "Then let's go kill it."

Back on my bike, the sense of wrongness bled away from me. I heard nothing more, *felt* nothing more than the warmth of a bright summer day mitigated by the shade of tall trees and a breeze ruffling through.

I pulled back onto the road with a pickup truck behind me.

CHAPTER TWENTY-FOUR

At the turn off to Wupatki, I cut the engine, rolled to a stop. The road that led to the ruins was blocked by a wide metal gate across the entrance, a three-strand wire fence, and featured a big posted notice stating the ruins were temporarily closed to visitors. Apologies for the inconvenience.

Yes, having four people killed by—*something*—would indeed be inconvenient.

Remi got out of the cab, climbed up into the truck bed, and opened one side of the big hinged tool box, which ran from one bed rail to the other. Kind of like steel saddlebags, in a weird sort of way.

He jumped back down, brandished a pair of wire cutters, and proceeded to cut away the fence beside the gate. He bent it back so that my bike and his truck would fit through, then motioned me onward.

I took the bike off asphalt onto deadfall made up of pine needles and other detritus, then returned to the entrance road. A little way down I came upon a parking lot, rolled into a space.

As I shut down the bike, I couldn't take my eyes off the ruins. Wupatki in the flesh, so to speak, was identical to photos that captured the place but not the *feeling*. Wupatki was old bones with an older soul.

Considering the builders cut stone into flat rectangles back in the twelfth and thirteenth centuries, and mortared them together with clay into stacked walls, I was damn impressed. The big building was built around massive sandstone rock formations swelling from the earth. The color throughout—stacked stones, the formations, and the dirt all around it—was a pale, dusty sunset gone rich beneath the sun.

We had the place to ourselves, since access was closed. I pulled helmet and gloves off as Remi drove in. I felt for the Taurus in my shoulder holster, decided to strip down to t-shirt, which left the gun and holster visible. Legal open carry is all well and good, but some people get nervous around guns. My ex hated them. Had we come where others, such as tourists, gathered, I'd have kept the jacket on even though the day was warm.

Supposedly the beast attacked at sunset, so we had some time. And no guarantees it didn't continue to hang around until well after dark. Lily seemed to think so; she'd said we would need the full moon in order to see.

I felt better for having my KA-BAR and revolver loaded with powdered iron shells. Remi checked himself as well: belt-mount holster, big damascened Bowie, the tri-part sheath of throwing knives.

Ghosts, as had been established, could be killed if shot or stabbed in the vulnerable parts of human anatomy. At the Zoo, I'd taken out the male ghost with a point-blank head shot, which certainly would have killed a normal human. Remi had thrown knives into a tight grouping in the heart, almost like arrows or darts in the bulls-eye, and killed the female ghost.

And he had exorcized the demon in the cop, leaving the host alive and unpossessed.

Now we faced an animal. Because black dogs had always been in the realm of folklore rather than reality as ghost-beasts haunting various areas, I wasn't quite sure what it would take to actually kill the thing.

"Well, let's get this checked out," McCue said, heading out. I hesitated a moment. Wondered, because I couldn't help it, if I would scream like a dying rabbit if the Churchyard Beast took us.

It wasn't a steep climb up into the ruins because the place was built on a modest plateau and twentieth-century contractors had put in wide, shallow, framed steps. At some point they'd also mounted hand rails throughout various parts of the trail in the ruins, and in some areas natural mortar gave way to modern cement to shore up the place.

A winding trail, converted to powdery red dust by the soles of thousands of shoes, led me inside. The ruin was open to the skies, though at some point a wood-pole ceiling had kept out the sun and rain, because the remains of those poles were scattered across the ground. And the walls were easily two stories high, no second floor. Again, I figured the builders had used wood to create a floor that now lay in ruins upon the ground.

The windows and doorways were shaped with great precision, considering the material was hand-hewn stone. I walked into a square tower-like room, saw the high second-story window. I tipped my head back to see what I could see. The sky beyond was a blistering blue.

I closed my eyes. Let my awareness of the here and now fade.

There was warmth in my head, like a banked fire, and the edges of my vision were a comforting green yet again. I caught the faint trace of fire, of ash, of water; of ground-growing plants such as squash, plus beans and tall, rustling corn. But that was not all. Piñon pines bore seeds that were roasted, or pounded into flour for baking. Wild plants offered flavor and spice, and there was meat aplenty from deer, rabbits, and prairie dogs, those weird little chipmunk-like animals who popped out of burrows and chittered to sound the alarm when children came hunting them.

It had been a vital, thriving community, a place where multiple native cultures came together to trade, until the climate changed. Water became less available, the land more arid, and eventually Wupatki could no longer support its residents. The tribes moved on, leaving behind them a massive structure surviving to this day, if depleted of roof, ladders, and flooring.

"Gabe!" Remi's voice snapped me out of it. "Gabe—come take a look!"

I followed his voice some distance, found a huge, round, deep dug-out area in the ground lined with stacked stone walls and mortar, plus a surrounding wall up top. Those top walls were probably three feet high; below the outer surface ring was a lower structure forming circular bench-like seating around a large area of flat, dusty ground.

I stood atop the wall, found Remi down in the—well, hole wasn't the right word. It was a planned and hand-built structure, not a natural opening in the earth. It struck me as incongruous to see a hatted modern cowboy standing in the middle of something built centuries before by Native Americans.

"It's a ball court," he said.

"Ball court?" That seemed unlikely. "How do you know?"

Remi stared up at me as if were too stupid to live. "I read the sign."

Oh. Yeah. Signs are handy.

"Anyway, come down," he called. "There's an opening about ten paces to your right."

And so there was, and so I walked through a walled entrance that struck me as similar to the entry tunnels football teams use to head out onto the field.

I strode toward Remi, until he told me to stop. "Look," he directed, and pointed at the powdery, gritty earth.

Boot prints all over the place. But overlaying them were animal tracks. Big-ass animal tracks.

"Too large for mountain lions," Remi noted, "And the shape's wrong, anyhow. Those prints weren't made by a cat."

Or a bear, I thought—though I doubted there were any out here in the middle of a waterless, very warm nowhere.

"Dog*like*," Remi continued, "but too large for a coyote or wolf."

I squatted, looked more closely at the paw prints. The depressions were clear. Even the holes left by toenails were well-defined. The creature had returned after the investigators departed.

I shook my head. "They're nothing more than folklore."

"Grandaddy and Lily said—"

I cut him off. I hadn't exactly meant for him to hear that. "I know what Grandaddy and Lily said."

Remi's expression was serious. "Then why do you want to deny it?"

It wasn't denial, exactly. More like an expression of hope,

but I didn't know how to explain it. From my squat, I looked up at the cowboy. "Because black dogs are *not supposed to exist*."

He was unsmiling; this was no joke. "Neither are demons."

I looked at the paw prints again. "This is a domicile. I can feel it, even if I can't quite do it in Grandaddy's way. You sense a demon in any form hanging around?"

Remi's eyes went blank and unfocused, but finally he came back to the here and now and shook his head.

I said, "It would be helpful if you did—" I gestured at the tracks "—but I guess not really necessary."

"I reckon that's the truth of it."

After a moment of quietude where all we heard was the buzz and whine of insects, I said, "I'll admit it . . . this scares the shit out of me. Some big-ass *thing* out of folklore killed four people."

"Yup."

I rose. "And it'll kill more."

"I would bet my horse on it."

That was stone-cold significance, coming from Remi. I stared across the high desert vista, saw endless blue skies. I was trying to convince myself that all this was real, when what I wanted was to forget the last few days.

It was a fucked up errand, maybe, but people had died. "We're coming back tonight and taking this thing out. One way or another."

CHAPTER TWENTY-FIVE

I n Arizona, I'd discovered, the curtain-fall of twilight came late. No wonder the state didn't do Daylight Savings Time. The light lingered much longer than in the Pacific Northwest, as did the heat of the day. Daylight here most assuredly did not need to be saved.

We were in Remi's bedroom back at the Zoo, and he was checking the slide of throwing knives in their sheath. The big Bowie was on his belt, as was his Taurus. The smooth efficiency of his movements made him dangerous. In a way I wished it otherwise—because then it made *me* dangerous, too. Maybe that was necessary now, but it played hell with memories of a quieter life. College student, college prof. Now ex-con and killer.

He glanced up. "How do you think we should kill it? I mean, what will work? Iron? Silver? Holy oil or water?"

After a moment's consideration, I remembered Lily's duffle. I placed it on Remi's bed, unzipped it. We both looked into an array of cardboard boxes containing bullets and shells, flasks, small bags of various herbs, a few bottles of God knows what. Also two of the twisted, silver-wrapped wooden stakes.

"It's not a vampire," I noted, "so we probably don't need to bring the stakes."

Remi's tone was subdued. "I'm not lookin' forward to the day we have to rely on those stakes. That's close work. *Too* close."

The black dog had been close enough to take down every member of the family. It could well try the same thing with us.

"We'll take a shotgun," I said, "but your rifle may be the best bet. I think it's advisable to keep our distance from this thing. You can play sniper. Or hunter. Whichever works for you."

McCue didn't buy it. "*You're* the one with the extra special, fancy-dancy gun skills."

"You're the one with the skills for *that* gun," I pointed out. "Later, I'll take the chance to learn its weight, its kick, check out the sights, the lever action. But not tonight."

Remi eventually agreed, then suggested we mount up. I shot him side-eye, grabbed a box of silver bullets and a second of iron buckshot shells. I opened it, considered the ammo, then blew a breath all over bullets and cartridges. It still felt ridiculous, but I wasn't going to argue.

"I imagine they were already dipped in holy oil," McCue remarked dryly.

"Let's just be on the safe side. Bless it with spit, you know?" Sexy image.

I handed him the box, and he followed my example as if he were blowing out birthday candles, then nodded. "Let's head 'em up, move 'em out."

"In case you hadn't noticed, I am not a cow."

"In all that leather you might as well be."

———

By the time we arrived at Wupatki, sunset was upon us. The witching hour, so to speak, but heralding instead the incipient arrival of a black dog, a barghest, a black shuck and all the other names.

I pulled off helmet and gloves, left them on my bike. McCue was taking down a shotgun and the Winchester from his gun rack. He handed me the shotgun. I broke it open, saw it was loaded with what we needed. I tucked more shells into my jacket pockets.

Remi's hunting rifle wasn't prepped for killing demons; he took the time to eject the old rounds from the repeater, replaced them with breath-blessed silver.

Abruptly, in my bones, in my consciousness, I sensed it again.

Evil.

Malevolence.

But tenuous. Coy. Ephemeral.

Domicile.

I settled the shotgun in my hands and against my right shoulder, turned in a circle, twitched shoulders against a chill. "You getting anything on the demon?"

McCue paused, and his eyes went distant. After a moment he shook his head. "I got nada. I don't understand how come your heavenly engine is running while mine isn't."

"*Half* running," I said. "It's still—intermittent. But as to why, maybe it's an alpha thing. And maybe in five minutes you'll know exactly where the demon is and what it's doing."

The moon was rising as we walked the path toward the ruins. My chest felt constricted, breath ran short. We'd killed two ghosts, exorcised a demon, but all had been wearing human form. This was a dog, and black dogs could indeed pull down humans from the heights, even those of us with sparkling little celestial beacons.

When McCue, in his drawl, said that he was fixin' to break off from me and circle the ruins from one direction, suggesting I go the other, I declared that idea horror-movie stupid. "If we do that, and I was watching this at home, I'd be yelling at the screen about how stupid we are. We stay together."

"And give the surrogate a tight-grouped target? Once we get in there and spread out, at least one of us'll get 'im."

Well, he had a point. "I really, really wish you could sense where it is."

He shot me an annoyed glance. "So do I, but I can't. Yet. So let's do this thing. If the surrogate's not inside the building, I'll find a spot to set up with the rifle. If that sucker is inside, we corner it and take it out."

We walked up the trail leading to the ruins. We did not rush. We made our steps quiet.

Remi watched the left, I the right. Both of us employed a sweeping visual assessment, checked the immediate environment, then one of us swung around and walked carefully backward to check our rear while the one in front kept moving.

Shitshitshit. I wanted not to be here.

Beside me, Remi said, "I wonder where the kids were when the parents got taken. Or if the kids were killed first."

And that eased me, in kind of a sick way, because I had a purpose. It smoothed down the hair on the back of my neck, settled my belly. I blew out a breath and let go of the tension. I knew we needed badly to save other children. And we could.

Kids. Parents. *Kids.* Boy and girl, maybe seven, maybe eight. Or both at once, possibly twins.

Adrenaline ratcheted up. I wanted this done. Over. And it was enough to fuel me. As we reached the big multi-roomed building, Remi said he was going left to circle around, and I should go right. The plan was to meet after checking out the perimeter, then go together inside the ruins to investigate individual rooms.

The moon remained on the rise, not yet at its zenith, but already it illuminated my surroundings. Lily had been right; tracking a surrogate in a black dog's clothing required good light.

I was halfway around the perimeter when the beast showed. Beneath the moon, not shunning its light, the thing paced slowly forward. Its head was lowered as it scented track, the tail up and rigid.

It was sleek, and slick, and oily beneath the moon, as if colors could not stick. Thanks to the lunar illumination I could see it clearly: angles, muscles, curves, a startling definition even against encroaching darkness.

I like dogs. Dogs like me. But this . . . oh, hell. *This* wasn't a dog. It was the End of Days. The end of my life. The thing was Mastiff. Great Dane. It was pit bull and Rottweiler with Doberman thrown in. It was *huge*, and the sheen of its coat, beneath the full moon, the delineation of its muscles strung tight yet rippling, promised a strangely beautiful, economical killing machine. An almost elegant death even in the midst of horror.

If, that is, one didn't mind having a throat ripped out and the vertebrae, like knuckle bones, like *gristle*, chewed to powder.

It stilled. Lifted its head, air-scented, looked directly at me and lowered its head in a hackled, stiff-tailed threat display. Teeth glinted, but that's not what I was struck by.

White. *White* eyes. Not the red of legend.

The pupils ceased their roundness and bled into vertical slits. Cat eyes in a dog's body.

Well, hell.

Here it was, and here *I* was, and my throat was there for the taking.

CHAPTER TWENTY-SIX

Only a fool stands in front of his ending and does nothing about it. I might still die, but I'd go out with a bang. Literally.

Even as I brought the shotgun up to the hollow of my shoulder, I heard a rifle report. The black dog staggered, cried out, dropped briefly, then surged back to its feet. It drew its lips back in a ferocious snarl.

Well, Remi might could be a better shot.

The black dog leaped, and I took off running.

I dumped the shotgun; it encumbered me too much as I ran, banging against my hip as I clutched it in one hand. Dogs, as far as I knew, even with a demon aboard, lacked the capacity—and the opposable thumbs—to gather up a gun and fire it.

Please God, let Remi's shot, even if not center mass or buried in the brain, slow the sucker down.

The ground was a conglomeration of grass, grit, dirt clods, stone rearing out of the soil. My knees and ankles took the brunt as I scrambled to remain upright, worked to keep my footing. The moon bathed the earth, but behind me I heard the dog.

No. The *surrogate.*

The chant gained volume in my head. *Remi Remi Remi.*

Breath, all tangled amidst need and fear and effort, came up from lungs into the air. I sucked oxygen, hearing the scrape of it against my throat.

There, before me . . . the ball court wall, crouching in moon and shadow. It would hardly stop the beast, but it nonetheless offered an opportunity.

"Remi!"

I thrust weight upward, leaped, felt my boots hit stone, then crouched and planted a hand at the end of a stiffened arm, propelled myself outward and down. I most assuredly did *not* want to hit the circular bench built low.

It was horror-movie stupid. The ball court featured only two narrow entrance/exits. The walls surrounding the court were not insurmountable, but definitely a challenge to someone badly winded and running for his life. But I believed it might give Remi another chance.

I hit ground, went down, tucked and rolled, came up to my feet just as the beast leaped onto the wall. The moon painted its body, turned it a tarnished, silvered gray, slick sheen against the darkness.

Just as I pulled my Taurus from its holster, Remi's rifle shot took out the surrogate.

I stood there with lungs heaving. I wanted to swear, but I lacked the breath.

The black dog, struck through the heart, had tumbled down the wall, bounced off the bench-like structure, and landed in a heap on the ground. Blood spilled out of its mouth, attenuated, stopped. The heart was no longer pumping.

I bent over, planted hands against my knees, though one still clung to the gun. I felt my hair fall forward to obscure both sides of my face. After a moment, breathing better, I sat down all of a sudden with no grace at all. I was still not acclimated to the elevation.

"*Gabe?*" came the call.

I wanted to answer. Nothing in me could.

Remi jumped up onto the wall with its wide, flat rim and stared down at me. The rifle hung from his hands. "You okay?"

I waved at him, trying to communicate my okayness through the gesture, then kind of folded up, tipped, lay flat on my back against the ground.

Holy shit. Holy *Christ*.

I didn't feel anything like a scrap of heaven's grace, neither essence nor spark. I was just a man, no more. But Remi and I had killed a demon.

McCue came into the ball court opening, walked over to me. He didn't squat, didn't kneel, didn't even bend down. Just stood over me with a rifle in his hands.

Then, waxing poetic, he said, "You scrambled like a chicken tryin' to outrun a fox."

I presented him with an eloquent middle finger.

After a moment, as my arm flopped back to the earth, he asked if I would live. I said yes, levered myself into a sitting position, then with the help of a stiffened left arm, I thrust myself up from the ground and onto my feet.

Said I, as I recovered my breath, "Couldn't you have taken him out *before* I scrambled like a chicken trying to outrun the fox?"

"Hell, son, where's the fun in that?" He grinned, and added, "Betas *rule.*"

I was sore from my tuck and roll. Apparently I'd come down hard on my left shoulder before doing an imitation of a hedge-hog rolling itself up against a threat.

I looked at the sprawled dog again. Definitely dead. And since a black dog wasn't truly real, there was no host to save.

"You know," I began thoughtfully, "this is really, really weird."

Remi's eyes went wide. "Wait—wait. *Gabe—*"

He was supposed to get a sense of demonic presence and seemed clearly alarmed, so when a woman appeared atop the wall I didn't even think about it. On edge, jittery, trembling from an adrenaline high, I shot her five times.

CHAPTER TWENTY-SEVEN

S he didn't go down. What she did, with markedly angry eyes, was unfold a pair of huge, black, shimmering wings, then snap them forward to meet and emit a thunderclap of sound so powerful that it sent Remi and I both to the ground from the force of it.

She put up a fist with the forefinger extended and stabbed at the air. *"Don't* piss me off!"

Remi brought his rifle up, though he was seated on the ground.

I reached out and caught the barrel. "No. No, that's Greg."

She glared at me. "I am Grigori; my name is *not* Greg."

"Who?" Remi asked, and then he got it. "Oh, the angel from the Zoo Club? The one who told you angels have differing agendas and humans might end up as collateral damage?"

We were still sitting in dirt. "That's the one. She says she's not one of them, but at this point who knows?" I rose, brushed dust from my pants, tucked my revolver back in its holster and extended a hand down to McCue. He grasped it, and I pulled him up.

Black eyes glittered as she stared at us. The moonlight was

kind to the bone structure of her face, with its high, delicate cheekbones and wide mouth, though it was set very grimly at the moment.

"How did you not die from that?" Remi asked. "Heart high through the center of your chest."

"Apparently they don't," I murmured. "Die, that is." I reconsidered. "Then again, maybe they do; she wouldn't tell me how it might happen the last time we met." I looked up at her. "You know, those wings are awesome. Grandaddy never really did show us his, just kind of a rippling, an *impression*, and displaced air."

The wings were outstretched. Dressed in black and standing atop the wall with those things unfurled, she resembled a . . . well . . . yeah: an avenging angel, Asian style. Then she furled the wings back almost like an accordion. They dimmed into the darkness beneath the moon, then disappeared altogether.

She gazed down on us both. "Grigori watch. Grigori record. Grigori keep track of what others are doing, most particularly when they are infants, as we reckon age." Now she glared. "My name is not Greg, or Gregory, and I'll ask you to stop using them. My name is Ambriel."

I gestured, indicated the black dog, hoped to mollify her. "We took out a surrogate."

"I saw." Her black hair was glossy in the moonlight. "I was watching; that's my job. But yours isn't finished."

Remi asked, "Are we to bury it? Burn it? What do you want us to do with it?"

"You are to clear the domicile. The demon will go with it."

"Uhh," I said. "They haven't taught us that yet."

270

She didn't look any happier. "Can you not sort it out on your own?"

"Remi knows Latin," I pointed out. "Will that help? If there's a ritual, I mean."

"Latin will do," she said in bad humor. "So, Remi, what do you think you should say to clear the domicile?"

He gazed up at her, ruminating on word choices. I could see it in him. Finally he offered: "Out, damned spot."

Greg—*Ambriel*—looked no happier. "This isn't *Macbeth*, idiot boy."

Remi looked thoughtful. "Would a rite of exorcism work?"

"It's already *dead*," she pointed out. "But we can't very well leave the body out here for tourists or Park Rangers to find, so we must get rid of it as well as its lingering influence. Erase it from this place. *That's* clearing the domicile."

I looked at the very dead black dog, empty now of demon. "Why is it still here?" I asked. "Black dogs aren't real. Without the surrogate animating it, shouldn't it just disappear?"

"The demon *made* it real," she explained. "Therefore it is."

I looked at Remi. He looked at me. We both turned to Ambriel. I said, "We haven't got a clue."

She was annoyed, sent both of us a sweeping glance of sheer disgust. "You should be able to figure it out."

"Okay." I looked again at the very dead dog, gave it a command. "Scram."

Naturally 'scram' was not the magic word, any more than Lady Macbeth and her damned spot was. Ambriel finally seemed to understand that we really, truly didn't even know where to *start*.

271

"Watch and learn," she commanded. Dutifully, Remi and I did just that.

She remained atop the encircling wall. Though her elbows were bent, she lifted and extended her forearms, bent her wrists upward, displayed the palms of her hands. She resembled nothing so much as a fugitive surrendering, hands in the air.

Then commenced the Latin: *"Patri bonorum omnium creatorem omnium sanctorum deponentes pestilentibus locis visum vocemque bestias inferni."*

I expected bolts of light, or laser beams, or smoke, or *some-thing, anything* visible, shooting from her hands. Something dramatic.

Nada. Nothing at all came from her hands.

And then the black dog's body exploded.

It was literally blasted apart. Portions of the body were flung up into the air and across the ball court. Remi and I both ducked, hunching shoulders and protecting our eyes from flying blood, bone, and viscera.

All of the scraps, pieces, and traces of the exploded body were immolated. Fires burned here and there, illuminating the ball court rather like lighting up a baseball stadium. Each pocket of flame consumed the black dog's scattered remains.

When the body was gone, when at last it was truly gone, I caught that overwhelming smell of sickly demon deodorant. Remi and I both coughed hard enough that I thought I was going to puke. But I swallowed my belly back into its cavity.

"Oh," McCue said in a hoarse voice. "Yeah, I can recite that. I just don't know how to explode the thing without C-4."

She stood with hands on hips, looming over us. "You need to learn it. I suggest you do that very soon. Because so far there have been angels to clear the domiciles, but that won't last. You're being given a little latitude right now because you are infants, but next time—and there *will* be a next time—you will have to do this yourself."

I opened my mouth to ask another question, such as why was it angels couldn't do all of this on their own and leave us out of it entirely, but she was just—*gone*. Between one moment and the next. "You know," I mused, "it would be helpful to be able to do that. Just translocate our heavenly asses right out of here."

Remi was staring at the ash and grit now smeared across the ground. Then he looked at me. "Well?"

"Well what?"

"Is it clear?"

So I let myself go, lost myself, sensed nothing of malevolence, nothing of evil. Just an *absence*. No colors at the edges of my vision, no blurriness, only an impression of emptiness. Then a little of the now-familiar comforting green eased itself in.

"It's okay," I said. "It's gone. Nothing at all left here." I looked at the scuff marks, boot impressions, paw prints. "So, what was it?"

"What was what?"

"What she said."

"Oh, the Latin? It means *'Our father, creator of all things good, of all things holy, rid this place of the sight and sound of this pestilential beast of hell.'*"

I laughed. "Oh, *that's* good, even if it is a mouthful. I like that. Pestilential beast of hell. Very cool."

Remi lifted his rifle, tipped the barrel back against his

shoulder. "Let's go, pestilential human. I'm fixin' to go horizontal for a while, then eat half a cow."

I looked again at the absence of dog, absence of surrogate that had killed four people. The entire complex of ruins was free of demon, completely cleansed. Free, too, of the cloying scent of its perfume.

I followed Remi up the low ramp leading out of the ball court.

CHAPTER TWENTY-EIGHT

Fifteen miles up the road from Wupatki, my vision went black, then red. I blinked hard, eyes wide, then squinted, tried to clear away the colors washing across my vision. Eventually I braked, slowed carefully and veered off road onto shoulder. My eyes felt foggy, but I could see.

Swiftly I pulled my helmet, planted it on the handle bar, swung a leg over the saddle. Even as Remi in his truck pulled up I walked straight across the road, stood on the other shoulder. In the moonlight, against the stars, the huge cinder cone bulked black against the sky.

I heard the truck door open, heard Remi climb out, slam the door closed. He crossed the road to stand beside me, but said nothing. He seemed to know instinctively when not to speak.

My vision was clear again, but I knew all I had to know. "It's a domicile."

"What, the cinder cone?"

"I *think* it's another black dog, though I can't be sure."

"I don't feel it," Remi said. "I mean, I felt the angel, but nothing now. No sense of surrogate."

I looked at the top looming over us. "It's up there some-where. It owns this place."

Remi turned, walked back across the road, got into the truck and hauled out his rifle, a shotgun, another box of shells and bullets.

His tone was completely casual. "Well, then let's go kill us another demon."

The full moon helped us make our way. It bloodied the cin-ders, lit up swatches of yellowed grass, illuminated dark veg-etation upon the flanks and sentinel pine trees. I knew that surrounding land was always more fertile after an eruption, but above the treeline the cone was all cinders, nothing more.

We maneuvered across the broken lava field, trying not to sprain or shatter ankles in the process, until we reached the base of the massive cone. On the hike from road to base, Remi had nearly killed himself several times while Googling on his phone. Now that we had reached the cone, he was full of facts.

"It's one thousand feet high," he said, "and one mile in base diameter. It erupted twice in the twelfth century. One lava flow traveled *six* miles."

"Does your phone tell us how to kill a demon in a black dog guise?"

Remi sounded amused. "Well, I'd have to do a search on that."

"Do it," I suggested pointedly, "*after* we've killed this thing."

McCue carried his rifle, not a shotgun. He had tucked a few spare bullets into the pockets of his jeans. I, on the other hand, *did* have a shotgun as well as my Taurus. Blessed cartridges in the shotgun, blessed bullets in the revolver.

"Blessed" sounds a whole lot better than saying they were bathed in breath and spit.

"You're sure it's up there?" McCue asked.

"I'm sure one has been here, or *is* here. I'm the one who handles places, remember? You're the one who's supposed to identify demonic presence. Preferably from a significant distance."

Remi tipped back his head and gazed upward, following the line of the round-shouldered pyramid from base to top.

"We're not splitting up," I declared.

"Hell, no."

"So let's climb this sucker."

Okay, so climbing up a mountain of cinders is not the easiest thing I've ever undertaken, especially at night with only the moon to see by. It's like planting boots in dry, loose, pebbled sludge, and every time you try to push upward the cinders give way and you lose ground. It was one step forward, four sliding steps back. Slamming boot toes into the cone, as if we were climbing Everest with crampons, didn't do much, either, because the cinders simply crumbled away under our boot soles.

Remi said, in a breathy tone, "The elevation here is over eight thousand feet."

I was panting now, trying not to slide and lose ground I'd gained. "Do I need to know that?"

"Well, it explains why we're both breathing like a bellows." He sucked air. "We're not acclimated yet, either of us."

Plant—dig—slip—slide. Over and over again.

McCue was right. The altitude was sucking breath and strength from us both. "Anything?" My voice was hoarse. I wanted water badly.

"Hold . . . Gabe, *hold*—"

I stopped climbing. Felt myself slide a few inches. Remi was a couple of feet down from me. He brought his rifle up to cradle it across his right elbow, the barrel snugged into his left palm.

He shushed me when I tried to ask him a question, his face shadowed beneath the brim of his hat where moonlight couldn't reach.

"Oh yeah," he said at last. "It's here. And it's another of those big bastards."

"Black dog?"

"Yup."

"Two? They're traveling in *packs* now?" I lost another inch or two as a shift of my weight stirred the cinders afresh. "That's not like anything I've ever read. They are solitary beasts."

Remi said tautly, "It's coming."

He and I went down on our bellies. I hooked my right elbow back so I had access to the shotgun trigger. All I had to do was rise up onto my knees and blast the sucker.

That is, *if* it came close, and *if* it offered a large enough target.

Moonlight painted the cinder cone. I saw the beast upon the flanks, literally *slinking* downward. Like water, it flowed.

I saw, too, white eyes shining, broken now and then by a blink. And then it stopped blinking and just *stared*, even as it continued to flow like dog-shaped mercury down from the heights.

"Go left," I said tersely, "I'll go right."

Because if we stayed where we were, so close together, it would be nothing for the black dog to leap into the middle of us and shred both our throats with no effort at all.

As we split, it stopped moving, sat down on haunches and elbows, butt uphill, chest heading downward, and contemplated us. I saw it lift its nose to scent, as nostrils flared. Jaws opened.

And it leaped.

Remi stayed where he was, flat on his belly save for the rifle butt tucked against his shoulder. A Winchester '73 is not a sniper rifle, it couldn't be set up like a true-born sniper rifle, but it did fire bullets.

He got off two shots. Both missed, digging out divots and sending a spray of cinders into the air. As the black dog came down toward him, I rose up onto my knees and let go with one barrel, but as the beast fell sideways, too near Remi for comfort, I knew it wasn't enough.

"Keep your head down!" I shouted, taking huge sliding strides through cinders. And as the beast reared up, blood running black beneath the moon, I fired the other barrel and took out much of its head.

"Okay," I croaked, realizing how out of breath I was. I turned, sat down on my ass with boot heels planted downhill to arrest a slide, and tried to breathe. "By the way, *alphas* rule."

Cinders whispered, crunched, tumbled as Remi, on his knees, made his very awkward way closer to me. He collapsed on his belly, head uphill, rifle in one hand as he lay against the massive, mountainous pile of cinders.

He was breathing hard. "Do you think Greg will come?"

"Why would Greg come?"

"To clear the domicile. I'm assuming this place remains fouled by the demon."

Oh, it was fouled. Definitely unclean. "Well, you know the Latin for it now, right, since she said it? Can't you do it?"

Remi shook his head. "I didn't hear it in Latin."

"She said it in Latin."

"I didn't *hear* it in Latin. It was, I don't know, mumbo-jumbo."

"Aramaic?"

He contemplated that a moment. "Better learn it right quick, hadn't I?"

"*I* heard it in Latin."

"Maybe you can do it, then."

"And risk saying something totally wrong? I don't think so. We could end up clearing our own asses right down a rabbit hole." I inhaled, tasted that awful perfume of demon death and decomposition. It coated my tongue. I spat, spat again, gagged, finally was able to speak. "Okay, we have to figure out how to do this. Because if we don't, another surrogate will show up to re-establish a claim, people will die, and we'll have to come back to kill *it*, too. Can you sound out what she said by ear? Do you remember enough of it?"

Remi clambered to his feet. "I reckon I can try."

I summoned Yoda again. "Do or do not, there is no try."

"You're just a regular fanboy, aren't you?"

"Pot, kettle. You *get* those references."

"Okay," Remi said, ignoring that, "she assumed a specific position, put up arms and hands just so. Then she spouted the mumbo-jumbo."

We both set down our guns and stood facing upward, where we could see the body. I felt a little stupid putting my hands up in the air, and thought McCue looked stupid, too, but we copied what we'd seen her do.

It looked better on a woman.

So there we were, hands raised in the air, palms turned outward. Remi commenced chanting. And I heard it as Latin, even if he was trying out the Aramaic, or whatever language Greg had invoked. I waited for the whole *pestilential beast* part, but nothing happened. The body remained where it was, not exploding and not burning.

In the quiet of the night, we looked at one another. "Go again," I suggested.

Remi rolled out the chanting a second time.

Nothing happened.

"Well," I said, "apparently we need more schooling in the fine art of blowing up demons. I've got the magic phone; I'll call Grandaddy. If he can't come to clear the domicile, maybe he can at least tell me what we're doing wrong." Remi was frowning, not paying attention. "Earth to McCue. I'm calling Grandaddy."

"Wait," he said. He looked at the ring on his middle finger. "High-five me."

"What?"

"High-five me." He lifted his arm up in the air, displayed his palm.

I stared at it a long moment, looked at him, finally started the arc that would fulfill the gesture.

Remi caught my hand, flattened both, one against the other, began the chanting a third time.

Our rings met, clicked together like magnets, and the corpse blew up.

We were close enough that we could not escape the flying body parts. As portions slid down our faces, fell off our shirts, were kicked free of boots, all the bits of the exploded surrogate caught fire. *We* did not, fortunately, though I didn't understand why we hadn't been burned at Wupatki, either. Maybe it was more of our celestial energy.

Remi and I retreated as best we could, sliding in cinders. As the stench of the perfume rose, I pulled the top of my jacket across the lower portion of my face.

"This is downright *gross!*" Remi exclaimed, unsticking his shirt from his torso. "And we can't go around in public blowin' up demons. It might could be a tad bit obvious."

"We didn't blow up the ghosts at the Zoo. We didn't blow up the possessed cop. Maybe it has to do with the Latin. What you just recited was different from the rite of exorcism. This was about clearing the domicile. Rick, Dick, and Candy did it for us at the bar—though it was cockroaches, ash, and grit—and Greg did it with the other black dog. And yes, it *is* gross." I thought about it. "I guess if we kill a surrogate rather than exorcizing, we can just haul the body out of wherever it is, find a safe place, *then* do the Latin and blow it up there."

"We've got to ask more questions," Remi declared. "They've got to tell us more than they have. It's like going in blind. The guys before us who got torn to pieces? Maybe it happened because they didn't know enough. In which case, the angels set them up for failure, and now they're doing the same with us."

"*Why?* It makes no sense."

"How the hell should *I* know! Even Lily said angels were

secretive . . . and Greg tracked you down in the bar to warn us about differing agendas."

My hair was damp and tangled, my leathers slick with— monster goo. Though I guess I should be grateful that my clothes hadn't burst into flames. "Let's go," I said. "We've saved the world from two more demons, and I want to shower, have a celebratory drink, hit the sack. This whole sneaking around in the middle of the night is wearing." I held out my hand, palm down, looked at my ring. "That was pretty cool, though, the ring-thing."

Remi thought about it. "Grandaddy gave us rings that help us. That don't sound like a man who wants to get us killed."

"Maybe it's not Grandaddy. Maybe it's someone else." I turned, began the descent. McCue came along behind me, crunching cinders as he slipped and slid. Hell, maybe it was *everyone* out to get us.

But still. Greg was an angel—and it would probably piss her off that we called her Greg instead of by her true name, but Ambriel sounded too much like Ambien for me—and had indeed warned us. The angels with the porn star names helped us. Grandaddy had been helping us in one way or another since we were kids.

Yeah, time to have a talk with the man—

I stopped short, turned around, slipped a little, then fixed Remi with a glare. "*You* need to work on your aim."

McCue glared back. "You ever try to kill a charging black dog while lying on your belly praying not to slide down a volcano even as you do, *and* working a lever-action rifle?"

Well. No.

"Okay," I said, "maybe we both need the practice."

But not tonight.

CHAPTER TWENTY-NINE

We returned to the Zoo after last call, which meant an empty parking lot. Once again we pulled around back, found the door unlocked—needed to ask Ganji about this—and went in. I wanted to go straight to the stairs, but Ganji—man, the dude was *big*—appeared to be waiting for us.

"You have had an eventful evening," he noted, viewing the state of our clothing. "And also, this came for you."

On the bar lay another manila envelope.

"Well, damn," Remi said wearily. "This shit's startin' to make me feel meaner than a skilletful of rattlesnakes."

"Did you see anyone?" I asked. "I mean, did you keep an eye on the mailbox in case you could see the person delivering the envelope?"

"It was not in the mailbox," he answered. "It was placed just outside the back door."

This time Remi grabbed the envelope and tore it open. He read it, then handed it to me. Same as the first time: letters cut out and stuck to the page by Scotch tape.

But this message was different: *'I know **what** you are.'*

I looked at Ganji. "Can you give me a drink? And then

another one? Maybe even a third. Because I'd like to get some sleep, and now my brain will be making the jump to light-speed."

Remi turned down a drink, said he was going to shower and go bed. I made it through one drink before the activity of the night caught up to me.

Ganji said, "Go to bed. I, meanwhile, will go up the mountain and sing to her."

I rose from the stool. "Uh—don't wake her up yet. At least let me catch a few hours of sleep. Then you can do a Pompeii number on Flagstaff."

As I started to turn, Ganji said, "I was there."

I blinked, turned back to him. "At *Pompeii?*"

"I am at all eruptions. They happen because I sing them awake. I am their lord. But here, now—it is not yet time. You may sleep without fear."

I stared at him a long moment. "Give me another drink."

My brain eventually did slow down from light speed, and I slept. I dreamed about volcanoes erupting, black dogs exploding, and some whackjob sending us mysterious messages. And since I hadn't eaten before going to bed, just showered after Remi then collapsed, I awoke ravenous and starved for coffee.

Eggs, bacon, country potatoes, toast. I was feeling human again on my second cup of coffee when Remi showed up in the doorway. His face was grim. "The deep web's working again."

"Just like that?"

"Just like that. And it's talkin' to us again, so to speak."

I stuck the cutlery and plates in the sink, took the coffee with me as I followed him down the hallway to the common room.

This time a two-word opening message: **Consecrated ground.**

Okay. We looked at one another blankly.

Then Remi seemed to get it. "A church is consecrated. And *un*consecrated if the building is sold."

Before I could say anything, a series of photos appeared. Two churches, a mosque, and a synagogue. All were charred skeletons, but identifiable.

"Phoenix," McCue said. "Catholic, Protestant, Jewish, Muslim. All on the same night. *Last* night. They've ruled out hate crimes, because no one religion was targeted."

"We're supposed to go to Phoenix?"

Remi shook his head. "Grandaddy seemed to think we'd be busy in Flagstaff for a while."

I thought it over. "I'm pretty sure demons can't go inside a holy place. Consecration is its protection."

More text appeared: *Chapel of the Holy Dove.*

Nothing more came up. The screen went blank. "I guess that's our assignment," I said. "Find out if a surrogate is targeting it, stop him/her/it before the chapel burns down. A holy place can't be a domicile, but there's nothing to stop a demon from getting busy from the outside with gasoline and a lighted match or a Molotov cocktail."

First we had to find out what and where was the Chapel of the Holy Dove. That turned out to be easy. The regular internet was working again, so Remi typed the name into the search field. Photos along with info came right up.

There wasn't much to it. It was twenty miles from Flagstaff, neither large nor imposing. Just a small, simple A-frame build-ing, with a shingled roof and a red-painted door hosting a cross made of mirrors.

"It burned once before," Remi said, "Got rebuilt in ninety-nine, all volunteer labor."

"Demons?"

"In ninety-nine? The hell vents didn't open until recently. Probably just a careless human."

"Soooo, we go out there to see if you can get a feel for any demonic activity?"

Abruptly the screen went dead. Remi depressed the power button a couple of times. Nothing happened.

Well, until one word appeared: *Now.*

I ran a hand through my hair. "Well, at least it's daytime."

"Maybe not so good. Other people will be there."

I rolled my head back until I could see the ceiling, released a noisy breath. "Collateral damage."

Once again I said I'd take the bike. Remi mentioned that it was a waste of gas to use two vehicles. I just looked at him, threw a leg over the saddle, pulled on gloves and helmet. I fig-ured that was message enough.

The ride out U.S. 180 to the chapel reminded me of back home, which I was not expecting. Back home in Oregon with its great tracts of forests, yeah, but here? Ponderosa pines, fir, aspen, juniper. Brilliant blue skies. A winding asphalt road. I felt sorry for McCue, walled inside his big pickup. Bike and an open road. What more can you ask?

Twenty miles out, I saw the sign on the right for the chapel.

I pulled off, rolled slowly into a cinder parking area that was actually just a wide spot in the road. Tire tracks proved that people did park here, but with no delineated spaces. It was just dirt and cinders.

I was beginning to hate cinders. Maybe I should have a talk with Ganji about it.

Up close, you could see just how small the chapel was. And its simplicity. At the west end, the end with the red door, the entrance was quite low. Beyond, soaring upward on an angled line, the roof gave way to windows. The entire east wall was made up of glass. I climbed off the bike, waited for Remi to park his truck, and then we walked inside. The view was astounding. The windows and A-framed roof embraced the San Francisco Peaks, the volcano cluster Ganji wanted to wake. Meadow, wild flowers, scatterings of pines. And the A-frame shape was carried through with interior, sharp-angled upside down V-shaped beams marching from door to windows. No formal pews, just wooden benches with backs, the kind you'd find in parks.

Graffiti covered the interior. Every inch of wood contained commentary in markers, pens, even rough knife-blade carving, and notes pinned to the walls. People from all over the world had left their marks. At first I was shocked that people would deface a chapel so badly. But as I walked the gravel floor and read a few of the notes, the messages written on wood, I realized most were of hope, prayers for others, or requests asking for intercession. There was great respect for the little chapel built atop mortared natural rocks.

No one else was present. We stood alone within the walls of stone, wood, and glass, upon gravel in place of manufactured flooring. The chapel featured a modest wooden pulpit, also covered with graffiti, a low stone altar, and a rough-hewn wooden cross mounted high in front of the windows, as if it were floating.

Remi found handouts explaining how the chapel had come to be built, then rebuilt after the fire, information he naturally shared with me. He ended with, "Weddings are held here all the time."

I walked to the windows and stood there gazing upon the Peaks. As I had on the mountain, when Grandaddy had hiked my hungover ass up and down Fatman's Loop, I sensed the peace of the place, the sanctity. Here, there was no *koyaanisqatsi*—no life out of balance. Life in this chapel was very much *in* balance.

Which explained why surrogates wanted to burn it down. Out of chaos comes Lucifer. Burned churches, synagogues, mosques, even this little roadside chapel, would make people think less of worshipping God and more of Lucifer. And to think of him was to open the door.

I stared at the cross. Thought again about what McCue and I knew now of Grandaddy, of ourselves: That he was a seraph, and we were born of heavenly essence, of celestial energy.

I asked what the girl in that kid's book had: "Are you there, God?"

God did not, as far as I could tell, offer any answer.

Remi was wandering around the chapel, reading notes and carvings. "I don't feel anything," he said. "I don't sense any demons."

"But you're not running at full capacity yet."

"We're in a *chapel*," he clarified. "Consecrated ground. Any sense of surrogate activity around here ought to be obvious, regardless. It would be like a black stain on white linen."

I shrugged. "Maybe the demon hasn't arrived yet."

"Well, if it wants to burn down the place, let's make sure it can't."

As Remi turned and headed for the red door, I called, "How the hell are we supposed to do that? And wouldn't someone *else* have already thought of it?" But McCue was gone, so I followed and found him up in his truck cab, pulling out Lily's duffle. He dug through it, came up with two flasks I recognized: holy oil and holy water.

"It's possible." He shut the passenger door, "Maybe after the fire the new chapel wasn't reconsecrated. And even then, if they did, it may only have been the building *itself*, not the land surrounding it." He tossed me a flask. "You man the oil. I've got the water. Let's walk a large circle all around the chapel, say twenty feet out from the building, and dribble oil and water every three feet."

All things Biblical I left to Remi, so I didn't object, didn't ask questions. Just eyeballed the twenty-foot distance from the chapel, and began to walk in a large circle. Remi started on the other side. We met, passed, wound up back where we'd begun. Both of us stared at the chapel.

I asked, "What now? Anything more?"

Remi nodded, then spoke quietly. But not to me.

"We present this building to be reconsecrated for the worship of God and the service of all people."

I waited.

"This house shall be known as the Chapel of the Holy Dove."

It was markedly quiet all around us.

And finally, after a fair bit in Latin, he added, in English:

"By the power of your Holy Spirit consecrate this house of your worship.

Bless us and sanctify what we do here,

that this place may be holy for us and a house of prayer for all people."

And that was that. Remi said the land around the chapel was consecrated, and the chapel itself *re*consecrated.

"So nothing inside the circle will burn?"

"Nothing inside the circle will burn."

A minivan pulled up. I glanced at it, saw Remi concentrating, eyes distant as he went inside himself. "Anything?"

He shook his head. "There might could be a demon—but there also might not."

The minivan doors slid open and a family got out. Man, woman, older woman who was probably a grandmother, three kids. I thought of the family the black dog had killed, and I wanted none of *this* family to be at risk—nor did I want any of them to be a demon in disguise.

They all went into the chapel, which answered *that* question.

A moment later the mother came back out. Petite, brown-haired, wearing a University of Arizona football jersey. She looked at the truck, the bike, and us. Clearly noticed the motorcycle leathers, the cowboy attire. In her eyes was reticence, confusion, a hint of shyness, but also a need to know something.

"This is going to sound really weird," she said, "but are you by any chance Gabriel and Remiel?"

I felt a cold finger at the base of my spine. "Why?"

"Are you?"

"Yes," Remi said.

"Wait." She put up a delaying forefinger. "He gave me something for you."

Remi and I exchanged concerned glances as she went to the minivan, unlocked it, reached in and pulled out a manila envelope. She relocked the vehicle, then walked back to us.

"We stopped for gas," she explained. "Just on the outskirts of Flagstaff. A convenience store. The cashier told us about this chapel, said it was very pretty, and added that if Gabriel and Remiel were here—cowboy and biker; he was explicit—I was to give this envelope to them." She held it out, eyes doubtful.

I tamped down foreboding, managed a smile. "It's a scavenger hunt," I told her, manufacturing a false amusement. "The clues come in the envelopes." I took it from her. "Thank you so much. The cashier's in on the game, too."

That eased her concern. "The kids love scavenger hunts!"

And then one of those kids started yelling inside the chapel, and she excused herself to deal with it.

As before, our names were written on the outside. Nothing more. I glanced at Remi, who nodded solemn encouragement. I was wearing gloves, so I used my KA-BAR to slit the envelope open.

A note, prepared as all the others were. The message was simple: 'More to come.'

I looked inside the envelope again, discovered something else. Pulled it out, held it so both of us could see it.

Oh, holy shit.

Remi was swearing also.

The 8 x 10 color photo was of a young woman, very dead.

Blood obscured her face, soaked half her clothing. Her limbs were sprawled.

I turned the photo over. In red ink, two scrawled words: *Mary Ann.*

Remi wasted no time. "We've got to go to the cops."

"Wait." I thought back, recalling the other two notes. "The first said, '*I know who you are,*' the second, with bolded emphasis, '*I know **what** you are.*' Whoever this is—I'm assuming a demon, as Ganji noted—it's playing a game *with us.* If we go to the cops, there will be all kinds of awkward questions we can't answer—and I'm pretty sure we'd become suspects. After all, I've got a record."

"Then we mail it," Remi's words were clipped, his drawl reduced. "Clean it of prints, send it to the police. Let them take it from there."

I held up one hand, wiggled my fingers. "Wearing gloves."

"So let's go back into town, get it done."

I nodded, slipped note and photo back into the envelope, placed it carefully in one of my saddlebags. I had no affinity for cops, after eighteen months inside, but McCue was right. This was police business.

CHAPTER THIRTY

As we headed down the road with its elegant asphalt curves winding through the forest, I found my mind making the jump to lightspeed again.

It had to be a demon playing us—unless it was an angel. I hated the latter idea, but Greg had sounded absolutely certain Remi and I were in pretty deep, that we'd be used by anyone who wished to manipulate us. Then again, what if *she* were the one playing us? Some Grigori had fallen, she claimed, and made Nephilim by sleeping with human women. For all I knew, *she* was a fallen Grigori with an agenda all her own.

I thought again of Grandaddy. There was nothing in the man now, nor had there ever been, that made me distrust him. But he himself had alluded to Lucifer's greatest trick—convincing people he didn't exist. Because then he could work in private, observed by no one until it was too late.

What if *Grandaddy's* greatest trick was convincing us he was working to save the world, when he wasn't?

And why on earth wouldn't he?

I thought of the magic phone tucked into my jacket. Perhaps

it was time we summoned Grandaddy, instead of him summoning us.

And then a woman on the right-side shoulder darted out into my lane.

Oh, *shit*.

Laying down a bike is not something anyone ever wants to do. You veer, you swerve, you do everything you can to keep it upright, especially a big twin Harley weighing over seven hundred pounds. Laying down a bike also is *nothing* like in the movies. For one thing, it hurts like hell. And a human body can break. The late Evel Knievel could attest to this after his attempt to clear the fountains at Caesar's Palace in Vegas. He broke more than forty bones.

So I veered sharply, then again even more sharply as the woman, who apparently had a death wish, or was drunk, or high, or just downright *stupid*, took three more steps into the road, turned toward me with her hands up. I hit the brakes, tried to keep the bike upright with sheer strength and balance, but I lost it.

I lost it.

You can't perform miracles with a big twin Harley, can't stop as short as with dirt bikes and the like. I really, really wanted not to hit her, so this meant I needed to control the machine the only way I could: laying it down in order to avoid her, and also not destroy myself in the doing of it. I hit the rear brake because now I *needed* the bike to go down, in hopes of sliding by without clipping her, rather than plowing right into her.

In seemingly slow motion the rear tire locked up, the bike slid sideways, tipped, leaned over—gravity was winning—and the rear assembly rotated forward. Both wheels now faced the way I'd been going because the bike was turned sideways across the lane.

I saw her face, very pale, surrounded by clouds of black hair. She appeared to be in shock. Well, yeah; I would be, too, with a huge motorcycle bearing down on me.

All I could think about were two things: Getting my left leg free before it got turned into ground-up hamburger sandwiched between road and bike; and keeping my head up. Helmets do a lot of good, but they're not impervious.

So as the bike went down I yanked my left leg out of the way. Metal hit the ground, sparks flew as the foot peg dragged. I slid with the bike a few feet, then got loose from it and commenced an awkward, involuntary series of tumbles.

I flipped, flipped again, rolled, strained my neck as I tried to keep my head off the ground. Asphalt grabbed at leather, which slowed me, but also changed the arc of my body, this time me *without* the bike, and thus considerably lighter than I was with the Harley. I flipped off the road entirely. I ended up on the shoulder of the lane across from mine.

Oh crap. Oh Jesus. Oh shit.

A woman. A *woman* in the road.

I tried to lever myself up. Saw my bike, uncontrolled, miss a curve and slide straight ahead at 50 mph, where it disappeared into trees and underbrush.

By this time Remi had stopped and was out of his truck, running across the road toward me. I pushed myself upright with my left elbow until I realized that was not wise, since I'd gone down on my left side. I tried to suck back the pain on a series of stuttered breaths.

As Remi arrived, I blurted, *"Woman.* She okay?"

McCue knelt at my side, eyes frantic. "Hey—hey . . . don't move. Okay? Just don't move. I'm calling 911."

"Wait," I said urgently. "Go find the woman. See if she's okay."

"What woman?"

"The one in the middle of the road. I didn't—didn't just fall over, you know. Go look. I'll call."

McCue was unconvinced and focused strictly on me. "I didn't see any woman."

I moved a little, wished I hadn't. "Well, *I* did. Go look. Go back and look. I'll call, I'll call. If she's hurt, the ambulance can pick up both of us."

I didn't want to think about her actually being *dead.* But I didn't recall contact. Maybe she'd jumped out of the way even as I swerved and laid the bike down.

Remi stared hard at me, assessing, reluctant. He still didn't move to follow my instructions, and now I was frustrated.

"I'm okay! I don't think I broke anything. Bruises, scrapes— I'll live. Got my left leg out, kept my head off the ground. *Go look for the damn woman!"*

He didn't like it, but he rose and started jogging back the way we had come. I fumbled at a jacket pocket, pulled a phone free, hit the Contacts screen.

I didn't call 911. I called Lily.

After five minutes or so, Remi jogged back. Once he reached me he knelt and said, "There was no woman. Nothing, Gabe. No scrap of clothing, no tracks—nothing. It was the right place—I saw your skid marks."

"I saw her, dammit!"

"Well, I didn't."

I let it go. We could come back another time. If she wasn't lying in the middle of the road, or unconscious on the shoulder, I probably hadn't hit her. Or else, if I *had* struck her, she'd been rescued by a Good Samaritan, though I didn't recall any vehicles going by.

"Okay." Damn, I hurt. "Get my helmet off. Everything moves okay; there's no back or neck injury. It's okay to take it off."

Remi freed me, set the helmet aside. "Don't get up!"

Because I was trying. I got as far as sitting, stared down the road. "My bike."

"Forget about the bike! You need a hospital."

I made an awkward attempt to climb to my feet. Remi called me all kinds of names, but in the end he helped me up.

"I'm okay," I told him again, holding myself stiffly and trying not to overbalance one direction or the other. "I'm—I'm gonna hurt like hell tomorrow, a few days after, but this is why I wear all the leather and a helmet. This isn't the first time I've wrecked."

Though none of them had been this . . . this extravagantly dramatic.

McCue said nothing, just stared at me.

I ran a gloved hand through my hair, scrubbed, unstuck it from my head. "Let's go look for my bike."

"We're *not* looking for your bike, dammit! We're waiting for the ambulance."

I improvised. "They said an ambulance is thirty minutes out. And it'll take twenty or so back."

"Christ," Remi muttered. "Okay, let's not wait. I'll take you to the hospital myself. Can you make it across the road?"

I made it across the road. Remi hovered, but saw I was walking okay, if stiffly. I managed to haul myself up into the passenger seat, and McCue closed the door for me.

As he turned the engine over, I inspected my left-side leathers. Sleeve was badly scuffed, but the pants showed significant damage with leather scraped thin from hip to knee. My left boot was deeply scuffed. I rubbed a hand up and down my left arm, checking for pain, then pulled off my gloves.

Yup, I hurt like hell already. Bruised underneath the leathers, probably some scrapes as well, but I wasn't broken.

We were about ten yards down the road when I asked McCue to stop, and it pissed him off. I'd never seen him angry before, just irritated.

He shot me a disbelieving glance, then turned his attention back to the road. "I'll come look for your bike tomorrow, okay? I'm just thinking about *you* right now."

I explained the facts of life in Motorcycle Land. "If we leave it, even if they can't lift it—and they can't; it's a heavy son of a bitch—people will steal parts. Strip it. I need to see where it is, see if it's hidden well enough until we can get someone out to collect it." I paused. "It left the road right about here. See the broken branches?"

"Will you shut up if I stop?"

"Yes."

McCue pulled over on the shoulder and parked. "Stay here. Wait here. *I'll* look. I don't need you staggering around in a forest and keeling over when it all catches up to you. Don't want to haul your tough-guy black-leather ass back to the truck."

I shut up. Remi scowled at me, then went off to track the path of my bike.

I leaned my head against the window. Okay, yeah, the truck seat was better than hiking around a forest. The aches were ramping up.

Remi remained gone for some time, and I began to fret. And when he showed up, his expression verged on blank.

"Nobody can strip it," he told me. "No one can *reach* it."

"What?"

"There's a ravine."

I was horrified. "My bike's in a *ravine?*"

"And there's a creek at the bottom. Lots of boulders."

I felt numb. "No. No no no. You're shitting me."

He shook his head. "I'm not. I'm sorry."

I planted my elbow on the arm rest, stuck my head in my right hand, and closed my eyes. I wanted to mourn my bike. But I hurt too much, and I was concerned about the woman.

The woman who *had* been there.

And then it occurred to me that maybe she hadn't been there at all.

Or, at least, not a human.

CHAPTER THIRTY-ONE

It was quiet in Remi's truck. I heard only the engine, the rumble of the road. I'd carefully shifted positions any number of times, uncomfortable. I'd become more certain that I hadn't broken anything, but skin and muscles were definitely insulted, and it was difficult to remain in one position for much longer than a few minutes.

I was biding my time before I told Remi we weren't going to a hospital. I had my ammo ready to go.

I shifted again. Needed distraction. "How about some tunes?"

Remi shot me a glance, smiling, then reached forward to turn on the radio.

Sure enough, shrill, twanging country. Should have known it. I thought about asking him to find another station, but it was his truck, after all, and I'd learned long before that, in the succinct words of a TV character: Driver picks the music, shotgun shuts his cakehole.

Then that song came on. "Okay," I said, on a stuttered breath, "tell me the truth."

He glanced at me, frowning. "Yeah?"

"Mamas and cowboys and babies. You know—*this* song. You know it?"

"Willie Nelson, Waylon Jennings. It's a classic."

I thought about it a minute. "Doesn't it bother you? A song suggesting babies should never grow up to be cowboys? I mean, isn't that against the code, or something?"

Remi smiled for the first time since I'd wrecked my bike. "Well, that's not actually what the song is about. And a lot of us flipped it."

I started to turn my head toward him, stopped because my neck hurt. "Flipped it?"

He was looking through the windshield, but his smile grew wider, broke into a grin. "Mamas, don't let your cowboys grow up to be babies."

Hah. Very clever. And it provided the perfect opening. "So, you've been hurt a lot riding all those animals?"

"Bulls and broncs? Well, for me most injuries have been bruises, maybe a couple of broken ribs now and then, stretched ligaments in an arm. Other cowboys sometimes run into something a little more serious, but for the most part it's nothing we can't take care of ourselves after a quick look-see with paramedics at the arena."

"You all opt for the hospital when it's bumps and bruises?"

He rolled his eyes. "Okay, okay. I get it."

"Suck it up tough, huh? Cowboy tough?"

"We *are* tough."

"Okay," I said amicably, "the same can be said about bikers. And that's why I called Lily, not 911."

He shook his head. "You're an asshole."

I grinned. "Yes. I am."

———

By the time we reached Lily's rig at the RV campground, I could barely move. Remi opened my door, took a good look, said he'd get me down.

I told him to go to hell.

He ignored me.

And so it took Remi's aid to get me out of the truck no matter what I preferred. Lily descended the motorhome steps part way through the attempt. She eyed me up and down, assessing my condition, then told Remi to take me into the garage and have me sit on the cot.

The first order of business was to learn medication allergies. I said I had none. Then it was family medical history— and I told her, rather sharply, that the history probably didn't matter because, hey, I wasn't *human*, was I?

Then she told me to take off my jacket, which I did with great care. Followed by holster. Then, I was told, it was t-shirt and leather pants.

I stared at her. "What?"

"Take off your t-shirt and your pants. I need to check out bruises, scrapes, etc."

"I'm bruised, and I have scrapes. Okay? Nothing new."

She was adamant. "T-shirt."

Remi stood all of two feet away, watching over Lily's shoulder. He'd put his hat elsewhere, and his head looked naked, hair standing up from his efforts to undo hat hair.

I sat on the edge of the cot, let down from its position against the wall. "I just want a hot shower, then ice."

"And you shall have them," she said. "But first let me treat the contusions and scrapes. There is no weakness in it; d'ye think many brave men have scorned a women's touch after battle?"

Well, me laying a bike down wasn't exactly battle. "I really only need a hot shower and a bed. I'll just head back to—" And I stopped. Because now I lacked the freedom of my own transport.

Remi wasn't laughing or smiling. "Let her take a look," he said, "and I'll chauffeur us both back to the bar."

I'd lost eighteen months with the bike, a year after I'd bought it. And it wasn't just the *bike* in and of itself, but what it represented: the me who had been, the me I yet might be. The me I'd never be again.

I made a valiant attempt to shed t-shirt, which was seriously uncomfortable since it required lifting my arms. The true difficulty arose as I realized that I simply couldn't *do* for myself. I needed Lily. I needed Remi. They worked me out of the tee, and I was bare-chested.

Okay, so a few bruises and scrapes. Minor road rash, seeping lymph-diluted blood a little. My left elbow, a strip down the side of my forearm, tenderness low on the left-side ribs. Red bruises were blooming as broken blood vessels made themselves known.

Lily used alcohol wipes on the scrapes, which only added insult to injury. I sucked in a hissing breath, then glared.

She smoothed antibiotic ointment over the scrapes. "All right. Off with the pants."

"I'm not taking off my pants!"

She shook her head, scoffed. "I've slept with a thousand men. D'ye think you've got anything they hadn't?"

I looked at Remi in appeal, but he was no help at all. In fact, he was studiously looking elsewhere.

I caught Lily's eyes and glared. "You may have slept with a thousand men, but none of them was *me*."

After a startled moment, she laughed in joyous abandon. Then she told me I could take off my pants willingly, or she'd cut them off.

Okay, taking them off was going to be a challenge. I was stiffening more and more by the minute. But I got them unzipped and shoved down past my hips, refusing help. Fortunately my boxer briefs were intact.

More contusions. Point of hip, knee, also seeping a little. I had a few dings on my right side from tumbling, but most of the damage was confined to my left.

"Aren't you the fortunate man," Lily observed, wielding wipes again, followed up by the ointment.

"Considering what could have happened, yeah." I worked the pants back over my hips, asked for my t-shirt. It wasn't easy to put on, but I managed it.

Lily looked me up and down. "You know the RICE protocol?"

"I've been banged up before, you know. Rest, Ice, Compress, Elevate. I can't very well elevate my whole body, but I'll go for the others, okay?"

"You can stay the night here," she offered.

Just what I wanted; sharing grunts of effort, the hissing expulsion of breath if I moved too quickly, with a woman who reveled in war. And I was pretty damn sure her offer wasn't an *offer*. "Thanks, but no. I'll head over to the roadhouse." I looked at Remi, hating my lack of freedom. I'd only just gotten it back.

He looked back. "If it were me, you wouldn't fret over giving me a ride. Well, I'm not frettin' over giving *you* a ride."

He didn't understand. Unless he'd been in prison, he couldn't. Everything there was regimented. *Everything.* Now I was free of it. Riding the bike almost 1,300 miles had given me myself back.

Lily dug something out of one of the cabinets, handed me two pill bottles. "Tramadol," she said. "Painkiller. Be sure to take it with food, otherwise you'll vomit all night. The other is Flexeril, a muscle relaxant. You'll be stiff tomorrow."

In the movies, the hero would turn down medication, intending to tough it out. But I was no hero, and I knew how I felt now, how I'd feel the next day. I took the bottles.

"RICE," Lily reminded.

"I got it." Now I was getting testy and tried to soften my tone. "Thanks, Lily."

Remi pulled the truck remote from his pocket and walked back into the RV living quarters with me on his heels. I didn't wear either holster or jacket; less to take off when we got to the Zoo.

McCue had the RV door open when he stopped short on the first step. I started to ask him what the hell he was doing, since I almost walked into him, but then he descended the rest of the steps, and I saw at the bottom a manila envelope.

Shit. *Shit.*

I turned, walked back into the living room and eased myself into the recliner. Remi came up behind me, pulled the door closed.

Lily looked perplexed. I warned her this wasn't going to be pretty.

McCue tore open the envelope, removed a note, read it then handed it to me. Once again letters cut from various sources. Two words only: *And another.*

Remi slid the photo from the envelope, looked briefly, closed his eyes. I took it from him.

Another woman, messily dead. I didn't linger on the image, just turned over the photo. Again in red ink, a name: *Annie.*

Lily took the photo from me and studied it. I remembered then that as Goddess of Battles such images were familiar and probably would not bother her.

She said, "This is not new to you."

"The envelopes began arriving a few days ago," Remi explained. "At first just notes. Said 'I know who you are,' then *what* we are. Now two photographs. We were going to mail the first to the police, but it was in Gabe's saddlebags and the bike's in a creek at the bottom of a ravine. Though now we have this one. You see anything in the local papers?"

"No," Lily said firmly. "Nothing at all about murdered women, and you know the news would be full of it with reporters descending on us. The time is spent on the killings at Wupatki." She handed the photo back to Remi, who slid it and the note back into the envelope. "I don't think this happened locally."

Remi nodded. "I'll get on the computer, try a few searches under various keywords. I might turn up reports."

I shook my head, anxious. "How is this guy finding us? It's almost like he's tracking us with a GPS unit, or stalking us. Two envelopes delivered to the Zoo, one to us at the chapel outside of town—" And then I remembered. "Our beacons. Grandaddy said hell could find us."

Lily's expression was solemn. "And so you are found. And followed. You are safe here, safe in the Zoo. And at Wupatki, because you cleared it."

Well, no—Greg had. But I opted not to say anything.

"Sunset Crater," Remi said, sounding tense. "It was a second black dog. We killed it, then cleared the area."

"The chapel," I added. "We installed a protective circle. Remi reconsecrated the building, then consecrated the earth surrounding it. It can't be burned."

"And so the photos." Lily nodded. "I believe this is called *gaslighting*. Psychological manipulation."

"But why us?" I asked. "I mean, we're barely born. Newbies, as you said."

"Oh, not just you," Lily replied. "I'm sure this is happening elsewhere, if not in the same fashion. But *especially* you, yes. Newbies or not."

"Especially us?" Remi asked. "Why especially us?"

Lily looked at each of us. "You were born on the same day, at nearly the same hour, minute, second. That is of significance."

"Again, why?" I asked.

"Because it's never happened before. No one, including the angels, quite knows what you are, or who you'll be. I imagine you are at the top of the demon hit list for no reason other than that."

I felt a chill pimple my flesh. "And the angels? Are we on their hit list, too? If no one knows what or who we are, including the angels, wouldn't it be safer just to kill us?"

Lily shrugged, utterly matter-of-fact. "Oh, I'm sure some will try." She flicked a bright glance at Remi. "Might could even succeed."

CHAPTER THIRTY-TWO

The ride back to the bar, a mile away, was short. The only thing said at all was a comment Remi made. "Guess we don't have to mail the new photo to the cops."

Remi's computer search might turn up something. I thought at first it would indicate the surrogate's whereabouts, then remembered we received the notes and photos locally. I supposed it might be two demons, with one doing the killing while the other delivered the envelopes. Hell, if we were at the top of a hit list, maybe dozens of demons were after us. It all began the night Remi and I put on the rings; the next night the hot blonde with the whackjob eyes had nearly killed me.

Or maybe it was angels.

I didn't want to think about that. I just didn't. Angels were supposed to be the good guys. But Greg had planted the idea, and it hadn't gone away. On one hand, if Grandaddy were right, it made no sense that angels would want to kill us—unless what Lily said was true, and Greg, that none of them knew what McCue and I were capable of.

Then again, *we* didn't know what we were capable of.

The parking lot was crowded as we turned into it. At

twilight, bar-goers headed out, even on weekdays. It was a social activity, and offered escape for many into beer or the hard stuff.

It was now habit for us to park in the back, though this time it was only the truck. And that made me anxious all over again. Landing in a creek might have softened the bike's impact. It would most likely need a lot of work, depending on the damage, but some motorcycle mechanics are wizards.

I opened the passenger door, looked at the step down. Oh, this was *so* not going to be fun. Remi offered to help, but I just shook my head, reached carefully for the overhead handle, began to slowly lever myself out.

As expected, and despite the brevity of the ride, I'd stiffened. I felt a hundred years old as I worked my way down from the seat to plant feet on the ground.

With great care I stretched, rolled my neck. Muscles and bruises protested, but I needed to move. While bedrest was recommended, I knew from experience I'd feel better if I didn't just lie around.

Since I had no desire to spend the night puking, I did indeed intend to grab some dinner so I could take the tramadol. But as we walked into the bar, with billiard balls clacking, loud country music playing on the jukebox, people laughing and dancing, I resolved that dining in one of the booths downstairs was not a good idea.

Remi realized it, too. "I'll have them fix something, and I'll bring it up to you."

I nodded my thanks. "Something juicy."

"Steak, or burger?"

"Definitely steak. Medium. Baked potato, loaded. Corn on the cob if they've got it."

"It's a cowboy steakhouse/dancehall. They'll have it."

"Okay. Just don't flirt with the waitress and let my dinner go cold."

He grinned. "Only if she flirts first."

Not fun climbing the stairs because it put pressure on my body in different areas. But I made it, dropped off the holster and jacket in my room, walked down the hall to the common area. I figured while I waited for dinner I could start Remi's search for murdered women.

It booted into a black screen. I thought maybe the video card had gone bad, but then a name appeared: *'La Llorona.'*

When Remi brought dinner he had two of everything, set the plates down on the table. He saw me staring at the screen and looked himself. "La Llorona? Well, it's Spanish for *weeping woman*, but after that I've got no clue."

I remembered he spoke Spanish, so he knew to turn the double 'L' into a 'Y' sound. "It's a legend," I said.

"I figured."

"Hispanic in origin, but has since been adopted by others. There are variations, but the basic story says a woman killed her two sons by drowning them in a river, then felt terrible remorse and now wanders around looking for them. Mourning them. Weeping."

Remi collected a beer out of the fridge for himself though nothing for me. Painkillers and booze don't mix. "So she's a ghost," he said.

"So she's a demon."

He stopped dead, saw the expression on my face. "What? What is it?"

I'd been thinking about it, knew I was right. "The woman

who ran out into the road. White shirt, white pants, black hair. La Llorona is always seen in white." I looked at him. "She came out of nowhere, ran right into my lane. It's why I wrecked the bike, why she wasn't hurt, why you couldn't find her."

Remi took off his hat and set it on the table upside down, away from the plates. He deliberately avoided meeting my eyes.

"I saw her." I was absolutely certain. "It was her, Remi."

"I'll take your word for it, but I didn't see anything."

I shrugged, wished I hadn't. It hurt. "I don't know the reason for that, but she was there. White clothes, black hair."

Remi pulled out his chair, sat down to start in on his steak. When I didn't move, he glanced up, stilled. "You want to go back there tomorrow."

"Apparently we're supposed to," I pointed out. "The name was sent to us. If we weren't intended to look for her, why would the name appear? She's a ghost, a demon, and we're supposed to take her out. But not exorcism; if the story is true, the host is much too old to survive. So it's guns or knives."

He paid deep attention to cutting his steak. "Not tomorrow. You need the rest."

"I'll be fine. Painkiller tonight, ice, the muscle relaxant tomorrow. And anyway, we need to kill this demon before it can cause more havoc."

"I'll go. On my own."

Something rose up in me, something imperative. Not just a wave, but a tsunami. "No." I didn't know what it was, just that I *couldn't* let him go alone. Even the idea of it was highly unsettling. *Primogenitura*, maybe, that need to protect. "Besides, she's not visible to you. I'll be your seeing-eye dog."

In consternation, he stabbed his fork so hard into a piece of steak that tines scraped on the plate. He told me to type in a simple question, said what I should ask.

I stared at him, then did as he suggested. *Gabe too?*

The screen replied: *Always both.*

I thought that over, typed in something else. Kept it clean. *And if we are entertaining? Ladies, that is?* Because I sure wasn't going to have an audience.

After a delay, the screen blanked, flickered, then disappeared and left me with a normal website.

Remi's tone was philosophical. "Well, I reckon that can be taken as either a 'yes' *or* a 'no.' I prefer the latter."

I dragged the chair back to the table, sat down with care. "And while we're out there, after we kill the demon?" Remi asked a question with raised eyebrows. "I want to find my bike."

He opened his mouth to protest, saw my face and took the better route. He didn't try to talk me out of it.

Smart man.

The tramadol took the edge off and, thankfully, did not make me sick. I didn't want to contemplate how that would feel after my contact with asphalt earlier. I left Remi doing a search on missing and dead women who fit his parameters and went to bed.

The only one sharing it was ice.

Remi had promised to wake me. He didn't. I woke up on my own, discovered it was ten o'clock and levered myself out of bed. Yup, very stiff, very sore. I wobbled my way into the hall, swearing I'd kill McCue if he'd gone by himself after the message on the computer: *Always both.*

Then I found him in the kitchen making coffee, and revised my intention. "I thought you were waking me up."

"I let you sleep in. We've got time."

"Did you find anything about murdered women online?"

"I found *too* much about murdered women online. But nothing identifying a Mary Ann or Annie. Well, that I saw. I didn't have much to go on."

I cracked multiple eggs into the skillet, pushed two pieces of a sliced bagel into the toaster, poured myself coffee.

"How you feelin'?"

I couldn't resist. "It's not the years, it's the mileage."

"You got pills for that."

"So I do. And I will not shirk them."

Remi opened his mouth to ask something more, then we heard the familiar five tones from *Close Encounters*.

"Yours," I said. "My cell's in the bedroom."

Remi answered, went very still as he listened, then said, "Thanks, Ganji."

His expression was odd. I got a funny feeling. "What is it?"

"Another envelope. This time tucked under one of my windshield wipers. Ganji saw it when he took the trash out."

I pulled the skillet off the burner and slid it onto a cold one, popped the bagels up, said, "Let's go find out what this one says."

"You eat. I can bring it up to you."

"I've lost my appetite." And I had.

I took the muscle relaxant first, which had the effect of oiling my rusty joints, then got myself downstairs without falling. Remi was behind me.

Ganji was sitting on a stool in front of the bar. We joined him, and without speaking he slid the envelope down to me.

I dreaded it. I just knew what was coming.

I opened it, pulled the note free. Just like all the earlier ones. This time, it said: *And another.*

I couldn't look at the photo. I just couldn't look. I handed off the envelope to Remi. After a moment he removed a photo, glanced at it quickly, then turned the picture over. Red ink, a woman's name: *Elizabeth.*

I dropped an F-bomb, and Ganji's brows rose. Remi set the photo face down atop the envelope. "Mary Ann, Annie, Elizabeth. Not exactly unusual names," he said. "Without last names, I doubt we'll find them."

"If he isn't killing locally, how is he putting the envelopes all over the place?" I asked. "Can demons translocate, or is there an accomplice?"

"Not only that," Remi said, "but the duration between deliveries is getting shorter and shorter. He's escalating."

I paced because I had to, and because it knocked more rust off my bones. I was loosening up but not quickly. "What's the end-game? What do these photographs *mean?* Why involve us?"

"Maybe he figures that's what he'll do to us," Remi said. "He's previewing his work."

"We're not women, so probably not targets."

"Seeing photos of women dead is worse than seeing photos of dead men."

He was right. I didn't want to look at grisly pictures of dead men, but it definitely bothered me more that the victims were women. "Maybe he thinks it'll flush us out," I ventured. "We're safe here, at Lily's, those other places. But that doesn't make sense. If we keep taking assignments, doesn't that make us vulnerable? And easy to get to us, I'd think."

Remi shrugged. "Maybe he doesn't want to get to us yet. Maybe he's just screwing with us. I mean, who knows what kind of games surrogates play, or how their minds work?"

I thought about it. "Maybe he figures it'll unnerve us, be easier to take us when the time comes, as the anxiety builds and builds. He's playing with his food."

Remi look vaguely ill at that.

"We've got to find him," I said. "Or her. Kill the mofo before we get nailed, before the death-toll hits double digits."

"How do you reckon we can do that?"

"Clues," I answered. "We can talk to people. Details on the envelopes, the paper used for the notes, the cut-out letters, even the ink and handwriting. Even the photo paper the image is printed on."

"We're not the police," he said skeptically, "and this sure as hell is not *CSI*."

"No, but there are specialists. And maybe, with a nudge from Grandaddy, they'll cooperate with two guys who aren't angels yet." I paused, stared at Remi. "Hell, why didn't we think of this? We should have asked Grandaddy first."

Remi pulled his the magic phone from a pocket, hit "Contacts." His cadences suggested no one was on the other end. "Grandaddy. Hey. Remi. Listen, Gabe and I got some questions. We need a little help. Can you come over to the Zoo tonight?" He disconnected, slid the phone back into his pocket. "Eat something, Gabe. Take a shower. We don't know how long it's going to take to kill off La Llorona *or* get down to your bike. Which proves you've got a big hole in your screen door."

"*What?*"

"Texan for crazy," he said. "Cuz that's what I reckon you are."

CHAPTER THIRTY-THREE

ily's starter kit provided another box of cartridges and bullets. To be on the safe side we bathed them in holy water, then oiled them. No spit was necessary this time.

My Taurus, shoulder holster; his Taurus, belt. My Taurus, iron buckshot; his, silver bullets. Then I rubbed holy oil into the blade of my KA-BAR. It wasn't silver, wasn't iron, but now it was half-assed blessed.

"Should I make the sign of the cross over it?" I asked, thinking of a little more celestial backup.

"You Catholic?"

"No. I'm not anything."

"Well, I was raised Southern Baptist. We don't do that."

I thought about it. "I guess it doesn't matter. I mean, God is supposedly everywhere. Maybe he's even in our guns."

Remi was feeding rounds into the chambers. His tone was dry. "Yup, I don't doubt at all that God is a bullet." He closed the cylinder, tested the rotation. "Now let's get ourselves on down the road and take care of this woman you saw."

"And my bike."

He slanted me a glance from under lowered brows, then headed toward the stairs.

When I told Remi again to make sure he reacted as soon as I said I saw the woman, he suggested I shut up.

I protested. "Well, *you* can't see her."

"We have established that," he said. "As you've told me *three times*: You see her, you tell me, I hit the brakes. Hell, it would be easier just hitting her with the truck."

"The truck's not iron or silver."

"You sure you didn't clip her with your bike?"

"It's not iron or silver, either."

Remi had latched onto a topic. "I mean, can ghosts feel things? The demon inside, I mean. And then if it's exorcized, does the host feel pain?"

I shifted in the seat, hid an involuntary grunt of discomfort. The shower and muscle relaxant had helped, but I'd be creaking a while longer. "Mark that down as another question for Grandaddy."

McCue took us back to the chapel to be certain we wouldn't miss the area where the woman caused my wreck, then headed us back toward town. We passed a few cars, but not many. McCue suggested I get online with my phone and see if there were reports of car accidents along this stretch.

I checked. Was astonished. "Four in two weeks. Nobody died, but they're all pretty banged up. But the accidents didn't happen in the *same* location. Close, but not the same."

"What's a few yards matter to a ghost?"

"Or a surrogate." I thought it over. "In the stories, she's

always near or in a river. She drowned her kids, so she doesn't travel far from water."

"There's no river here."

"But there *is* a ravine with a creek in the bottom. You said so."

"*Why* did she drown her kids?" Remi asked. "Does anyone know? That is, if the story were true?"

"It varies. But she was reported to be so beautiful that all men lusted after her. She attracted a rich man, who married her, and she had the two kids. Then the husband admitted he never wanted kids and was going to leave her. La Llorona drowned them to hold onto her husband, but he left her anyway. So she died, and her ghost grieves to this day."

Remi shook his head. "What mother drowns her own kids?"

I thought of a couple who had. "Andrea Yates drowned five in the bathtub, including a six-month-old. Susan Smith rolled her car into the lake and killed both children. Smith did it because her lover didn't want kids and was going to leave her."

Remi was silent a moment. "Awful lot like the legend, ain't it?"

"And if it happened now—*now* now, I mean—I'd say both were possessed. But back then, the hell vents were closed and no surrogates were loose on earth."

"So she wanted you to wreck, but not necessarily to die?"

I thought that over. True that no one had died. Then I remembered something Grandaddy had said about the master plan of heaven and all the Celtic knotwork. "Chaos. It's *chaos*."

Remi took his eyes off the road long enough to shoot me a glance. "Chaos?"

Counting off, I stuck thumb and two fingers into the air

one by one. "It's mythology, it's philosophy, it's religion. Chaos is said to be the first formless matter that existed before Creation. It's cosmology. Chaos magic is a branch of occultism."

Remi got on board. "So this demon in ghost's clothing doesn't care if people die, only wants to cause chaos?"

"I think so."

"So she won't be actively trying to kill us."

"Well, she might if we actively try to kill *her*."

La Llorona, as hoped, eventually darted out in front of Remi's truck. I blurted that information, and he didn't try to swerve, as swerving and overcorrecting is probably what caused all the wrecks. He drove the pickup right through her.

She was not corporeal. Therefore not killed or injured.

And then, to my shock, she ran in front of the truck again. When I shouted, he didn't swerve. Or, well, he did, but it was an intentional, controlled swerve. He took the truck to the side of the road, threw the gear shift into neutral, yanked on the emergency brake, told me to start driving as soon as he got into the bed of the truck. Up and down, back and forth.

He was out by the time I shouted after him, "But you can't *see* her!"

"Then tell me where she is! Use a clock face!"

I climbed across the console, which wasn't particularly easy or comfortable, slid in behind the wheel. Dropped the emergency brake. Threw the truck in gear, goosed it to roll it off the shoulder into a turn without laying down rubber, drove back toward the chapel, turned around again. Heading toward town, she'd so far run into the right-hand lane, never the left.

"She'll be on the right!" I shouted. Saw in the mirror Remi's body shift over.

She ran onto the road. I slowed, shouted, *"Two o'clock!"*

I saw a throwing knife zip by the truck, but she did not fall. And now we were heading right by her. *"Three o'clock!"*

He missed again, but she nonetheless paused for an instant, eyeballed us, stared hard at Remi as if evaluating him, then turned and ran back toward the trees.

"I can see her now!" McCue pounded on the truck roof. "Stop! I'm going after her!"

I stopped. Before I could say anything Remi swung himself over the bed rail, jumped down, and ran after her. Amidst an array of blistering curses I shut down the engine, got out of the truck without falling flat, and ran stiffly after *him.*

She led us a chase. It wasn't merry, that's for sure; in fact, it was painful. Remi was a fair distance ahead of me, and I had no second gear. The body just wouldn't give it to me. But I did my best to make my way over fallen trees, through screening branches, and dodged stumps.

"Remi! *Wait up!*" But I was pretty sure he wouldn't.

And yet, he did. He was waiting at the lip of the ravine, poised to take off again at any instant. "She went down here," he said curtly. "There's a way, but it's chancy. I don't think you can make it."

"I'll make it. Don't *lose* her!"

He took off his hat, spun it onto the ground, went over the lip.

When I got there, I saw why he called it chancy. It wouldn't even qualify as a true trail, but there were opportunities to make your way down if you were careful.

Even as I started descending, my brain worked overtime. Why would a surrogate run from us? They wanted us dead. All of them, I assumed. But this one apparently wanted nothing to do with us.

Chaos. *Chaos.* A state of utter confusion, disorder, total lack of organization, unpredictable behavior.

We had a demon on our asses who was very methodical, mostly predictable when it came to notes and photos, and certainly organized. Maybe chaos demons were only good for causing mayhem, not committing murder.

Shit, the climb down was *not* fun. I clung precariously to rocks, brush, grass, leaned close to the wall of the ravine. I could see Remi's boot prints in patches of soil and followed them. Granite outcroppings allowed for safe handholds now and then, and dirt-filled crevices permitted very careful steps.

McCue was now down from the trail, hastily stepping toward the creek over water-polished rocks. I caught a glimpse of white above the water, as if La Llorona was floating there. And then she was. White clothes, black hair, a strikingly beautiful face with large dark eyes.

Dark eyes, not white. Not like the black dog.

According to the legend, she now and then left rivers to visit people, which explained why we'd tangled with her. Now she was back in the river, more or less, and I wasn't sure if it would provide additional power, additional chaos.

Remi splashed into the creek, took a stance.

"Twelve o'clock!" I shouted. "Straight on!" Then recalled he could see her.

He let loose of the third and last throwing knife.

It went home in her heart. As had the ghosts in the bar, she pixelated, groaned like a deflating bagpipe, then fell right down into the water, where she dispersed. Remi hesitated, then waded out farther.

I slid down the last step before level ground. "What are you doing? You got her. She's dead!"

"Lookin' for my knife!"

"Do you think you can *find* it in the water?"

"It's clear and still," Remi called back. Then cried *"Hah!"* and bent down, pulled the knife from water. He was grinning to beat the band. "Okay. Now we go back for the other two knives."

"Well, they're on the road somewhere."

"I'll find 'em. And my hat."

I stood stiffly by the river rocks, trying to ignore overtaxed muscles. I waited until he was almost out of the water. "Don't *do* that again!"

"You would."

"That's beside the point."

"That *is* the point." He glanced back at the creek as if searching for remains. But La Llorona was gone. "Hey, look yonder!" Remi exclaimed, pointing. "Your bike!"

Indeed, my bike, in water close to the bank. Wheels submerged, left side in shallow water, gas tank visible and part of the saddle, one handle bar sticking up.

I wanted to cry. Of course, it was possible the bike was yet salvageable; we needed to get to it so I could take a look. But still.

I waded through the water and reflected that at this moment I was behaving more than a little like La Llorona, hunting and mourning my drowned child.

CHAPTER THIRTY-FOUR

As we stood in calf-deep water, Remi bent and spread his legs, braced, reached down to grab part of the bike.

"What are you doing?" I asked.

"Don't you want to get it out of here?"

I agreed. "I'd *love* to get it out of here, but even working together we can't lift a bike weighing over seven hundred pounds."

Remi, who had straightened, gazed down upon my drowned child. "Then—what do you do? I mean, you're hardly the first who's totaled a bike."

"First, it may not be totaled; and second, a wrecker. Here, though . . ." I shook my head, vastly unhappy. "I don't know if they've got a winch cable long enough, and I seriously doubt anyone can drive down here. And a helicopter—"

"*Helicopter?*"

"—doesn't have enough room to maneuver," I finished. "But I can't just leave it here."

Remi was exasperated. "You just named all the things that can't be done! Is there anything that *can?*"

I stared down at my half-submerged bike, then looked up at Remi. "Levitation?"

McCue remained exasperated. "Then let's levitate our asses out of here, and we'll figure out what to do with the bike later."

I looked back once again at my poor motorcycle, reached down and patted the part of the saddle that wasn't submerged. "We'll be back."

Remi and I turned around to begin the sloppy walk back to the bank, when two white-swathed figures abruptly burst upward from the water and floated in midair. McCue and I both took a couple of steps backward made ungainly by the water.

Children. In christening gowns, despite the fact they were much too old for the ceremony. Five? Six?

They stared at us out of dull black eyes rimmed with blue bruises, faces a sickly pallor. As one, mouths moving simultaneously and tonal pitch identical, they said, *"You killed our mother."*

It took me no time at all. "La Llorona's sons."

Remi was almost stupefied. "But she *drowned* them! Why are they mad at us?"

"Because ghosts are pissy, and they're not really ghosts anymore." I eased a hand toward my shoulder holster. Two sets of eyes fastened on the movement. "Okay—if I distract them, can you shoot them? Or whatever?"

"They're kids, and considerably smaller than we are," Remi said. "What harm can they do?"

"They're *not kids!*" I shouted, and then one of them came at me while the other flung itself at Remi.

Oh, hell. I grabbed the gun out of the holster as I went down to keep it out of the water, managed to push myself into a seated position, snatched a quick look at the kid-ghosts to figure the angles, and fired twice.

One of the shots went off-center. The other did not.

I fought my way to my feet, bracing against submerged rocks, and saw Remi handling the big Bowie as if it were a butter knife. He sliced *his* kid-ghost across the throat, then stabbed him in the heart.

Kind of overkill, you ask me.

Black blood flowed down the ghost's christening gown. Then, merely bodies in the water, he and his brother-ghost simply dispersed and disappeared. No sound. No smell. They just—became threads that were spun by the water into nowhere.

I straightened, water running from me, still-dry gun held in one hand. "Okay," I said, "Mom and the kids are one big happy family together in—hell. Can we go home, now?"

It was the most uncomfortable ride I'd ever experienced, and I was willing to say it was the same for Remi. Both of us were soaked from mid-chest down. Our boots, so waterlogged, weighed a hundred pounds apiece. And jeans, when wet, adhere to the body, even feel like they are shrinking through an area where you really don't want them to. And leather is worse. Neither of us mentioned it, but we were vastly uncomfortable.

Remi rolled the truck behind the roadhouse and parked. As the evening before, plenty of customers. And since the back door led us into and through the pool tables, we got plenty of weird looks. Both of us tromped upstairs and disappeared into our respective rooms to shed clothing, particularly the boots, and dry ourselves off. I wanted a shower, but I was too hungry to wait. In dry clothes, sock feet—I really didn't care—I left my bedroom to check out the common room, see if the man behind the curtain was sending us messages again.

I found plenty of normal websites, but the deep web didn't come up again.

It had been some time since Remi had left that message for Grandaddy. I didn't know that I'd have any better luck, but I called him. Reached a voice with a one-word command: *"Speak."*

So I spoke. Told the phone that Remi had already called him, got no answer, and now it was me. Would two calls work better than one?

But it was early yet, as time is measured in establishments serving alcohol, and it was entirely possible Grandaddy didn't respond to phone messages. I'd never thought of calling him before. He just showed up now and then, without any advance warning.

I'd never once wondered what he might be doing when absent from my life. For as long as I remember, he came and went. Never any explanation other than a nebulous *I have business.*

Now I knew what that business was.

R emi and I ate downstairs. For some reason the crowd of patrons provided a certain amount of relief. They were *normal*. They weren't black dogs, or a ghost woman hunting drowned ghost children, or a Grigori, or a surrogate.

Grandaddy did eventually arrive, and he carried a manila envelope. Remi and I both stared at it. Neither of us moved to take it.

I was seated. Grandaddy was not. Ordinarily it was a deliberate positioning that might intimidate the ones who remained seated. In this case, whether or not that was his intention, it simply wasn't successful.

He dropped the unopened envelope onto the table, just shy of landing in our plates. "A young woman," he said, "came to me as I arrived and asked me to deliver this to you."

I looked at the seemingly inconsequential envelope. Our names, as always, were printed on it. Gabriel and Remiel, not the shortened forms.

McCue shoved his chair back and stood up abruptly. "Best do this in private upstairs."

I followed his lead. Grandaddy, with the envelope, brought up the rear. We went into the common room, where all three of us sat down at the table.

"We need to know," I said plainly. "What our roles are, what this war is, what the true agenda is—and how many angels are opposed to Remi and me specifically?"

The light was kind to his silver-white hair, kind to his face. I had no idea how old he was. I had no idea if angels aged, or if they remained as they were, stagnant. "The agenda is to stop Lucifer from returning."

Remi's tone was cool. "And just how do we do that?"

"You *are* doing it," Grandaddy said, "by being who you are, and by your actions."

I shook my head. "Not good enough. A Grigori came to me, warned us that we may be used for other purposes than the one you just stated."

His head came up, and his blue eyes burned. "A Grigori." When we said nothing more, he looked at each of us individually, weighing us. He'd always done that with me, and I assumed also with Remi, but this time there was a sharpness to his gaze. "Who?"

"Ambriel," I told him.

He pushed away from the table, rose, took three steps away, then turned back. "Your job, the one for which you were conceived and trained for, is to kill as many surrogates as is possible. Legends, mythology, tall tales, fictional characters, historical figures, and so forth. We must gain control before they do."

"Aren't you omnipotent?" I asked.

"God is. The rest of us are not."

I flicked a glance at the computer. "And just where *is* God in all of this? Hiding behind a dark web and feeding us a few scraps now and then? Is this *Mission Impossible*, with orders filtered by unseen beings? *Charlie's Angels*, where Charlie was never seen, only heard?"

Grandaddy neither confirmed nor denied. "In a handful of days, you have removed from the devil's chessboard eight pawns. You did this working with very little information and only part of your powers; and be assured, they will grow. *No one* has accomplished what you have in so short a time. Yes, it's true you will threaten some, even angels, because we are a political hierarchy as well as a celestial one."

Remi's tone was very clear. "Are we targets? Targets of our own kind?"

"No."

I stared him down. "Are you sure?"

The lines in his face deepened. "What precisely did Ambriel tell you?"

"That humanity may be caught in the middle of this heavenly battle, and instead of being the beneficiaries of a world without Lucifer's threat, humans become collateral damage. Irrelevant."

"Irrelevant," he echoed. Then he was back at the table without us seeing him move, and he bent, slammed a fist down upon the surface. *"Who do you think we are doing this for?* Not us; *we* hold heaven. But to save humanity, to keep the sacrifices of humans to a minimum. To stop Lucifer, to kill his children. *That* is your job."

"Then what exactly is Ambriel? Has she any stake in this?"

He shook his head. "Grigori are to remain neutral. They are not to interfere. They have caused enough trouble in the past."

"When they fell."

Grandaddy was more than a little annoyed. "God doesn't kill his children. Even Lucifer was merely flung out of heaven, not killed. But the male Grigori, who were merely to watch, began providing information to humans long before they could possibly be ready for it, and then they lay with human women and got children on them."

"Nephilim," Remi said.

"They should not exist," Granddaddy said flatly. "They were never *meant* to exist. The Grigori in effect created a new race, and did it without permission."

Absently, I rubbed fingertips against the table. "Ambriel said—"

"I don't care what Ambriel said! No, she is not one of the fallen, but she takes their side. She wishes the Nephilim to live."

Both Remi and I stared at him, stunned. After a moment McCue took his hat off, set it upside down, ran both hands

333

through his short hair and fixed Grandaddy with hard eyes. "So much for saying God doesn't kill his children."

"He doesn't. But the Nephilim are not his. They are not the children of God, nor are they the children of man."

I shook my head in disbelief. "So they are expendable."

"They should never have been born in the first place."

"Yeah, well, they're here now," I said. "That horse is out of the barn."

He was stone-faced. "Your job is not to hunt Nephilim. Be glad of it. When one dies, a piece of heaven dies, and it damages us all."

I assessed him. "So Ambriel is the enemy?"

"Ambriel has been misled. What she doesn't realize is that Nephilim may at any time turn their backs on God and join Lucifer. They owe no allegiance to anyone."

"Mercenaries," Remi said.

I rubbed fingertips against the wood again. "If that is true, why doesn't heaven pay the Nephilim, either to fight for heaven or at the very least to stay out of the argument. Then you wouldn't have to worry about them joining Lucifer."

Grandaddy said, "That is not our way."

"But sending us off to kill for you is?" I shrugged. "Maybe it should be. Desperate times, and all that. I would think the End of Days is the most desperate time of all."

Remi indicated the computer. "If it's not God on the other side, is it you?"

"It is not. What I have to say to you can be said in person, not through a computer."

"Then who is it?" I asked.

Grandaddy shook his head.

The lazy drawl was back in McCue's voice. "Either you can't, or you won't. Look, it ain't no shame to admit you can't *when* you can't."

Grandaddy shook his head again. "I can't, because I don't know. I suspect, but I don't know the truth."

I looked at the sealed envelope he'd dropped onto the table. "Do you know what's in there?"

"No."

"We do. Go ahead. Open it."

Grandaddy studied us both a moment, then picked up the envelope. He slit it open with a fingernail, removed the note. As he unfolded it, read it, his eyebrows rose. He dropped the note to the table where Remi and I could see it, cut-out letters once again: *And a fourth.*

I felt a crawling in my gut. Grandaddy removed the photo, was clearly concerned by what he saw. "Who is this poor woman?"

Remi said, "You want to know her name, turn it over. It'll say."

Grandaddy did so. "Catherine."

"She's the fourth," I told him. "Two notes without photos, followed by four additional notes *with* photos. All women, all butchered—and each manner of death worse than the one before."

My phone went off. Remi and I both jumped. I answered.

Ganji said, "There is a delivery for you. A package."

I looked at the note, the photo. "Do we—do we have to sign for it?"

"No. The delivery man is gone."

I looked at Grandaddy. "But you're sure the delivery guy is not a surrogate?"

He shook his head. "This building has been cleared. No demon may enter here."

I said into the phone to Ganji, "Grandaddy says no."

"Shall I bring it up?"

"Please."

I disconnected, looked at Remi. "I take it you weren't expecting a package."

He shook his head. "And I take it *you* weren't."

I looked again at the note, the photo. "Catherine" was nearly unrecognizable as a human.

Ganji knocked at the door at the top of the stairs. Remi rose, went to open it. He came back with a small parcel and yet another manila envelope.

God, I did not want to open it.

I said to Grandaddy, "You really don't know what's going on with the notes and photos?"

He shook his head. "This is not the work of angels. It's the work of Lucifer's children."

Remi set the package on the table. He stared at it as if it might be a rattlesnake, every bit as reluctant as I to discover what was inside, what the note said.

Grandaddy unsheathed his knife, cut open the package. It was a styrofoam container much like doggie bag boxes. That, he opened as well.

Holy Christ. A recognizable—and recognizably human—body part.

I recoiled. Remi looked appalled.

"Oh, man," I muttered. "This is—this is fucking *sick*."

After a glance at Grandaddy, who seemed as ignorant of answers as we two, Remi slit open the envelope, looked inside, then pulled out a note.

This one was not made up of cut out letters from multiple sources. This one was handwritten in red ink, just like the names on the back of the photo.

McCue read it quickly, color fading. Then, in a squeezed, uneven voice, he read it aloud.

"From hell.

Gabriel and Remiel

Sirs
I send you half the kidney I took from one woman,
preserved it for you the other piece I fried and ate it was
very nice. I may send you the bloody knife that took it
out if you only wait a while longer."

Remi let the note drop from his fingers. He lost his tan entirely, swallowed convulsively. "Oh my God. It's the text of the original letter . . . and the names are right. The first names of the women in the photos—they're the same. Mary Ann *Nichols*. Annie *Chapman*. Elizabeth *Stride*. Catherine *Eddowes*." He drew in a breath, still pale. "The next one—I think the next one will be a woman named Mary Jane. For Mary Jane Kelly."

"*Who?* How do you know that?" I picked up the note, scanned it quickly—old-fashioned cursive writing and filled with spelling errors, almost indecipherable—then saw there was more writing on the other side. Four lines only, printed with careful clarity.

Call me Legion.
Call me Iñigo Montoya.

And the final two sentences:

Call me Jack the Ripper.
Catch me when you can.

Original in the Records of Metropolitan Police Service,
National Archives, MEPO 3/142

AUTHOR'S NOTE

It's believed, of the thousands of letters received by police that were purportedly written by Jack the Ripper, the one most likely to be genuine was indeed accompanied by a human body part identified as a kidney. And while most of us tend to misquote the letter's famous line as *Catch me if you can*, the actual text says *when*.

Urban fantasy began for me, as it did for so many of us, with Charles de Lint. I read most of his work before the subgenre had a name. Read more urban fantasy by other authors over the years since de Lint's work first appeared.

After three decades of writing novels set in imaginary worlds of my own devising—the Cheysuli, Sword-Dancer, and Karavans series—I got an itch to try my hand at fantastic elements set in our world, relying on reality as a backdrop to the *un*reality I would serve readers. I wanted to play with the paranormal, the supernatural, as well as legends and lore, myth and magic, history both oral and written. And to use modern slang and pop culture references was great fun.

I did ask my editor if I could use the occasional F-bomb. It's not a regular part of my personal lexicon, but I felt it would definitely be part of Gabe's. She was fine with it. Said she was born in New York City and f*** was her middle name. Unfortunately I could not quote song lyrics word-for-word because of copyright and licensing issues. It's a shame, because country music lyrics are the most colorful on Planet Earth.

My minor is in British History, but cultural anthropology also fascinated me in school. I loved learning about different civilizations, religions, rituals. I very nearly switched my major from journalism to anthro, but to do so would have required me to take a statistics class, and that meant the arcane and incomprehensible rituals and recipes of mathematics would be involved. Thus, my BS in journalism.

The initial impulse was to make my two protagonists a male and female pairing. But I realized it would probably end up sounding very like Tiger and Del of my Sword-Dancer series, and while I love writing about those two characters, I didn't want to do a knock-off of my own work.

I had Gabe already in mind, reflecting my interest in folklore and mythology. As for Remi, well, I grew up in Arizona and, for many years, owned horses and attended rodeos frequently. This even led to three rodeo queen titles in the '70s: Scottsdale Parada del Sol, Phoenix Rodeo of Rodeos, and Miss Rodeo Arizona.

I spent pretty much every Friday night dancing to country music at cowboy bars, and Wednesday nights after Rodeo Club when attending Northern Arizona University in Flagstaff. The latter venue included the Museum Club on Route 66, which is the model for the Zoo Club. So when Remi talks about powdered tobacco tucked inside his lip—well, yes, I tried it a few times. And I did shots of tequila, and have eased my way through good single malt *uisge beatha*. (*Alba gu brath!*)

As for guns, I've taken classes, hit the shooting range (revolver preferred to semi-auto), researched, repeatedly picked the brains of gun experts James Kosky and Simon Hawke. As for motorcycles, I've ridden but never driven, and certainly never laid one down. There, Simon Hawke's experience with All Things Motorcycle was invaluable to me. But all errors, always, are mine and mine alone.

Upcoming projects, in addition to the further adventures of Gabe and Remi, include a new Sword-Dancer novel and the final installment of the Karavans series. I can be reached through my website, www.jennifer-roberson.net.

—Jennifer Roberson
Tucson, Arizona